D1189790

11-9-22

For Brenda,

Cry Murder, Baby

You're next...

Mary Monroe

authorHOUSE®

AuthorHouse™
1663 Liberty Drive
Bloomington, IN 47403
www.authorhouse.com
Phone: 833-262-8899

© 2022 Mary Monroe. All rights reserved.

No part of this book may be reproduced, stored in a retrieval system, or transmitted by any means without the written permission of the author.

This is a work of fiction. All of the characters, names, incidents, organizations, and dialogue in this novel are either the products of the author's imagination or are used fictitiously.

Published by AuthorHouse 04/07/2022

ISBN: 978-1-6655-5604-0 (sc)
ISBN: 978-1-6655-5605-7 (e)

Library of Congress Control Number: 2022905857

Print information available on the last page.

Any people depicted in stock imagery provided by Getty Images are models, and such images are being used for illustrative purposes only.
Certain stock imagery © Getty Images.

This book is printed on acid-free paper.

Because of the dynamic nature of the Internet, any web addresses or links contained in this book may have changed since publication and may no longer be valid. The views expressed in this work are solely those of the author and do not necessarily reflect the views of the publisher, and the publisher hereby disclaims any responsibility for them.

This book is dedicated to
Michelle, Mark, Marcie and Melody
Who gave me the gift of being a mother

"All power tends to corrupt and absolute power corrupts absolutely."

- Lord Acton

Prologue

She heard her cell phone alarm ring. An annoying sound that pierced her deep slumber. She had just been up with the twins at 2 a.m. for their night feeding. Her husband rolled over and put his arm around her waist, a familiar gesture. She felt his warmth. Away, she heard one of her babies in a sharp cry. *Oh, no. Let me enjoy just five more minutes.* She knew it was inevitable. Like clockwork, the babies awoke around this time, but she was hoping they would sleep in a little to give her five precious minutes to herself. *Just five minutes, please!* Oh well. She lumbered out of bed. 5:30 a.m. God, it was still dark. She went into the nursery and placed the pacifier in the crying baby's mouth. Her husband was up. He was in the shower. She went into the kitchen, made the coffee. A full pot. Enough for his Yeti thermos that he took to work, and two (or three) cups for herself. Her arms smoothed over her sides, noticing the lumps that had stubbornly refused to go away after her pregnancy with the twins. She knew she should do her pelvic floor exercises her doctor prescribed, but instead chose to plop in the living room rocking chair. She was glad the babies had gone back to sleep. The coffee brewing smelled intoxicating. He came into the kitchen dressed in Levi jeans and a freshly washed work shirt. He looked tired, so much more tired than his 37 years. She knew it was hard for him to get up this early every day, but he never complained. To her, he was still ruggedly handsome.

"Morning, babe," she said, as she watched him get his coffee. He still made her heart flutter, even after five years of marriage. His strong physique hadn't changed much from his college years of playing soccer. "How'd you sleep?"

He came over to her and gave her a morning kiss. "With you next to me? Never been better."

She giggled that laugh that he always seemed to emit from her, no matter how tired she was.

"Were you up during the night with the twins?" he asked in a caring tone.

"Yep, two o'clock. Andrew was just starving for his bottle, but little Anthony just went back to bed after I got Andrew his bottle," she shared with her husband.

"Well, it won't be long until they're sleeping through the night."

She shuffled in her cozy slippers to the refrigerator and gave him the lunch she had packed after she couldn't go to bed right away at 2 a.m. – ham on rye with mayo, an apple and a ready-made chocolate pudding in his insulated lunch bag.

He said, "You are my world. Everything you do for our family, and you still find time to make my lunch."

At 6:00 a.m., with their customary goodbye kiss, he was off. She lay down on her bed. The bed covers were cool and crisp against her skin.

A baby's cry. *Oh, please, not yet. Just a few more precious moments of peace. I guess I shouldn't complain; the babies had been less fussy since they started on the Nature Plus Formula program.* She was glad her mom's friend who worked at SynCor, had recommended it. Only seven weeks old and both were sleeping through the night at least a few times a week. She went into the nursery. Who's awake? Was it little Andrew or Anthony? Andrew, of course. The bigger one. And now he was peeling out a scream she hadn't heard before. Sharp and high-pitched. She turned on the night light, a little lamb with pink-colored cheeks. It cast an eerie glow to the room. She lifted Andrew out of his crib. His face was cherry red and tensed up in the delivery of another high-pitched wail.

"Hush, little baby, momma's baby. Hush now, everything's okay. Were you having a bad dream?" Andrew was wet. As usual. Dear little Andrew. The first twin out. A big boy, 7 lbs. 8 oz. Then little Anthony,

6 lbs. 7 oz. More fragile. As if he had wanted just a few more weeks in her dark, warm womb, but had been, reluctantly, coerced into birth by Andrew's readiness. She wondered if she would ever know a day again without an avalanche of wet and soiled diapers. She changed Andrew. But still the piercing cry. Not his "wet" cry, which she was accustomed to. Not his "hungry" cry, which she could determine. An unusual cry, tinged with what? Fear? Genuine fear? How could little Anthony be sleeping through all this, she wondered. Sweet baby Anthony. How she loved the twins so. Not that it was the abundant, unconditional love that she had thought she would feel when she became a mother. At least not yet. It was more an overwhelming tumbling of responsibilities, feelings, and finally, just plain old physical work that she hadn't anticipated. If only she could stop feeling so tired all the time. It did help now that the babies were on Nature Plus Formula.

Ever since they had started on it, they began to sleep through the night a few times a week, as promised, and even – unless if it was her imagination – were less fussy. She was glad her mother's good friend had gotten her admitted in the SynCor program. The best part of the whole thing was that it was free. And that certainly helped with things. Her husband, as a lineman for the telephone company, made a good salary, but between the loss of her salary and added expenses, she had to watch their budget.

Well, Andrew was changed and beginning to quiet down. She swung him onto her hip. She went into the kitchen and took out two bottles and placed them in the warmer. Little Anthony would soon be up and hungry, as usual. It was odd that even though he was smaller than Andrew, he was a much greater eater. It was as if he was making up for lost time, trying to catch up to Andrew. She fed Andrew. He gobbled the bottle down hungrily and fell back to sleep in her arms. She tiptoed into the nursery. She lay Andrew back into his crib. Andrew began crying.

"Hush," she said. "You'll wake up Anthony."

She glanced over at Anthony's crib. He looked so quiet, so calm. It amazed her how babies could look like little angels when sleeping, and just the opposite when in their moods. She stroked Anthony's jet-black hair. He was cool and moist to the touch. She turned on the dresser light. His skin cast a bluish hue. She felt her body freeze. She picked up Anthony in her arms. He felt limp, lifeless. She felt panic grip her, and gently shook her baby. "Anthony! Wake up! Wake UP!" she screamed. She placed her nose by his face – no breath! She laid him on the changing table and breathed into him. She saw his chest expand. She did it again. And again. And again. And again. She concentrated and prayed. *No, God, not my baby.* Her mind went blank—gray—and she breathed again into the tiny limp body. So channeled were her energies, she failed to hear little Andrew crying at a high-pitched decibel from his crib. Crying bloody murder for his twin brother.

Chapter 1

October 29

M ichelle Heywood loved her life and her career. It gave her an opportunity to play with big stakes, and if she played it right, win the big rewards. She was glad she had moved into the exciting world of advertising. It gave her a sense of accomplishment –even power—by seeing the immediate results of her work, her actions. For instance, at today's account meeting at 2 p.m. with one of Ackerly, Adams & Associates' largest accounts, Valu-Mart Drug Stores. Since she had been put on as account executive, she had single-handedly ironed out a lot of problems that had developed under (in her estimation at least) the haphazard account management of the senior account executive, Ward Thatcher, and even ad agency president, David Adams. In the past few months, she had cleared up all the problems with copy errors, incorrect prices, wrong pictures of products, inaccurate addresses, and had increased the accuracy of the preprinted flyers needed for each regional newspaper.

It had not been easy and had required long hours at the office, diplomatic conversations with the media buyer that had resulted in the elimination of overlapping newspaper coverage per region, saving the client money. Long hours with the printer and art department. Yes, long hours with Hawk Wilder, Art Production Director. Why did her mind always wander to thinking about Hawk? Sure, he was drop-dead gorgeous with his dark hair, tanned skin and tall muscled body. And he was available. Rumors were that he had recently broken up with his girlfriend about six months ago. But protocol meant she needed to keep everything on the up and up, professional.

All the long hours of hard work had paid off. Valu-Mart Company President Richard Johnson and Marketing V.P. Malcolm Campbell had reported 22%-32% sales increases at all Valu-Mart stores. Michelle's aggressive social media campaign, combined with new vivid point-of-purchase displays, were received by store management with high praise. Michelle had thrived on the positive feedback. It seemed to give her added impetus to present the newest layouts and campaign for the Christmas promotion.

She had surprised, even herself, by her smooth presentation of the newest design by Art Director Hawk Wilder. The Christmas campaign was quite a departure from the customary Christmas flyers the company had previously done. Instead of the bold product display with large sale prices popping off, she and Hawk had designed a picturesque cover photo design featuring several diverse families discovering an array of holiday presents, all of course at Valu-Mart stores.

Much to her delight, both Johnson and Campbell had flipped over the new campaign. As she had presented it, with much spontaneous excitement and enthusiasm, she had felt Adam's and Thatcher's reservations. But, she had continued onward as if she had been walking a tightrope and was relieved of all stress when she saw the smiles of the Valu-Mart company President and marketing V.P. It didn't surprise her a bit when, after their approval, both Thatcher and Adams had jumped on her bandwagon, saying they thought it was a super creative avenue, good "warm and fuzzy" advertising, etc., etc. Michelle wondered what had made the two of them into such spineless chameleons and hoped it would never be her cross to bear.

Bbrrmm. The internal office intercom on her desk phone buzzed. "Michelle, please stop by my office before you leave today. About 4:30."

"Sure, Dave. Anything special you want to talk about?"

"I'll talk to you at 4:30."

End of conversation. Hhmmm. Now he really had caught Michelle's curiosity bug – what did he want to speak to her about? Was he upset by her boldness? Had she overstepped some imaginary boundaries that she was supposed to uphold? Michelle looked at her watch. She had twenty minutes to kill until 4:30. Michelle's mom always told her she had a strong sense of curiosity. In fact, some of her adventures – or misadventures – of her 29 years could reflect the old saying, "Curiosity Killed the Cat." She looked over her notes from the Valu-Mart meeting. She could begin writing her notes from the ad meeting (a habit an old supervisor once taught her) or – because she knew she was too excited about the meeting to sit still right now – she could go to the art department and tell Hawk how Valu-Mart management loved his (their) campaign. It was an easy decision. She knew every nook and cranny of the ad offices, since she had spent most of her professional life there.

Ackerly, Adams & Associates would be considered in the industry as a small to mid-sized ad agency, with approximately 30 employees. Adams had become president after Thomas Ackerly had died almost two years ago. Ackerly had been a superb ad man – creative, insightful, and daring. Combined with management expertise and business acumen, he had been the guiding force for the direction and growth of A, A & A. He had hired Michelle Heywood seven years ago, right out Chicago's famous Northwestern University as his administrative assistant and had told her that he was going to teach her the "agency business."

She had learned about advertising from the ground up – how to communicate with clients, how to follow-up on projects, how to write copy, and how to purchase media. And in the seven years that Michelle had worked under Thomas Ackerly, she had witnessed the success of the agency – substantial profits, as well as local and national recognition for excellence in advertising.

It was all brought to a stark halt when Thomas Ackerly died of a heart attack about two years ago at the age of 55. Michelle had taken it hard. Since she had lost her beloved dad to colon cancer her sophomore year in college, her mentor had meant a lot to her. Her growth as a professional ad executive was a direct result of his mentoring and coaching. His partner, David Adams, had purchased Ackerly's half of the business and attained the title of President. Adams had kept the original corporate name of Ackerly, Adams & Associates (A, A & A), because of the excellent reputation it had earned in the Chicagoland area and beyond.

But during the two years since Adams had been "running the show," the agency had lost several major accounts and could be headed for financial problems. Michelle was determined to help build the image and profits of the agency – a legacy on behalf of Thomas Ackerly's name.

The agency was located on the seventh floor of 610 Michigan Avenue, right in the center of Chicago's professional businesses – the Sun Times, the Chicago Tribune, and the famous two-mile stretch of Michigan Avenue's ad agencies, home to some of the world's most creative and insightful minds – the minds of people who created brands of consumer products. The minds of people who determined which hair shampoo, which internet service, which mouth wash millions of people in the United States, and the world, would use.

Michelle reached the art department located at the west end of the seventh floor. It was a total departure of atmosphere from the sleek, professional stature of the account executive offices. Surrounding the art tables of Hawk and his staff of artists and computer geniuses were a potpourri of photos, folders, laptops, and of course, the artists' defenses against the barrage of work and requests that flood through their doors. She glanced over them: the poster that read, "Complaint Department. Please write complaints in the area provided below" and then a blank box about 1/16" x 1/16". And the wood plaques that read, "If you want it bad, you'll get it read bad," and "Clean up after yourself, your mother doesn't work here." She laughed at an aging poster of a turkey with the saying, "It's hard to soar like an eagle when you work for turkeys." And of course, the infamous, "You want it WHEN?" And then, Hawk's own personal saying, posted above his art board, a more serious quote by Muhammad Ali: "Impossible is just a big word thrown around by small men who find it easier to live in the world they've been given than to explore the power they have to change it." That was Hawk. Fearless to go that extra mile.

Michelle had always enjoyed the atmosphere of this freewheeling department of the agency and had always enjoyed working creatively together with Hawk Wilder.

"Hey, Hawk. What are you working on?"

"That new package design Adams wants for Syncor."

"Oh."

"Well?"

"Well, what?"

"Don't well what me. How did the holiday campaign with Valu-Mart go?"

"Oh, that. Okay."

"Just okay?"

"Well, not *just okay*," Michelle said with an air of mystique. "It went fabulous, wonderful, stupendous, you name it, we were a big hit!"

Hawk laughed, "I knew it! Just by looking at you when you came in. You do this thing with your eyes and your mouth."

"Hawk – you should have been there. Boy Thatcher never said a word. Nor did good ol' Adams through the whole thing. And I'm going on and on. Then as soon as Johnson and Campbell went for it, said it was the best thing they had seen from us in months, then ol' Thatcher and Adams were in love with it."

"Figures."

"Yeah, and now Adams wants to see me in his office at 4:30. What time is it now?"

"It's 4:20."

"Well, gotta run. Dying of curiosity to see what's up. Tell you later."

David Adam's office depicted his personality – safe, logical, dependable. Not particularly the worst of traits, mind you, but not necessarily the most desirable ones for a creative head of an ad agency. After Michelle sat in the chair facing his desk, he began: "Michelle, in the past year since you've been co-repping the Valu-Mart account with Ward, the account has really done well. Sales up, product looks good, client's happy, so I'm happy. I don't know if you heard it through the grapevine or not, but Ward Thatcher is leaving us. He accepted a V.P. position with Troots, Farr & Williams, and that's fine with me.

Frankly, Thatcher can't hold a candle next to you, and I don't need any dead weight on board. Michelle, I'm promoting you to Senior Account Executive. You'll be the lead on the Valu-Mart account. That new gal Tina Williams can assist you with the leg work on it. I think she's determined and with you as her mentor, I think she'll do well. I also want you to be our lead on the SynCor account. As you're aware, that was one of Tom Ackerly's bread and butter accounts, so when he died, I personally handled it. Now Bram Pavolich, who is President of SynCor, is introducing a whole new subsidiary to his food line, a division that produces infant formula. I've shown him a few ideas of mine, and, well, to be truthful, he didn't seem too impressed.

"He wants – in his own words – freshness, creativity, the right message to make *every* new mother want to purchase Nature Plus Formula for her baby. That's why I want you to handle the account. You're bright, fresh. If anyone can keep this account in house, you can. I told Bram I'd be bringing you to our meeting tomorrow at noon. So – what do you say?"

"Thanks so much for your confidence. I won't let you down."

"Okay. That's tomorrow at noon. We'll drive together."

"Great. Thanks again, Mr. Adams."

"You are receiving a substantial increase in your salary, profit sharing, bonus and a company car. You'll get Ward's."

The image of Ward's sleek, black Lexus came flooding into her head. Wow, what an upgrade from her well-worn Toyota with over 100,000 miles! Raise? Bonus? Her mind was spinning, but she managed to hold her composure and state confidently, "I'll do an excellent job for this company. I won't let you down."

"You have my full confidence," he responded.

Her mind was bursting with excitement. Unrivaled salary. A company car. Wow, she couldn't believe it! He had really come through for her! Tonight, she'd celebrate … an expensive bottle of wine, no – champagne! Some cheese. Maybe dinner out. It was a night to celebrate. A celebration of the beginning of an exciting career move. Tonight, Michelle would celebrate the beginning of a new and exciting part of her life.

Chapter 2

October 30

B ram Pavolich felt as if his life was at a grand turning point. For the past 20 years, SynCor Foods had grown from a humble beginning as a cookie factory into a multi-billion-dollar operation with a proven reputation as the leader in two important consumer categories – cookies and popcorn. Perky Plus Popcorn and Grandma's Butter Cookies had earned him the reputation as the #1 manufacturer/distributor of consumer popcorn and cookies. Yes, it was a tribute to his genius combined with the marketing skills of Thomas Ackerly, his ad man for 24 years up until his untimely death two years ago. Now it acted as an insult to his mastery of craft to have an idiot like David Adams creating the public brand for his products.

And it wasn't just his opinion. In the past two years since Adams had personally handled the advertising for Perky Plus Popcorn and Grandma's Butter Cookies, sales had dropped by 30%. Changes had come into the marketplace. Changes within the female consumer who was his target demographic that Adams had not taken into consideration. Today's woman was more independent and powerful, a highly intelligent consumer. Over 50% of the total labor force was comprised of women and more than 50% of women with children under the age of one worked outside the home as well. Yet, Adams had done nothing to adapt the old, battered sing-song jingle of Perky Plus

Popcorn that basically told women if they want to be "perky," all they needed was Perky Plus Popcorn.

Well, damn it, women didn't want to be perky anymore! They wanted convenience, ease, economy, nutrition, and yes, to please their families. The basics of human nature had not changed, but the approach had to be different. He had told Adams this for several months, but it seemed to go in one ear and out the other.

He had laid it on the line with Adams at their meeting last week. He was opening a new division of SynCor Foods, "Nature Plus Formula," and it was the apex of his 55 years. The climax to his genius career. Nature Plus Formula, the ideal product to accommodate the growing needs of the grown children of the Post World War II "Baby Boomers," who were now "Grandma" and "Grandpa."

Today's mothers wanted the benefits of breastfeeding but also the convenience of bottle feeding for their on-the-go lifestyles. They wanted the convenience and freedom bottle feeding gave them but wanted the nutrition and nurturing benefits of breastfeeding. And now, he had combined the best of both options into one highly-marketable product – refrigerated formula in cartons that contained 25% real mother's breast milk. It was the climax of his career that would not only bring up the losses of Perky Plus Popcorn and Grandma's Butter Cookies, but also establish him as the leader in feeding America's babies. And, in three to five years, the world's infants.

He'd be damned if he'd allow that bumbling fool, Adams, to market his newest creative genius.

Yes, he had laid it on the line with Adams: either a new Senior Account Executive would handle the SynCor account, or he would sign up with a new agency. It had to be the right person, preferably a woman, who was highly creative, insightful, intuitive and a master at words and images. He remembered how Adams had looked so shocked when Bram had told him this. He had anticipated that Adams naturally would not want to lose one of his biggest accounts. But could it have been more serious than that? Could his ad agency be in big financial trouble? Well, that was not his problem.

And then, just yesterday, he got a phone call from Adams saying that he had just such a person, a Michelle Heywood, to handle the Nature Plus Formula account, and she would be coming to today's meeting at noon.

Well, it was just a few minutes away until he would meet this young woman who, if she was the right person, would be a pivotal key to his company's success in his new venture.

Bram rubbed his hands together. Yes, the success of Nature Plus. The success he rightly deserved, and even needed, right now.

Isabelle "Izzie" Nick took pride in being, in her mind at least, the best administrative assistant in the world. Maybe other women wanted to "climb the corporate ladder," but she had found her niche in life. She had always had a flair for punctuality, precision, detail, and organization, and was able to profitably utilize these skills: first as the Executive and Confidential Secretary to Bram Pavolich of SynCor Foods and now as his administrative assistant. In her integral role, Izzie was privy to information that others didn't see. She was good at what she did, always having her boss's best interests as her priority. She had his gratitude, and he was generous with his praise of her special abilities, and yes, she even had drama and excitement. She would never tell him this, but she'd probably work for him for free for all the fun she had on the job. SynCor was a fascinating place to work, something exciting was always happening. Like today. In just a few minutes there would be the big ad meeting for the Nature Plus Formula line with some new gal from the ad firm.

Bram had told her that Adams had said she was really a dynamo when it came to targeting ad messages to get the right results. Well, Izzie hoped that this would be the right person. She knew sales of SynCor's two major products, Perky Plus Popcorn and Grandma's Butter Cookies, had been off and Bram was banking a lot on his new line of baby formula products. She wanted the success for Bram, for Nature Plus, and for herself. Since she had never married or had children, her job was everything to her. She had to know she was doing a superb job, so she could look in the mirror and instead of seeing a 51-year-old maid, she'd see a relevant, vital "Best Administrative Assistant in the World," a real credit to her company. She was, indeed, a company girl. Let's face it. She was no "spring chicken." She had worked her way up from the secretary pool when she was just a timid 18-year-old schoolgirl to an honored position with a rivaled salary – and she intended on keeping it.

Well, it was five minutes to noon. Hmmph. She would see if this new gal Michelle Heywood was prompt. Mr. Adams had been "sloughing off" as of late and coming to ad meetings as much as 30 minutes late and she didn't like it!

Here came Mr. Chet Hartman, and his new assistant, Pam Pritthouse. Chet was a good guy, Izzie thought. His new assistant was a college student intern majoring in marketing who wanted to learn "the ad world from the best." Bram had welcomed her to his firm, much to the dismay of Chet who declared he didn't want the responsibility of an intern, due to the "goodness of Bram's heart." Or, should I say, Izzie thought to herself, the goodness of Pam's heart (or the medically enhanced 38DD breasts adorning it!)

Bram had always been fond of large-breasted women. Even though, while glancing at herself, she felt that he didn't respect them. Izzie, with her tiny 34A chest, had Bram's respect and admiration that Pam Pritthouse probably could never earn due to no fault of her own, but her ample chest. Hartman had not wanted an intern; he hadn't wanted any additional responsibility, but Bram had insisted on "helping the poor schoolgirl" out.

"Mr. Pavolich, Mr. Hartman and Miss Pritthouse are here for the noon ad meeting."

"Very well, send them in."

"As well, here comes Mr. Adams and a young lady – probably Miss Michelle Heywood. Shall I send them in also?"

"Yes, Izzie, I've been waiting for her – I mean them."

"So, you're Michelle Heywood, superstar Account Executive and Advertising Wiz Kid," Bram said. "Are you going to be able to market my new Nature Plus Formula products so that every woman who has a baby under a year old or who is about to have a baby selects our formula over #1 Simi milk and #2 Lac-alike?"

"I don't know if I can do that. *Every* woman is quite a request," Michelle play-acted the demure ladylike woman. Then she spoke up in a clear, articulate voice that cut through the momentary tension that had filled the room. "However, Mr. Pavolich, would you be interested in acquiring a 50 per cent share of the 47 percent of women who choose breast feeding combined with 80 percent of breastfeeding women who supplement breastfeeding with bottle feeding plus a 75 percent share of women who elect bottle feeding as their feeding method? That would give you a billion, 100 thousand purchases in the coming fiscal year with an average purchase of one quart, totaling more than two million tons of Nature Plus Formula in the coming year."

Michelle smiled inwardly, her outer look one of total seriousness and sense of purpose. It had been a great delivery; her acting classes in high school often came to her professional rescue. She was glad she had received a dual major at Northwestern, Marketing and Financial, needed skills she used doing hours of research this morning.

"Girl does her homework," Bram said. "I'm impressed. But now, can you produce?"

"Mr. Pavolich, sir. I don't do anything less than perfection. We'll have consumers singing, dreaming and buying Nature Plus Formula. You can count on it."

"Good. That's what I wanted to hear."

Up to this point, the ad meeting had been a two-way "tennis match volleying" between Michelle and Bram. It was as if it were a battlefield between the two: Bram offering ad monies in exchange for brilliance in ad concept and insightful marketing; Michelle displaying her creative wares and capturing the prize – the SynCor account.

Conflict resolved, other team players were drawn into the strategic game plan: Adams, obviously relieved that Bram had accepted Michelle and that his agency would continue to have the needed revenue from the SynCor Food account; Chet Hartman, offering Michelle and the agency his knowledge of internal marketing set-up and sales distribution plans; Pam Pritthouse, absorbing every word as if in an intellectual and professional wonderland.

Michelle was thrilled to be part of the exciting world of advertising and to play an important role she had earned through years of hard work, determination, combined with innate talent of human insight and writing ability. She thought, I'm one of the key strategic planners in a marketing program that will affect millions – possibly billions – of people. A thought she found extremely exhilarating.

As was customary, Michelle set up her miniature, tape recorder to record the transactions at the ad meeting. It was a procedure that, at first, put some accounts ill at ease, but in the end, helped to clarify vital points discussed in the ad meeting.

Nature Plus Formula would be available to the public over the counter prior to the Thanksgiving season. A target date of Friday, November 25, the day after Thanksgiving, was established as the advertising campaign kick-off date. The deadline forced the agency to put together a full-blown national advertising campaign in just a little under one month with a multi-media saturation budget of 25 million from November 25-January 2nd, 100 million through the next fiscal year.

Bram had emphasized that he wanted the full impact of Nature Plus to hit the public prior to and during the Christmas holiday season, when many breastfeeding mothers would opt to quit breastfeeding if offered a viable, healthy alternative due to the many social demands of visiting friends, relatives, parents, and holiday get-togethers. Nature Plus would be the deciding factor for new mothers who were undecided about their chosen feeding method and, when the buying and excitement response was the strongest, would present the formula bottle mother a totally new and exciting method in infant feeding.

"Because" Bram Pavolich said with a definite note of triumph in his voice, "there has never been anything like Nature Plus Formula. It will take over the baby formula market like a tsunami."

Michelle had to agree. There certainly had never been anything like Nature Plus Formula products. Nature Plus would have a totally different distribution plan. It would be available in refrigerated pints, quarts, and gallons in the dairy section of the nation's leading supermarkets, as well as in freezer containers in the frozen foods sections. But the most striking differential factor of Nature Pus Formula was the fact that it was the only infant formula ever designed that utilized human breast milk as a component!

Michelle practically fell out of her seat during the marketing meeting when Bram had excitedly said, "Nature Plus has one very distinct advantage over all other traditional infant formulas. Nature Plus is 25% *real breast milk*! And not only does it contain real breast milk, but it will also be specially marketed and packaged to accompany an infant's varying nutritional needs from the first day of birth through one year. You see, when a baby is first born, its mother's breasts are not yet engorged with milk; however, it is advantageous for the baby to suckle at the breast to get the "colostrum," a clear odorless mixture which is nature's own vitamin-packed energizer for the newborn, which is secreted by the mammary glands for several days just before and after childbirth. Babies who do not breast-feed do not get this power-packed nutritional first start in life . . . until now, with SynCor Foods exclusive premiere 'Colostrum Cocktail'."

Bram went on uninterrupted for a full half hour outlining the Nature Plus Formula line. He described the "Baby's First Colostrum Cocktail" as a 3 oz. refrigerated carton of formula with the added nutrient value of real mother's colostrum. It would carry a stiff price tag of $27.95, due to the limited availability of colostrum. But, if Bram's calculations and instincts were spot on, this price would be of no concern to non-breastfeeding mothers who would jump at the chance to give their baby this natural wonder energizer.

Following the Colostrum Cocktail were four distinct formulas specially designed to supply the changing nutritional demands of the one- to three-month-old, four- to six-month-old, seven-to-nine-month-old, and ten months to one year old.

Michelle interrupted Bram's lengthy monologue with the question, "But where do you get the mother's breast milk?"

Bram answered, "Right here, in our own production plant. Come on, I'll take you and Dave on a tour of the facilities. Chet, Pam, that will conclude our meeting. You may join us if you wish."

They were greeted on the second floor with a bold sign that read, "SynCor Foods Production Plant" on the first line, and under that, "Nature Plus Division." As Michelle looked over the facility, it reminded her of a nail salon setting with rows and rows of reclining chairs. Everything was pastel! Pink chairs, violet tables, like a Barbie dream house come to life. Each doner woman had her own area, complete with a comfy recliner, color TV and side table for eating or hobbies. And she couldn't help noticing the array of foods on the table for the mother. Fresh fruits, nuts, and a carafe of fresh water, adorned with orange and lemon slices. It looked like something out of a luxury spa! The temperature was a cozy 79 degrees.

Excitedly, Bram continued, "Look here," as he pointed out a computer chart that was encased in plastic and hanging outside one of the stall doors. "This computer read-out contains all the information about this doner – name, age, medical history, children. See . . . Rosa Hernandez, 23, excellent health, immigrated here last year and couldn't find a job, so we are really helping her. She has had all her immunizations, including the Covid vaccine. She has two children: Victor, 3, and Amanda, 3 months. Victor is in our on-premises SynCor day care. Amanda spends time here with her mother, and then she goes into the nursery when Rosa is 'on duty.' She is well cared for in our baby nursery. Please note, this woman was in jeopardy of being sent back to her native country Guatemala but was able to get her work permit working for us."

Gleefully, he continued, "She has it made here! Free day care, someone taking care of her baby, free meals and up to 16 ounces of beer a day. Did you know, Miss Heywood, that the wet nurses of old used beer as a breast-milk stimulator?"

Not waiting for an answer, he continued in a somewhat manic manner, "Plus she receives a generous salary, a comfy chair to sit in to watch TV, a table where she can do crafts, all in return for three to four quarts of breast milk a day. The breast milk is then frozen in the appropriate quantities needed for both the frozen container line, which has an expiration date good up to one year, and the fresh variety, which has a shelf life of about one week."

Bram knocked on the entrance door of Rosa Hernandez.

"Hello, Mrs. Hernandez. Como estas?"

The young woman looked up from her seated position on the recliner and said, rather nervously, "Bien, Senior Bram." She held a sleeping Amanda in her arms against a rose-pink device that looked like a breast pump encasing both of her breasts. It was attached to a wall apparatus that looked like a refrigerated storing device. It was a cool stainless steel. The scene, although calming at first glance, held an eerie undercurrent to Michelle. *Was this ethical? Was using a human product for others' consumption right?* It was a new concept that rocked some of her values. She told herself she must keep an open mind. *If this could benefit women, who was she to bring her pre-notions to the project. She must remain open minded.*

Michelle thought Mrs. Hernandez looked older than 23. Her hair was matted, unbrushed, and she had a haggard look like she hadn't slept in days. Michelle smiled back with a nod of her head. She felt strange watching this young woman in a human production plant! This production plant whose products she was going to brand and sell to millions of mothers for consumption by millions of infants.

Michelle couldn't help asking Bram this question: "Mrs. Hernandez looks tired. Does the constant breast pumping tire her out? How many hours does she pump?"

Bram answered confidently, "Rather the opposite. Our new pumping technology is painless, delivering not much more than a gentle pressure. Because of the new advances, she can pump as long as she's able for up to six hours, take a one hour stretch and exercise break, and go back for up to 6 more hours, completing her 12-hour shift. She is then free to go home, be with her family and return the next day to relax in our comfortable reclining chairs, where she is fed throughout the day the most nutritious foods with ease of effort, knowing her children are being taken care of in our nursery. It's a once-in-a-lifetime opportunity for these women, who would otherwise not be able to support their families.

Back at his executive offices, Bram seemed very much in control of the situation, in direct contrast to how Michelle was feeling.

"Well, that's my product. Bet you never saw anything like that before! It took my genius to create it, so now my question to you, Miss Heywood, are you able to sell it? Can you market it in a little less than a month to selected markets with the highest percentage of pregnant mothers and new mothers of newborns and infants?"

Any reservations Michelle had about what she had seen selfishly took a back seat as her mind floated over that new Lexus she would be getting for securing this account. "Yes, sir, we can, and we will! I'll have a creative ad multi-media social-media package ready to present at next week's meeting, with our multi-media strategy for your review. Let's say, latter part of next week," Michelle volleyed back to him.

"Excellent, Michelle. Glad to have you aboard. Now, in summary of what has transpired, this is what I need from you . . ."

Michelle made sure she had enough tape left on her recorder to safeguard important details Bram was going to lay out. Yes, it was all secure, and then a loud knock on the door. A man in a white lab coat stepped inside the private office.

"Excuse me, Mr. Pavolich sir."

"Richardson?" Bram's tone of voice indicated that he did not appreciate being interrupted.

"I need to talk to you, sir. Right away. It's of drastic importance."

"Richardson, can't you see I'm busy?" Bram growled with impatience. "Make an appointment with Izzie."

"She's not here right now, sir, and I must speak to you as soon as possible. I have made certain –"

"Richardson, I would like you to meet our marketing people – Dave Adams, President of Ackerly, Adams & Associates; Michelle Heywood, one of the brightest young ladies I've ever met. She is our new account executive, and of course you know Chet and Pam. Everyone, this is Dan Richardson, chief of research."

Michelle noticed that Richardson struggled to smile and nodded his head through an obviously disturbed attitude.

Bram continued, "We'll only be a few moments longer, Dan. However, I have an outside appointment immediately following. Do you have something you can leave with me?"

"Yes, sir. It's all here. It's all here," Richardson said, as he waved a large manila envelope in the air.

"Fine," Bram said with an air of dismissal. He wanted this pencil pusher to leave what had been a fine upbeat vibe of his marketing meeting. "I will take it with me to review. Please leave it in my incoming basket. Good night Richardson," he said, in a decided voice, leaving no doubt as to the finality of the conversation.

The door closed. The executive addressed his marketing group. "Frankly, I don't know if I'm running a business here or a kindergarten. A personnel problem, someone wants a day off, they all feel they can interrupt whatever I'm doing for their concerns. Thirty years in the business and I've seen it all. Well, where were we? In summation, oh yes, this is what I will need from you by no later than next week . . ."

As Michelle watched the lips of him recite off the list of required items from marketing and advertising, she was glad that her hands worked automatically in taking down the necessary data. Plus, she had the added backup of the meeting being taped on her recorder. Because, somehow, she could not hear or see Bram. The desperate look in the eyes of the intruder permeated her consciousness to the point of distraction. Instead of seeing Pavolich, all Michelle could see were the eyes of Dan Richardson: fearful, desperate, horrified.

Isabelle "Izzie" Nick knew her personality trait of meticulousness and attention to small details to be a two-edged sword. For example, it was because of her keen instinct for organization and thoroughness that she had achieved her coveted position as administrative assistant to Mr. Pavolich. The fact that needed papers could always be found at a minute's notice, and appointments carefully maintained were a credit to her name.

But then, there were those times (like right now) that her blessed (or cursed was it?) characteristic only caused her trouble. Like right now, when after she had returned to her desk from the ladies' restroom. There was a slightly ragged oversized manila envelope jutting out from the incoming basket of materials for Mr. Pavolich. Scratched over the envelope was sprawling writing, "Bram Pavolich. Confidential Information. Dan Richardson."

Izzie knew by the words "Confidential Information" that that dictated to her, "Hands Off!" Izzie prided herself on being a real "company girl." Whatever was good for the company, was good for Izzie. She had always respected confidentially marked packages, letters, and correspondence to any of her bosses that she had ever served. Not that there was ever an overabundance of such materials. In fact, this was one of the very few pieces she had ever seen so marked for Mr. Pavolich.

And now, she knew that she should leave well enough alone. But her "meticulousness," if you will, would not permit that ragged unkept piece to reach the desk of her boss. Bram was still in the ad meeting with that new ad girl and Mr. Adams. It was almost 5 p.m. Better to leave well enough alone. But, in a fleeting moment, the envelope was in her hands, being opened. She threw the ragged manila envelope in the trash.

"Mmphh!" she said aloud. How could people be so sloppy! Especially a man like Dan Richardson, head of research, who should be a scientific man, a man who took pride in small details. Not that he was a bad guy. Izzie rather liked him and often chitchatted with him about his two little girls – Mallory, 6, and Taylor, 8. Oh well, Richardson may have been in a hurry when he addressed it.

She opened the materials that were in the envelope to see how many pages there were and how large they were. Richardson had the materials in a much larger envelope than was needed. It was a good thing that she paid attention to such details that saved the company money. The difference in the large size envelope and a smaller size one was substantial. Her thriftiness throughout the years, Izzie thought to herself with pride, really contributed to her feeling of self-worth to her company. A penny here and a penny there added up to lots of money.

Izzie typed on the brand new #10 size envelope, "Bram Pavolich. Confidential Information. Dan Richardson." Now all she had to do was refold the report (was that what it was?) to fit this new neatly typed envelope. She had to re-crease out the folds on the original piece. Five pages. She pressed on the sheets. As she looked down, she noticed that parts of the report were capitalized and underlined. Her keen eyes seemed to be riveted to those phrases

DANGER TO BABIES...ANTIBODIES...REACTIONS CAN BE SEVERE...ONLY A MATTER OF TIME, BUT IT'S A MATTER OF LIFE AND DEATH! MUST STOP NATURE PLUS DISTRIBUTION AND MARKETING IMMEDIATELY!

Her curiosity got the better of her. Fleeting thoughts of company loyalty were bombarded by her overwhelming urge to read this report! She heard shuffling sounds from Bram's office. The meeting was probably over, and they would be out in a few seconds. Izzie folded the five-page report to fit the new envelope she had just typed, whisked the envelope flap to her mouth for a quick seal, and tossed it into Bram's incoming business box.

The door to his executive office opened.

"Great meeting, David. Michelle, glad to have you on our team. Izzie, Michelle will be contacting you in a few days to arrange our next advertising marketing meeting, so please schedule accordingly."

"Yes, sir," Izzie said, somewhat with hesitation. And then she continued, "Good to meet you Miss Heywood." Izzie was surprised at her feelings of jealousy as she saw the powerful young woman, commanding respect from her boss. Michelle was a striking young woman, with reddish-blond hair curled into a ponytail knot on her head. Her size 8 professional outfit looked like something straight out of Neiman Marcus. She probably buys her clothes from the exclusive store on Michigan Avenue. But more than her clothing, Michelle emitted an air of confidence with her erect posture and direct eye contact with the men! *Her* man! Wasn't the success of SynCor's Bram Pavolich a result of her constant care and concern? Behind every great man was a great woman. Izzie didn't feel too great, however. She couldn't help comparing herself to Michelle. Izzie's clothes were purchased from QVC, the daily special. They were perfect for her, comfortable, practical, and able to cover the extra 20 pounds she had put on over the years.

After Michelle and Dave Adams left, Bram scooped up his incoming materials.

"Any messages, Izzie?"

Izzie watched the envelope she had just retyped go into the hands of Bram.

"Izzie?"

"Yes sir?"

"Any messages?"

"Oh, no, there's nothing."

"Good. I'll be in my office for a few minutes. Please don't let anyone disturb me. Have a good evening, Izzie."

Izzie's mind was spinning. What had she just read? My God, it hadn't been meant for her eyes. Yet, she had read it. She realized her pulse was raising and her chest felt tightened. Now calm down, it is not your business. How many times in the past had she been a party to confidential company matters, here at SynCor Foods and at other prior companies? She had learned through the years that a good secretary had to be a good company person. What was good for the company was good for her. How many times had she heard that? She had to keep company matters to herself. How many times had she heard, "Loose lips may sink ships?" Let all the gossipy young gals blow off their mouths and stay in the secretary pools. Yes, a top-notch executive assistant learned to mind her own business, and her bosses would respect her for it, and reward her. Just as Izzie had been rewarded throughout the years. Yet, what had it all meant?

It had read, "<u>STOP NATURE PLUS DISTRIBUTION AND MARKETING IMMEDIATELY</u>." She was sure that Bram would take care of whatever was necessary. But she couldn't rein in her mind. The all-cap underlined words she had read kept floating over her thoughts like a rolling headline on a media ad. "<u>DANGER TO</u>

BABIES … ANTIBODIES …ONLY A MATTER OF TIME, BUT IT'S A MATTER OF LIFE AND DEATH!"

What about the babies who were on the free formula program for Nature Plus right now? What about Sofia Ruiz, whom Izzie had recommended enroll in the free formula program for her twin sons?

And at the thought of it, Izzie froze. Yes, Sofia, the daughter of her best and oldest friend, whose sweet little baby, Anthony, had just died two days ago of Sudden Infant Death (SID). Izzie froze in her seated posture, gazing straight ahead, looking at nothing. Her thoughts were frozen on the prospect of seeing Sofia at baby Anthony's funeral, tomorrow, Halloween, October 31, 10 a.m.

Chapter 3

October 31
Halloween

S ofia Ruiz felt depressed. She wondered why people wore black for funerals. It only served to make her feel more depressed and sadder than she had ever felt in her life. The last three days seemed like a vicious nightmare that just never ended. Her eyes burned with tears as she looked at the gray suit that her husband would wear to their son's funeral. Black and gray.

Oh, God. Why did this happen? She had searched her heart repeatedly for a reason. Why had God taken her son? Antonio's and her son? And what about little Andrew? How could she tell him when he grew up that his brother died while he cried out in warning to his mother? Andrew's piercing cry of what? Murder? His scream would always be permanently imbedded in her mind. Everything that had happened after . . . calling Antonio, telling family and friends, making funeral arrangements . . . could never erase the haunting memory of holding little Anthony in her arms and breathing into his mouth, over and over again, to no avail. And she would never forget her phone call to Antonio. "Our Son is dead! Little baby Anthony is dead!"

"What are you saying? It's not true, it's not true!"

And now, at 10 a.m., she would be going to the funeral of her son. How would she survive? How could she survive? How could she go on with life? But she had to for little Andrew's sake. She was still a mother and wife. And Andrew would need her now more than ever, just as she would need Andrew and Antonio now more than ever. She had decided not to take Andrew to the funeral. Her aunt said she would be happy to watch him. Sofia had at first rejected the idea, because she wanted to hold her only son in her arms always. But she had then decided that it would be a good idea. She wanted to spare Andrew the pain she would be feeling.

"Hey, babe," Antonio said as he wrapped her in his arms. "How are you holding up? Your aunt just arrived. Can I help you get anything ready for Andrew?"

"He's all set. But could you make up a couple of bottles for him? I still must finish my hair. The Nature Plus Formula is in the refrigerator in the back on the left."

"Sure, honey. Anything else I can do to help?" Antonio hugged Sofia close.

"End this nightmare."

"It'll be over soon, honey. It'll be all over very soon."

Mary Tillman somehow knew that she was going to have a girl. Call it wishful thinking or just female intuition, but she knew she had little Amanda Michelle inside her and ready to come out to see her new world any day. And the sooner, the better! She was already seven days past her due date, and with every day she grew more and more anxious. Mary had always wanted to have her family completed before she was thirty, and her life plan was in good order. At 27, she already had two fine sons, Jack, five and Jeremy, three. While her sister Michelle had always been the sister with the "brains" and the ambition to go to college, Mary had always wanted to marry a great guy and have a family.

And Jack, (or J.T. as everyone called him) was great. He was a caring father, loving husband, and, as a prominent dentist in the southwestern suburb of Chicago, a very good provider. And now, Mary thought, if she had her little girl, her dream life would be complete. By being young with her children, Mary would be only 40 when she could resume her career in her chosen profession as a dental assistant or enter some other field. Wouldn't it be something if she went into labor at their Halloween party tonight? She hoped not. She had planned too long for this party to not enjoy herself.

Halloween had always been special to her and Jack. During their five years of diaper changing, bottle feeding, and tending to the needs of the children, they looked forward to their big annual Halloween party where they could let their hair down and act like free-spirited kids themselves. Last year, she and Jack went as Fred and Wilma Flintstone, and this year he was going to be a farmer and she would be a pumpkin! Logical choice!

She went over the details of the party. She would have a lavish charcuterie board filled with a sumptuous variety of cheeses, salami, nuts, grapes, crackers; platters of decadent desserts, and two crock pots full of yummy pulled pork for sandwiches. She had to remind Jack to pick up the beer and ice. She wondered what Michelle was coming as. She had been so busy lately she hadn't had a chance to touch bases with her. Now, where was that phone number for her ad agency? She knew she turned off her cell phone during work. Here it was – Ackerly, Adams & Associates, Michelle Heywood, Account Executive. 988-4295.

"Ackerly, Adams & Associates. Good morning!" said a cheerful voice at the other end of her phone.

"Ms. Heywood, please."

"Thank you. Just a moment please."

"Michelle Heywood speaking."

"Hey, sis! What's up? You're coming to my Halloween party tonight, aren't you?"

"Wouldn't miss it for the world! Your annual Halloween party is my big night of the year."

Mary laughed. "Are you bringing a date? There's going to be quite a few eligible bachelors here if you're interested."

"Sounds tempting. However, I am bringing someone. The Art Director, Hawk Wilder. It's the first time we'll be "officially" going on a date, and I can't think of a better first date than one of your parties. They are infamous, you know."

"That's for sure. Remember that year Stanley McKormick was dancing with that carved pumpkin over his head and then he couldn't get it off when it got stuck!"

"That was a riot. Hey, guess what? I was promoted to senior account executive. I got a new company car, a Lexus, a big raise, bonus and profit sharing!"

"Whoa, now you're a Big Shot. Good for you, sis."

"Well, I gotta run."

"Me too. I still have some shopping to do."

"See you later."

"Chow."

Yes, their parties were infamous for crazy happenings. Mary Tillman was looking forward to a wild and wonderful night.

Michelle was glad to have heard from her sister. She had been so busy lately that she hadn't had the time to keep in touch with her. She was excited about Mary's pregnancy. Soon she would have three children, and she was Michelle's little sister! It was hard to believe. And now, Mary would soon give birth to the little girl that she and Jack dreamed of to complete their family. Her sister also offered her a very good sample of the market she was going to try to reach with her advertising messages for Nature Plus Formula. She knew that Mary wanted to breastfeed, so it wasn't exactly that she would try to "sell" Mary on the formula, but it helped Michelle to focus on a particular person when writing her headlines and copy for a campaign. Michelle knew that the basic premise of good advertising and marketing was to focus all efforts on the demographic you were trying to reach with your advertising messages.

In other words, if you were trying to reach new mothers, you should use advertising copy that they would relate to, feel comfortable with, trust, and would offer solutions to needs they have. That was perhaps the biggest error in ineffective advertising. Some ad firms and marketing people got so hung up with "clever" headlines, striking color schemes or artistic effects, that they lost sight of exactly who they were trying to reach. Good copy, in Michelle's mind, connected directly to the customer, made a convincing impression, and prompted action. So, she thought, what would be this fabulous advertising slogan that could influence "millions" (had she *really* told Bram Pavolich that many!) of women to purchase Nature Plus products?

She had a big job ahead of her and until Michelle focused exactly on what strategy would work, she was always filled with an ever-present need to ponder, think. Okay, she said, what does a new mother want in her newborn? A healthy baby, of course. That is always #1. A happy and beautiful baby. Also, a woman would want other factors in a chosen feeding method for her baby. Convenience, for one. Ease of preparation. Nature Plus had all these benefits. Okay, she thought. What is the Unique Selling Proposition (USP) of Nature Plus products? In other words, what makes Nature Plus stand out from the rest of the multitude of products on the marketplace? Michelle knew that the Unique Selling Proposition was the second important key to good advertising. Most products are very, very similar to their competition. However, it is up to the smart marketer to find, or as the case may be, "invent" a decided difference to a product. In the case of soft drinks, for example, there is very little difference in the taste, per se. But that is why successful commercials feature the "created" benefits of a product . . . people enjoying life, couples in love, nature, beautiful things.

The consumer equates these beautiful things to the product. A product is therefore highly desirable, and, if the conditions are right, purchased.

Of course, then there was the whole area of media – 50% of the ad budget would be on social media, such as Facebook targeted ads, Twitter, Instagram, TikTok, and LinkedIn for the professional market. Michelle was aware of the advantages of paid social media including message frequency and targeting her audience. Again, who was she trying to reach? Women 18 – 35 who were pregnant, planning on getting pregnant, or had infants under one year of age. Traditionally, this demographic was not a big newspaper reader. Michelle felt that the campaign could include some medium-space newspaper ads, simply as a complementary part of the whole campaign. Michelle felt that TV and radio would also be used, backed up with a few awesome 4-color ads in magazines targeted to new mothers: *Parents, New Baby* and *American Baby*. Outreach to pediatricians and ObGyn doctors was of utmost importance, and products must be available in hospital maternity wards as soon as possible.

The Unique Selling Proposition for Nature Plus Baby Formula was simple. It was the fact that real human mother's milk was used in Nature Plus. Of course, this would have many positive benefits like fresh wholesome natural ingredients, natural antibiotics from the breast milk, freshness of product, ease of purchase in the dairy or freezer departments of grocery stores.

But would it have any negatives? Would mothers resent the fact that another mother's milk would be going to their babies, and somehow make them feel inadequate? Michelle remembered reading about marketing studies that pointed out that when cake mixes were "improved" so all a mother would have to do was add water, they were rejected by the consumer. It turned out that the studies found out that making a cake was equated to women filling their family with happiness. When she no longer had to add fresh eggs and milk to the boxed product, the joy of creating something was taken away, and the product was no longer desired. And therefore, not purchased.

Could a similar effect happen when she would try to market real breast milk in a formula product? Michelle had to think of the perfect campaign to eliminate all the negatives and emphasize all the positives of Nature Plus to make it the hottest selling thing since sliced bread. Michelle found herself thinking so hard, she could feel her forehead start to burn.

Bram felt as if he had a sliver in his hand, and he had to get rid of it. Here he had the perfect product that would help him gain the high position in the industry he rightly deserved. With Nature Plus, he had the whole world in the palm of his hand. Adams had finally come through for him with that new girl, Michelle, whom he was very impressed with. She was the needed key in the whole picture who, he felt confident, would come up with the perfect promotion for Nature Plus. And then this Richardson comes along like a jagged sliver to splinter all his efforts. He held the typed sheets from Richardson in his hand and read them again. The man sounded desperate. He had found the report in the typed envelope last night in his "in" box. He had taken it home to read in the privacy of his home. He knew he had to take steps to eliminate the thorn. He had thought about his problem last night, and now this morning. He wondered if Richardson had told anyone else about his "discoveries." He doubted that. From what he knew of Richardson, he was a company man. He had a pretty good hunch that Richardson would have approached him first before sharing his information with anyone else.

But what about his wife? Was he one of these guys that told his wife everything or was he a private man? Bram knew he had to eliminate the sliver from his palm.

What was that song? *He had the whole world in his hands, he had the whole wide world in his hands, he has the little bitty baby in his hands, he's got the whole world in his hands.*

Yes, Richardson would have to be dealt with.

Izzie hadn't slept well last night. Somehow, after she had read, or just glanced at, Richardson's report to Bram Pavolich, she had felt horrible inside and could not shake the feeling. It was as if his words, *Matter of Life or Death*, repeated themselves in her mind over and over. And now, while at Sofia Ruiz's baby's funeral, she felt worse. A death is always a tragedy, but the death of a baby seemed like a cruel twist of fate on so many people.

Why Sofia? Why the daughter of her close friend who looked to her almost as a second mother? What words could she tell her? What could anyone say to a mother who had lost a baby?

It was a wicked day for a funeral. Halloween. She couldn't wait to get back to work, and the day to be over.

Dave Adams thought to himself, Michelle Heywood is the best thing that ever happened to A, A & A. Bram seemed really impressed with her at yesterday's meeting, and she came off like a real superstar. Now if only she could produce. Adams felt confident if there was one thing Michelle was, it was a producer. Bram was ready to spend 25 million in advertising and media between Thanksgiving and Christmas, and that was just fine with him. Based on the 15 percent commission, art and production charges, Adams computed that the SynCor account would bring in about $3,750,000.00 in the next few months. The raise, bonus, Lexus he had given Michelle was a mere pittance compared to the substantial profits the new division of SynCor Foods would bring to his agency.

And it couldn't have come at a better time. The agency had been in bad shape for the last year. They had lost a few accounts, leading to a steady decline in cash flow. As of late, Adams had been "borrowing from Peter to pay Paul." The TV and radio stations, newspapers, and printers were threatening not to extend any more credit to his agency and were beginning to implement cash on order policies.

But now, with over three million in cash revenue coming into the agency between now and the new year, it was going to be a very merry Christmas indeed.

Yes, Nature Plus Products would get Ackerly, Adams & Associates back on its feet again.

Hawk Wilder, Art Director, was a craftsman of visual language. He indeed believed in and had conquered mastery over this language and felt it to be his chief asset. When other people would see an advertisement and comment, "Isn't that a great ad," Hawk would know why. The balance of white space to type. The leading of type. An ad must seduce the readers, connect with them, and motivate them to buy!

For his talents, he was rewarded quite well: he made a substantial salary, he saw direct results from his "talent," making it a career both fulfilling and satisfying.

Now, however, he couldn't focus on much of anything except Michelle Heywood. His mind kept thinking of her easy way with him, how she tossed her hair back with a hearty laugh over a little joke they shared. Her smile brightened him until he found himself smiling along with her. Michelle's visits to the art department were becoming more and more the highlight of his day. He respected her mastery of the written word, a talent when combined with his, resulted in beautiful creations. He was anxious to know how the SynCor Foods ad meeting, held yesterday, went. He dialed her extension, 218. He knew she didn't have her cell phone turned on at work, one of her quirky habits he had noticed.

"Michelle Heywood speaking."

"Hello, Ms. Heywood. Happy Halloween."

"Hawk? How's it going? I was just planning on coming over. Do you have some time to discuss the SynCor account? We've got a lot of work to do, and you won't believe our product! Baby formula made with real mother's breast milk!"

"You're kidding!"

"No, full blown campaign – social media, TV, ads, radio, the whole nine yards. 25 million beginning the Friday after Thanksgiving through Christmas."

"Wow. 25 mil? Not bad. Come on over. I've got time now."

"I'll be right over."

Hawk could feel that thrill of excitement that he experienced whenever he was challenged with a new project. It was an excitement that was enriched by the prospect of working and being with Michelle.

Dentist Jack (J.T.) Tillman had his last appointment at 3:30 p.m., so it worked out that he could be home early to help his wife with the party. Mary had things organized well, so now he would do the finishing touches on his Halloween decorations. J.T. had a storage unit devoted to Halloween animated caricatures, including demons, goblins, ghosts, Freddy Krueger, and dozens that he had collected throughout the years. For weeks, their home had looked like a Carnival House of Horrors. His signature piece was a Zombie walking dead character that he had improved on over the years. The guests looked forward to seeing it yearly as they entered the Tillman family home, and he knew this year's addition of sound effects and motion were fabulous.

"Mary, honey, come check out my masterpiece," J.T. called out as he demonstrated the slashing motion of a very realistic looking knife chopping down, combined with new horrific grimaces and lights on the zombie's face.

"Jack, it's the best. I love it."

"What do you need my help with? I'm your loyal servant," he joked.

"Nothing, really. Everything's well set, and Ashley Richardson is coming over soon to help me with the final food prep, so I'm good. You just enjoy your monsters." She laughed in that good-natured way that was music to his ears.

"Ashley Richardson? Isn't Dan coming?"

"Oh, sure. He'll be here. He's going to come over about nine."

"Good. I haven't seen Dan for a long time. In fact, not since his last six-month checkup."

And now, he "played" with his new zombie character, slashing potential victims with a piercing knife.

Bram Pavolich had perfected his plan for tonight. He knew that in matters with such great consequences like this – a murder – that nothing could be 100%. Something could always go wrong. But he had gone over his plan to murder Richardson over and over, and had finally decided that it was perfect, or as humanly perfect as possible. He was ready to carry it out because he had to. Nature Plus products were that important. Nobody could stop them. Step one. Call Richardson, Ext. 472.

"Dan Richardson, research."

"Hi, Dan. It's Bram. I know it's late in the day, I can't believe it's almost five, but I must talk to you in person about the report you gave me yesterday. Naturally, I'm very concerned about your findings. Of course, I reach the same conclusions you do. We must terminate the Nature Plus product line." Bram heard a long sigh on the other end of the line.

"I'm relieved that you feel that way, sir. Frankly, I respect you very much because to discontinue the line at this late stage will be a very costly venture; however, who can put a price on human lives? Particularly helpless infants."

"Richardson, I would prefer it if you would not mention anything like this over the phone. You never know who could overhear you. There's no need to cause unnecessary rumors, panic. Have you told anyone else about your findings, Dan?"

"No. In all due respect, I felt I should speak to you first."

"Smart man. Have you told anyone? I mean *anyone*. Your wife, perhaps? A relative? Close friend?"

Richardson responded, "No, no one. That's not something you just tell anyone you know. And my wife and I had decided a while back to keep our work lives out of our home lives."

"Good. Well, Dan, I have a dinner engagement tonight; however, I think we should talk this over. Is there somewhere we can meet in total privacy? Perhaps your home, tonight, say about 7 p.m.?

"In fact, that would work out perfectly. My wife is helping a friend set up a Halloween party that we're going to tonight. She's probably already left for the night, and the girls are at a slumber party. I was just going to go home, have a few beers, and then leave for the party about 8 p.m. We'll have a whole hour in total privacy."

"Fine. What's your address, Dan?"

"7585 Oak Park. It's about a half hour drive after rush hour."

"Great. Seven o'clock tonight, then. And Dan, I have just one request of you. You and I know about our meeting tonight. No one else should know. Not even your wife, if she should call you. I have my reasons."

"No problem."

Bram looked straight ahead thoughtfully. Yes, it should work. Step one accomplished with honors.

Richardson had made it unbelievably easy.

Michelle felt inspired about the Nature Plus campaign. Talking to Hawk about the new project seemed to crystallize in her mind the direction the campaign should take. She felt as if she was on the brink of coming up with the perfect campaign slogan for Nature Plus. Michelle was aware of the creative process: hard, fast, and determined conscious thinking on a topic, followed by a resting period. This allowed the subconscious mind to do most of the creative work by combining and re-combining all the aspects of the subject, until, when you least expected it, the subconscious mind would present the conscience mind with a beautiful slogan, or idea, like a gift on a silver platter, and Eureka! One of the highest feelings a person could achieve. Right now, Michelle could feel her brain "cooking" the ingredients and was excited about the anticipated outcome.

She was also excited about Hawk Wilder going to her sister's Halloween party with her as her date. It would be the first time she and Hawk had ever been together on a personal level. Oh, a few drinks after work with other people a couple of times. But this was their first official "date." Well, she thought, as she looked at the clock on her desk. It was 5 p.m. and time to end the "professional" Michelle and enter the personal. As Michelle walked through the door of the ad agency, she said, aloud, to no one in particular, "It's time to party!"

Bram's mind worked methodically. First, he would walk to the costume shop a few blocks from Syncor headquarters. It was a long walk, but he was in fine shape. That would take about 30 minutes. He'd take two briefcases: one for the stolen Halloween costume, one for his copy of Richardson's report. After he got the costume, he'd walk a little further to the little greasy spoon called The Bee Hive, call a cab, and then go into the men's room and put on his costume. In the meantime, he'd discard the extra briefcase in the alleyway between the two buildings. He'd tell the cabbie Richardson's address, tell him he was going to a Halloween party, give him a big tip. The dumb cabbie would be happy. But what about the murder weapon? A knife? No, too messy. Something heavy to knock Richardson out. Maybe a sprinkler showerhead. Or a brass door knocker. Or a hammer. Yes, perfect, a hammer! And gloves – he'd have to make sure his costume had gloves. He'd get the murder weapon from a common drugstore. Innocent enough purchase. He'd pay in cash. He would make sure it was a smaller mom and pop store without indoor security cameras. Sure, his plan had a few flaws, but basically the plan would work. The flaws would be ironed out. What if Richardson had a friend there? What about the bloody Halloween costume? How would he get home? Yes, there were still certain aspects to work out. But now it was time to go to the corner drugstore for the relatively innocent purchase of a hammer. He'd then clear his head to perfect his plan, after a trip to Mandy's Magic House or as he called it, Mandy's Cat House. Yes, a massage by that blonde with the huge tits, followed by a rapid fuck would clear his mind to clarify the perfect plan for the elimination of Richardson.

Sometimes Mandy wondered why she ever got in this business in the first place. Sure, she had worked her way up the ranks from being a common street prostitute to managing a first-class operation. The money she made was generous enough – beat working in a laundromat – and now she could be selective about who she "serviced" and who she didn't. But there were times, like tonight, that the whole thing depressed her. Here it was 6:30 on Halloween, and it seemed the men got crazier than usual. Several of her girls had complained of "kinkier" requests tonight, and frankly, she couldn't wait to close at 1 a.m.

Bram Pavolich, one of the regulars, seemed like he was in a hurry. "Mandy, how's it going?" he said.

"Usual, but kinkier tonight. Halloween fever, I guess," she responded.

Bram mumbled, "Who's on tonight?"

Mandy responded, "Antoinette, Marie, Janice will be done soon."

"Marie, the blond with the big –"

"Yes, she's the one you like, Bram."

Bram fumbled out some bills.

"Yes, Marie. She'll do just fine. Just the inspiration I need tonight."

"Inspiration?"

"I'll take Marie. But make it fast. I have to be out of here before seven."

Hawk Wilder would be at Michelle's apartment any minute to pick her up for her sister's Halloween party. Michelle had dressed as a ballerina with a long flowing dress with full skirt and fitted bodice. She inspected herself in the mirror. With hair atop her head, she felt a little like Cinderella going to the grand ball. But was Hawk her Prince Charming? Tonight would be the first time they would ever cross from the professional to the personal. Was it a mistake? Would it ruin their working relationship? Michelle felt her mind drifting, imagining. If two people could create such beautiful ad masterpieces, imagine what they could do with life?

Michelle looked at her watch – 7:30 p.m. She couldn't wait for Hawk to arrive and see her costume. It would be a wonderful night. A night she would never forget.

Bram Pavolich felt refreshed. Marie had revitalized his mind as well as his masculine vitality. He relished his two-mile walk to the costume shop, walking with long strides, breathing deeply. He swung two briefcases in perfect rhythm to his stride. One contained Richardson's report and a large solid steel hammer he had purchased at that little hardware store before going to Mandy's. The other briefcase was empty, waiting to be filled with a disguise for murder.

Dan Richardson appreciated the silence in his home. It was a definite change. Between the two girls and Ashley, his home was usually a hub of activity. But tonight, he reflected, as he relaxed in his easy chair with a beer, Ashley was at Mary Tillman's house, helping with party arrangements, and the girls were at a Halloween slumber party. He was relieved that Bram had seen his point of view concerning Nature Plus products. Frankly, Richardson hadn't known what to expect. He really didn't know Bram "the man." He knew he was like any successful owner of a national company . . . smart, ambitious, aggressive. But when a product could hurt the public who bought it; in this case, kill innocent babies, well, that was murder. And after today's telephone call from Bram, Richardson was damn glad he was no murderer.

"I know this is late – I mean, Halloween night at 7:30 p.m. – but do you have any costumes in my size? I guess I'd take an extra-large. I'm not fussy. Any costume will do," Bram spilled the words out.

The salesgirl looked about 16 years old. Bram figured she was a high school student just helping for Halloween.

"Well, all our larger sizes are back here."

The salesgirl led Bram to the Southwest corner of the shop.

"Here's our fitting room."

"I won't need that."

Bram was getting nervous. How could he shake the girl so he could steal the costume? He pulled out a cigarette. He lit it with the matches he had picked up at Mandy's cat house. He waved the hand with the matches.

"Looks like the owner is looking for you," he gestured.

"Sir, I'm afraid you can't smoke in here," the girl said.

"Sorry," Bram said, while crushing the cigarette out on the concrete floor.

"I'll be fine here. I'll need to browse for a while," he said, dismissing the young salesgirl.

Bram sighed in relief when the girl finally left his side. He spotted a Frankenstein costume with a mask! Perfect. The costume would allow him to blend in, but he needed a mask to conceal his identity. Carefully, he placed the empty briefcase between his legs and opened it with one hand, while pretending to inspect the costume. He glanced around. The owner was ringing up a sale at the register. The girl was flirting with a young guy.

Good, he thought, opportunity. Life was opportunity. He slipped the costume off the hanger and stuffed it in the briefcase. Gloves! What about gloves! He saw white gloves that went with a butler's outfit pinned to the sleeves of a black tail jacket. He carefully unpinned them and tossed them onto the Frankenstein costume. He snapped the briefcase shut. The girl was still talking to the guy as Bram walked out of the doors of the costume shop with step two of his murder plan successfully implemented.

Taxi driver Pete Wrangler felt all the nuts came out on Halloween. He was only on his taxi shift since 3 p.m., and already he had picked up a man and his secretary who just wanted him to drive around the city and make out, a guy dressed up as a dame, and now, this guy dressed up like Frankenstein – mask and all! He could barely hear the address of the destination. The only way he was sure it was correct was when he repeated it to the guy, and the amazingly realistic mask nodded up and down. What the hell. It was a long easy ride: $45 tab, and the guy had already pre-paid with a $100 bill. Maybe he would forget the difference. Damned if Pete Wrangler would remind him. Yep. It was going to be a long night.

Richardson was becoming impatient. Here it was 8 p.m. and no sign of Bram Pavolich. He had told his wife he would be at the Tillman family Halloween party by nine. After a hellish week, he was looking forward to it. It was a 30-minute drive. What would Bram say to him? Would he pull the Nature Plus line and sacrifice the projected 45 million annual profits because of his research discovery?

Still, how could Bram sell formula that would inevitably kill 2% of the babies that would use it? And the causes of death would be totally impossible to link to Nature Plus. They would be natural causes due to a breakdown of the baby's own antibiotic system.

Some babies would die of pneumonia. Some would die silently in their cribs, seemingly victims of Sudden Infant Death (SID). Some would die of leukemia. Only through Richardson's comprehensive investigation and research did he discover the one flaw in Nature Plus Formula. Because the formula was 25% natural breast milk, it contained mothers' natural antibodies. In approximately 98% of the babies, these additional antibodies would make them super healthy, a new breed of uncommonly strong infants who would be resistant to colds, and other illnesses. In about 1% - 3% of the babies; however, their own antibiotic systems would reject the additional ones, react to them as a cancer, and work over their capacity to try to repel them from their little bodies.

Eventually – sometimes within six weeks, sometimes up to three months – the baby's own antibiotic system would completely break down and leave the baby defenseless to common germs. Eventually the baby would die. It was incredibly fortunate that Richardson had discovered this. He had thought intently on how to handle his findings. He analyzed his options: contact the federal government agencies, contact the media, or finally, the option he had selected, approach Bram Pavolich. He felt it was the honorable thing to do, and he was decidedly grateful Bram had agreed with his conclusion – Nature Plus Products must be stopped.

A cab pulled up to his house. Richardson checked his watch. 8:04 p.m. Could it be Bram? A figure dressed in a – what? – Frankenstein Halloween costume with mask emerged. Was it Bram? The cab drove off, and "Frankenstein" walked to his door. The doorbell rang.

"Yes? Can I help you?" Richardson asked.

The mask was lifted off by white gloves. It was Bram Pavolich.

"It's me, Dan. I'm going to a Halloween party after our meeting. I hope you don't mind?"

Dan laughed. "Of course not, Bram. In fact, I have a Dracula costume waiting for me. I'm also going to a party; I think I told you? In fact, I should leave shortly. Come in, come in."

Bram sat on the living room couch. He looked at Richardson intently. He said, "Before we begin, I want to express to you my sincere gratitude for your superb scientific research. I'm an honest man, Dan. A man must live with himself. You know what I mean? No amount of company profits is worth harming innocent babies."

"I'm totally relieved you feel that way, Bram."

"Have you told anyone of your findings, Dan? Co-worker? Friend? Family?"

"No, not a soul. I've worked for SynCor Foods for over 10 years, and I felt I owed you that out of respect."

"I appreciate that. These things must be dealt with on a confidential basis. A rumor begins, riot, the press, you understand what I mean."

"Indeed."

Bram opened his briefcase facing himself.

"I don't seem to have my copy of the report. Do you happen to have yours, Dan?"

Dan Richardson opened a large portfolio.

"In fact, I do. I brought the case studies, also, for your review."

As Richardson turned, papers in his hand, he saw Bram facing him. He had a strange look on his face. A look resembling, what? A trapped animal.

Suddenly, with startling swiftness, he saw Bram's arm swing back and up. His gloved hand was holding a large object, shining menacingly. A hammer!

As his mouth gaped open, poised to scream out, Bram's free gloved hand sealed it shut. In a fleeting moment before he felt the blow on his head, Richardson realized the terrifying truth.

His face froze in blinding horror, stifled in crying out for the babies of the world. Stifled in crying out murder.

Ashley Richardson felt a wave of panic. Call it female intuition, or whatever, she felt an incredible feeling of danger. She told herself, don't be silly. Everything is fine. The girls were at a Halloween slumber party. Dan was probably putting on his Dracula costume and getting ready to leave for the party. People had already started to arrive. She had helped Mary with all the final preparations. Still, a call to his cell wouldn't be unreasonable, just to ease her mind and erase this sudden feeling of panic. It rang. She counted the number of times, four, five, six. Then, Dan's voice mail message. She didn't bother to leave a message. He might be walking up right now. He would arrive soon. Yes, Dan would be here before 9 p.m. to join her at the Tillman's annual Halloween party.

Isabelle Nick awoke with a start. For a few moments, she was totally disoriented. *What had happened?* A nightmare. She had fallen asleep while watching TV and had been startled into wakefulness. She wiped her eyes. What an awful dream! She couldn't remember much, but she remembered it scared her. She was at the funeral of Sofia Ruiz's twin, and as she was looking at the living twin, baby Andrew, he shrunk up in front of her eyes and dissolved into an unsightly skeleton.

She looked at her watch. 8:20 p.m. *Halloween, hmph. Too many goblins and Halloween gook.* What an awful day *for* Sofia Ruiz to bury her son. A tragedy that somehow her restless mind would not let her forget.

"Hawk, that's it! The Nature Plus ad campaign will be amazing," Michelle said, as they walked up the sidewalk to her sister's house.

"They don't call you the creative whiz kid for nothing," art director Hawk Wilder responded. "I can see it now. Ten second commercials featuring a real happy baby and the announcer copy, 'Why is this baby happy? She has the advantage of real mother's milk with the convenience of a formula. A new era in baby formula is on the horizon: Nature Plus, our name says it all.'"

"We'll do a whole series of them. Why is this baby healthy? Why is this baby so alert? We'll blast the market with teasing curiosity for a week, and then climax it with full 60-second spots featuring all the advantages Nature Plus has over traditional formulas."

"It has all the elements of a successful marketing program. A product answering a need in the market," Hawk said.

"And with our combined talents, the campaign will be world class."

"You look world class tonight, Miss ballerina," Hawk said. "But 'nuf of shop talk. Let's party."

It was almost 10 p.m. and Dan Richardson had not yet arrived at the Tillman's Halloween party. Ashley Richardson was restless. Where was Dan? It wasn't like him to be late. She had tried his cell phone several times, but it had always gone to his voice message. That wasn't too surprising. Sometimes Dan turned his phone on silent at work and forgot to turn it back on. Ashley had an eerie feeling something was wrong. After 20 years of marriage, she felt things about Dan on mere gut instinct. And now, she was worried. Was he in an accident? Should she call the hospitals? Emergency?

Maybe he had fallen in the shower or something and was unconscious. She decided to call Maureen Sanders, the one neighbor whom she trusted with a spare house key. She would call Maureen right now and ask her to go to their home and see if anything was wrong.

Maureen Sanders had just washed her hair and was about to curl up in her bed to read the latest issue of *Family Circle* magazine when

Ashley Richardson had called. She had sounded nervous. Not at all like her usual cheerful self.

She carefully jotted down the phone number where she could contact Ashley. She stuffed her feet in her worn fuzzy slippers, wrapped herself in a long, quilted robe, and walked across her damp front yard to the Richardson's home. She knocked and heard no response. Poised with the key to open the door, she found it unlocked. As she stepped in the Richardson's foyer, she saw a body lying on the carpet in the living room.

Instinctively, she ran to the body which she immediately recognized as Dan Richardson. His head was streaked with blood, mottled through his dark hair. His eyes looked at her, frozen in a look of terror, reflecting light.

Suddenly, aware of her own immediate danger, Maureen screamed and ran out the open door, into the dark.

In the ten years that detective Marcus Harris had been assigned to homicide, he had found that Halloween brought out the mysterious and dark underbelly of society. This year was no exception. The phone call from Maureen Sanders that he just received was the fourth murder for the night, not to mention six reported rapes and countless muggings. The location of the murder was just 10 minutes from the station in a nice suburban area, not known for crime. Well, in a few minutes, he'd be an integral link in another Halloween horror of the worst mode. Murder.

Michelle had never experienced anything like tonight in her life. Amid the laughter of her sister's annual Halloween party came a piercing scream from a woman she later learned to be Ashley Richardson. Silence prevailed, then huddles of people questioning. The air seemed to float in limbo. When her sister had asked if someone could drive Ashley Richardson to her home, it was Hawk who had volunteered.

It was in the car on the way to the Richardson's home that Michelle realized that she had a link to this bizarre situation. The husband of Ashley Richardson, whom they had just found murdered in his home, was the same man Michelle had seen yesterday. The research man from SynCor who had interrupted their marketing meeting with what he had called an "urgent matter." The same man whose look of urgency had haunted her. And now he was dead.

Bram Pavolich was quietly pleased with himself. It had gone well. Better than he had imagined. The several blows of the solid steel hammer had proved to be fatal, without as much as a whimper from Richardson. Then, he had quickly gathered the materials from Richardson's portfolio into his briefcase. The telephone ringing had temporarily startled him, especially with its seven rings. But then he had regained his composure. Nature Plus products had been protected, as he knew it had to be. Nature Plus had to regain his position in the industry, at all and any costs.

Chapter 4

November 1

Michelle had heard about La Leche League International groups before but had never experienced them firsthand. Her sister, Mary, was ready to have her third baby any day now and was determined to make her third baby special by breastfeeding. It was Mary who had asked Michelle to join her for this Saturday afternoon meeting of the group. Michelle had not totally recovered from her eerie experience last night when she and Hawk had driven Mrs. Richardson home to the scene of her dead husband. And the odd discovery that this dead man, staring up at the ceiling, was the same man she had just met – even for a moment – at SynCor's marketing meeting was even more uncanny. She had learned from her sister that the Richardsons and the Tillmans had been friends for years. Dan Richardson's family had gone to Jack's dental practice for years. Michelle was in awe at how life intermingled people into each other's lives, mysteriously, and with, what? Perhaps purpose.

Michelle felt an undeniable feeling that she was "meant" to have met Dan Richardson – even briefly – before his tragic death. But why? Now, here at the La Leche League meeting, Michelle was reminded of the breastfeeding mothers at the Nature Plus production plant. She couldn't deny that something about the way they were positioned in cubicles producing milk for Bram's company gave her the creeps. It was almost like the Stepford Wives. Everything looked warm and cozy on the outside, but underneath, it seemed a façade. *Was it ethical taking milk from mothers for products to the public?* Was Michelle dismissing the horror of a new mom in a pumping device for ***12 hours at a time?*** Was she only focused on the success of Nature Plus and her own success in the process – complete with new company car, a gorgeous Lexus? *Who was she turning into?*

Now, she focused on the women in the La Leche meeting. In a large circle in the group leader's living room, about 20 women, most with infants, some pregnant, were chit-chatting amiably. At least seven of the women had babies nestled to their breasts, shielded by the upper fabrics of their blouses, sweaters or a light blanket. Mary was one of about six pregnant women seeking advice and guidance about this new womanly experience they would be engaging in.

Michelle, absent of both infant and pregnancy, felt like an observer looking in. The group leader, the woman at whose home the informal meeting was being held, called for everyone's attention.

She said, "Welcome to our La Leche League monthly meeting. For those of you who may be newcomers, I'd like to explain, briefly, the purpose and function of La Leche League. Our national association was founded by a group of mothers whose goal was to share and help in the continuation of one of the best experiences available to a woman – the art of breastfeeding. It has been scientifically proven that breastfeeding is beneficial to both the baby and to the mother. In a society that does not always accommodate the breastfeeding mother, we find it beneficial to share experiences, both good and bad, about this experience we all share.

"Briefly, breastfeeding is the most natural way to nourish one's child. It was created by nature to benefit both baby and mother. Baby benefits by the close bonding with mother, and by receiving the highest nutritional food available, which contains mother's own antibiotics. Scientific research has proven that breast-fed babies are healthier, have fewer allergies, and are less fussy. They also develop a close secure bonding to their mother.

"Benefits to the mother are many. The uterus contracts faster and gets into pre-pregnancy shape faster when the mother breastfeeds. There is no middle-of-the-night bottle to warm. A breastfeeding mother simply holds her child close to her, while nature has heated her milk to the exact temperature the baby needs. A special hormone is also released while breastfeeding that serves as a mild tranquilizer for the mom, which enables her to relax and feel at one with her child.

"There are some demands that a new breastfeeding mother must cope with, like, how do I breast-feed when other people are present? How can my husband share in the nurturing process of my baby? How can the breastfeeding mother leave her baby for personal free time? These special situations breastfeeding mothers must face are one of the reasons we meet as a group. We share personal experiences and successes with breastfeeding to help others. So, enough of my lecturing, this is a meeting for all of us to contribute to. So, may we start to my left? Please introduce yourself and your infant, if appropriate, and please share with the others, why you are here, what you like about breastfeeding and what you don't like about breastfeeding, and hopefully, how you coped with your dislikes. Would you like to begin?"

Michelle turned to the woman to her left. She was a dark-haired woman, in her mid-twenties, who was presently breastfeeding an infant, tucked under a red angora sweater.

"My name is Celeste Roman, and this is Sarah, who is almost six months old. I'm here because I enjoy talking with adults who are sharing similar experiences. I need the escape and adult companionship. Prior to having Sarah, I worked in a professional position full time. The best thing I like about breastfeeding is that it has helped me to substitute a purpose to my life. I feel I'm really contributing to my baby's life when I feed her. I know I'm doing the best possible thing for her that I can. The worst thing about breastfeeding is that it is quite demanding, and I have little personal time for myself. But I feel this is a temporary time of my life, and worth the investment in my baby. I'm glad to be here."

The circular group smiled at her, some clapped, and then a brief silence.

"Next," the lecturer said in a soft voice. Eyes fell upon Michelle. She felt suddenly awkward.

She said, "I'm a guest of my sister seated to my right, who is about to have her third baby any day. It will be her first experience at breastfeeding, but I'll let her explain about that. I'm not married, and not pregnant, but the matter of breastfeeding is still of great importance to me, both as a woman and a professional.

"You see, I'm working on an advertising campaign for a new line of baby formula that contains real breast milk, Nature Plus Formula, which will be on the market in just a month. The more I learn about your feelings and experiences, the more I will be able to tailor my advertisements to your needs."

The group leader addressed Michelle directly.

"But didn't you know, a breastfeeding mother never supplements with formula feedings."

Michelle answered, "I'm responsible to change that, if I'm to accomplish my professional goals. But, please, let me hear more about why you all feel breastfeeding is the only way to go. My mind is not 'etched in stone.'" Michelle turned to her sister, as to transfer the discussion on.

Mary said, "You see, she, my older sister, was always the brains of the family. I'm the one with two boys and my little daughter is on the way."

Mary's candidness cracked the stillness that had prevailed during Michelle's introduction. Mary chattered amiably to the group as Michelle observed the women in the informal circle. The "target market," if you please, that she had promised Bram Pavolich a 50% share turnover to Nature Plus.

Did she even know what she was talking about? These women wouldn't use a formula supplement. Or would they? Michelle decided to listen carefully She could learn much. It was a beautiful situation for first-hand marketing research. The research she desperately needed to make the Nature Plus campaign a huge success and pave her road to professional achievement.

Chapter 5

November 2

Michelle was a spiritual person. She often felt God's presence as an active influence in her life, leading and directing her actions. It was not a pious, fearful relationship, rather just a quiet, inner acknowledgment that came from outside her own self. She had first experienced God back when she was in fourth grade and she was writing in her diary. When, quite without notice, her mind became blank and she received an unspoken message which clearly stated, "You will be a writer." Michelle, even at her young age, was quite taken with this extraordinary experience, and somehow, ever since that time, her energies seemed channeled to accomplish that feat.

And now, as Michelle reflected in the peaceful solitude of her neighborhood church on Sunday morning, she was filled with a sense of pride and accomplishment that she was, indeed, making a living on her writing ability. But she was still haunted by an eerie foreboding that God's presence was more prominent in the last few days. She felt a strong impression of God observing her, and it was both comforting and unsettling to her. So much had happened to her in just the past few days. Events that had heightened her feelings of everyday life.

She said aloud, softly, "I don't know what you have in store for me, God, but please don't leave me."

A quiet sense of peace settled over Michelle.

Chapter 6

November 3

B ram Pavolich had not anticipated the press' reaction to Richardson's murder. Who would have thought that upon his arrival to his company this morning that he would be bombarded by newspaper reporters, photographers, and yes, even homicide officials, asking SynCor employees, and even he, President of the company, if there would be anyone who would have a motive to kill Richardson? One loud-mouthed pushy dame had gone as far as to shove a TV microphone in front of his face, posing him with the question, "Dan Richardson, who was brutally murdered on Halloween night, was the top researcher on your new product line, Nature Plus Formula, which we have heard through the grapevine is 25% real breast-milk, and scheduled to be available to the public in a few weeks. Mr. Pavolich, as President of SynCor, what, if any is the connection between your company and Dan Richardson's untimely death?"

Bram was startled by this unforeseen intrusion on himself and had simply stammered, "No. No. No connection whatsoever. No comment."

He had worked up quite a level of perspiration when he had placed the call to his ad agency for Michelle Heywood. When his new "ad whiz kid" answered her line in a businesslike manner, "Michelle Heywood speaking," he had barked: "Get to my firm fast. And take any PR professionals with you. The press is determined to cause trouble for Nature Plus."

Izzie was quite exhilarated by the flurry of activity that surrounded her. TV reporters, newspaper writers, even a reporter from the renown national news network CNN was there. Many had requested to speak personally to Bram Pavolich. Some had been apprehended by security while snooping around in the research labs. *What link would Richardson's murder have with SynCor Foods?* Apparently, when the major outlets read the local newspaper's story on Richardson's death and his link to SynCor and a revolutionary new line of baby formula, it struck as gold for a juicy slant on a rather mundane murder. Izzie thought they were foolish. Richardson's murder had nothing to do with SynCor Foods. Or did it? Didn't Dan Richardson give Bram a report just the day before his murder, which said that Nature Plus products must be stopped. Didn't Izzie see the words, MATTER OF LIFE AND DEATH when she had opened the confidential report to retype the envelope? But they, the media reporters, didn't know anything about the report. The only people who had known about the report were Richardson, Bram, and herself (unknown to Bram.) She didn't dare leak a word about the report to anyone – particularly the nosy media people. But she couldn't help wondering if it *had* meant anything. Was there any connection between the two? Maybe if she had the chance, she'd mention it to Michelle Heywood, that new ad agency girl. But could she trust her? She was on her way here because she had overheard Bram barking at her to get here as soon as possible.

No, she better not even mention it to Michelle. You can't always trust women in business. It could get back to Bram, and he might question her company loyalty. No, it was best to keep these things to herself, Izzie decided, as she smoothed the creases from her new beige silk suit from Neiman Marcus. She smiled to herself. Yes, she would look crisply professional and important on her TV screen during tonight's evening news.

Danny Wingfield, crime beat reporter for the Chicago Sun Reporter, the newest competitive morning daily that was achieving remarkable success in the traditional two-daily newspaper Chicago market, knew his chief attribute in being a writer of recognizable talent, was his ability to sense a story. Sure, a good university like the one he had attended, Loyola University Chicago, could teach you the elements of journalism – how to interview, how to make news judgments, how to write. But unless a news reporter had an innate sense for understanding people, being cognizant of patterns in human behavior, and reading between the lines, they would never reach the tops in their field.

And, today, judging the scene at SynCor Foods, Danny knew he was on the tip of a monumental story. How? First, it was the President of SynCor, Bram Pavolich himself of Grandma's Butter Cookies and Perky Plus Popcorn, both household names. Just by observing him, Danny could sense that he was a man who enjoyed power. He had researched SynCor Foods in the newspaper's "morgue," as it was called, as soon as he had read of Richardson's death in the local newspaper. He learned that SynCor was one of the foremost outstanding food production companies through the '50s and '60s into the present due to the phenomenal success of Perky Plus Popcorn and Grandma's Butter Cookies.

But, since the advent of the new health-conscious consumer, SynCor's profits and stock price had consistently slipped. Current financial reports indicated that most reserves had been tapped and the company was soon to report severe losses. Danny had found a few isolated news stories that indicated that the company was preparing to launch a major new product line, Nature Plus infant formula that contained human breast milk – unheard of in the billion-dollar industry!

Research on the innovative, and very important, new product line had been ongoing for the past 11 years. All indications were that this product was to hit the market just after Thanksgiving, in just a few weeks.

Danny had phoned Ashley Richardson early this morning and had learned that her husband had prepared a report that he gave to Bram the day before he was murdered. She knew nothing of its contents, however. She did say that he had been anxious to give him the report.

And now, Danny felt in his journalistic instinct that it was no mere coincidence that the man who headed up the research had just been murdered.

After the last newspaper reporter left, Michelle had experienced a deep sense of relief. She felt proud of herself and the way she had handled the reporters' questions.

"No, there is no connection between Mr. Richardson's death and our new product line, Nature Plus."

She must have repeated that statement a hundred times. However, as the day grew on, her mind felt doubtful at the truth of her statement. When a reporter named Danny Wingfield asked, "Does the report on Nature Plus research Mr. Richardson gave to Mr. Pavolich the day before his murder have any bearing on his death?" Michelle had paused, being caught off guard. She had faced Bram and whispered, "What report is he referring to?" Bram had responded, "I know nothing of any report."

Michelle had thought of when Dan Richardson had interrupted their initial ad meeting saying he had a matter of urgent importance to discuss with Bram. He had a large manila envelope in his hand. Was that the report this reporter was referring to? How had he known of it?

Michelle had noticed a surprised look on Isabelle Nick's face. She made a mental note to herself: talk in private to Izzie Nick about this look that revealed that she knew something. She remembered an old cliché, "Behind every successful man is a good woman."

She wondered if Isabelle Nick was the woman behind the success story of Bram Pavolich.

Bram Pavolich was haunted by the expression of Isabelle Nick after that short nosy reporter from the Sun Reporter, Danny Wingfield, had asked Michelle Heywood a question about Richardson's research report. How had he learned of it? Who else knew of that research report? His wife? A co-worker? Surely Izzie had never mentioned anything to the reporter. Or had she? He pressed his inner-office hot line number to Izzie.

"Yes, Sir?" Izzie still liked her old-fashioned manners when it came to addressing her boss as "sir."

"Izzie, I'd like to see you for a few moments."

"Yes, sir. I'll be right in."

When Izzie sat across from Bram's massive desk, he observed her as being very tiny, totally lacking power. A surge of power flowed through Bram.

"Izzie, I'd like you to attend the funeral of Dan Richardson tomorrow to represent the company. Also, send a large floral arrangement," Bram began.

"I'd be pleased to, Mr. Pavolich. There's something I'd like to ask you, sir. Did you ever read the research report that Dan Richardson gave you Thursday night?"

"What report?"

"Why, you should have received it Friday morning at the latest."

"I never saw the likes of any report."

"Why, I left it in your in-box Thursday evening."

"Perhaps Richardson picked it back up before I got it. I heard he was under a lot of marital strain lately and had been acting irrationally."

"That's odd. He seemed like it was very important. Well, perhaps he changed his mind."

"Exactly. By the way, Izzie. I'm going to raise your salary $100 a week. I think it's long overdue, and you deserve it."

"How very generous of you, Mr. Pavolich. I appreciate your confidence in me."

"Izzie, I respect and want to reward you on the basis that you are a company girl. Loyal. That's what makes a good administrative assistant. Yes, Izzie, don't ever forget that you are a SynCor Foods girl, first and foremost."

Michelle hated wakes. If Hawk hadn't persisted, she would never have attended Dan Richardson's wake Monday evening following her grueling day fielding newspaper reporters for SynCor Foods. The handshake his wife, Ashley Richardson, had extended to her was in such sharp contrast to the jovial contact she had had with her at her sister's Halloween party, before she had learned the awful truth. Her mind fixed upon the sight of Richardson's two little girls staring, standing next to their mother. Michelle felt shaky as she walked up the aisle to the satin lined coffin. When she saw Dan Richardson, face-to-face, her mind involuntarily became fixed on his expression.

His face emitted an impression of defeat, horror, and shock, frozen in a silent message. It was the same look of horror she saw on him Thursday when he had interrupted their advertising meeting. It was a look and feeling that clung to Michelle like a morning fog.

Later that evening at Michelle's apartment, she said to Hawk, "There's something more to Richardson's death than meets the eye."

"How so?"

"I don't know, but it's a weird feeling I have. Strangely, I feel his death is somehow connected with Nature Plus Formula."

"Michelle, that's a pretty strong statement, especially considering your position as account executive on Nature Plus for SynCor Foods."

"I know. That's what worries me. But I somehow feel there's some connection between Dan Richardson interrupting our ad meeting and what happened to him."

"What interruption?"

"During our Thursday afternoon ad meeting, Dan Richardson interrupted us, and told Bram he had something very important to discuss with him. He had an envelope in his hand. Bram told him to leave it for him to read. And this morning, Bram denied he ever saw any report. I saw an instant look of disagreement on his administrative assistant's face."

"What connection could there be between a formula line and a research man? Are you sure your creative imagination isn't getting the best of you?"

Hawk pulled Michelle into his arms, her back resting on his chest. This was a new intimacy they shared since their first "date" had turned so surreal. They had a new bond of caring and protection. She relaxed in his arms.

"Perhaps you're right. What possible link could there be between the two? I think my brain was just working overtime. It's been a long, tiring day."

Michelle's thoughts melted away as she lay in the comfort of Hawk's strong arms surrounding her shoulders.

Chapter 7

November 4

D anny Wingfield let himself enjoy the satisfaction every writer feels when they see their written word in print. He read the headline from today's morning paper.

SynCor Foods Top Researcher of New Infant Formula Murdered on Halloween

By Danny Wingfield

Chicago – Bram Pavolich, President and Chief Executive Officer of SynCor Foods, 200 S. Wabash, publicly disclaimed yesterday at a news conference any connection between his company and the murder of Dan Richardson, head researcher for SynCor Food's new infant formula line, which contains human breast milk. The new infant formula is expected to be marketed to the public on a nationwide scale within the month.

SynCor Foods is the manufacturer of Perky Plus Popcorn and Grandma's Butter Cookies.

Richardson was found murdered Halloween night by a neighbor after his wife, Ashley Richardson, had made repeated efforts to reach his cell. Richardson was expected at a Halloween party at 9 p.m. He was found dead at approximately 9:30 p.m.

He is survived by his wife and two daughters. Homicide detective Marcus Harris is conducting the investigation. Harris said yesterday, "We have reports that a tall person dressed in a masked Frankenstein costume was seen near the Richardson residence shortly before the time of the murder. Anyone with information regarding this murder should call homicide at 756-7800."

The article was adjacent to a photo of Bram Pavolich from yesterday's news conference. Danny knew that this was to be the first of many articles on Dan Richardson and Nature Plus Formula.

Yep. He could feel it in his bones.

Erma Krumple never forgot Tuesday was garbage day. Ever since she became a widow last April, the simple daily chores in her life had taken on new meaning. With Mr. Krumple gone after 41 years of marriage, Erma found it necessary to reschedule her daily life to give it meaning and purpose. Tuesday, November 4, was no different. Or seemingly so. As usual, Erma had carefully bundled her garbage in a pine-scented plastic kitchen bag with self-tie. As she approached her trash container in the alleyway, she noticed that the lid was slightly cocked, hanging off the aluminum can. How puzzling, Erma thought. She wondered if the city had hired new garbage workers who weren't as careful as the others. Erma removed the lid and was surprised when a dozen flies emerged. She was so mad! The City of Oak Lawn disposal system would hear from her. Erma prided herself on a neat and clean home. And that included garbage!

Erma peered into the can and was surprised to see that it was stuffed with a plastic mask. It looked like a Frankenstein mask!

"Kids," Erma said aloud. "Halloween tricks."

But as Erma pushed the plastic mask down with a stick, she noticed a splash of red that didn't belong. A spray of red right to the side of the front of the Frankenstein costume. *What the?* Dull red. Why, it was blood. Lots of blood. And this wasn't a kid's costume. This costume was big enough to fit a man. A large man. A fly landed on Erma's hand, sending cold shudders through her spine.

Izzie Nick took pride that Mr. Pavolich trusted her as a company representative in corporate affairs. However, in this case, by attending the funeral of Dan Richardson, she felt odd. After all, it was the second funeral she had attended in the past week.

First, she had attended the funeral of Sofia Ruiz's baby Anthony on Halloween, and now she was a company representative at Richardson's funeral.

She had arrived early, as was customary for her. It was 9:30 a.m. and the service wasn't scheduled until 10 a.m. As Izzie looked up from her watch, she was faced by a young man in his thirties, whom she recognized as a reporter who had been at SynCor Foods Company just yesterday. In fact, he was the one that had shocked Izzie when he had asked Mr. Pavolich about any possible link between Richardson's research report and his death. She was shocked because she knew that there were only three people who knew about the report – Bram, herself and Richardson. And only she, Izzie, knew of the contents of the report, since Bram said he never saw it. But where could it have gone? A report doesn't jump out of one's in-basket. Or perhaps he had read it, and denied it? Why?

"You look lovely today, Miss –."

"Hmmmph?" Izzie said, startled out of her train of thought.

"I said you look lovely today. I recognized you from yesterday. You work at SynCor Foods?"

"Yes, I do. I'm Bram Pavolich's administrative assistant, Isabelle Nick."

Danny's eyes lit up as if he had come upon a gold treasure.

"That's right. And may I commend you on your professionalism in keeping the day's events under control. It takes a very special person with a lot of talent to do so."

"Why, thank you," Izzy said, feeling herself warm at the compliment. "And you are …?"

"Danny Wingfield from the Chicago Sun Reporter, Chicago's fastest growing morning paper."

They shared a laugh.

"Rather unfortunate, isn't it?" Danny continued. "Healthy man with a family – and kabootz – he's murdered. I mean, who would want to kill such a nice man? What could be the motive?"

"I'm afraid I don't know," Izzie said. "He was a nice man. Loved by everyone. Mr. Pavolich said, however, that he had quite a few personal problems lately. Marital disagreements."

"Oh, Bram Pavolich said that? I suppose that's what was in the report Dan gave to him the previous day?"

"Oh, no. That had nothing to do with personal matters. It was pertaining to Nature Plus Formula."

"Oh, so you read the report, Miss Nick?" Wingfield said, casually, non-confrontational.

"Oh, no, no, no, no. I mean, I don't even know anything about any report," Izzie blurted out.

"I had learned during private interviews with Mrs. Richardson following her husband's death that she knew he was working on a report of great importance on Nature Plus products, and that, in her own words, he was going to present it to "the old man" – meaning Pavolich – the day before his untimely death."

"Oh, so she did know of it," Izzie found herself saying, despite herself. "Did she ever read the report?"

"That's the unfortunate part," Wingfield continued. "She never read it, and Mr. Pavolich denied seeing it, so I guess no one on the face of the earth – at least among the living – knows of its contents."

Izzie's mind went blank. No one living. Contents of report. Matter of life and death. Stop Nature Plus products at all costs.

"Miss Nick, are you all right?"

"Hhmm."

"I said, are you all right? The funeral service is about to begin." Danny exited to a seat in the back.

As Izzie watched the funeral service proceed, her thoughts were working in slow motion. She must still complete her corporate duties of expressing sympathy to Mrs. Richardson on behalf of SynCor Foods, her purpose for being here on company time. She must shake off these eerie thoughts she was having. Mrs. Richardson and her two daughters looked so sad. Hard to believe Dan could have had marital problems with a lovely family like that.

As she glanced around the people in attendance at the funeral, she noticed that that nice reporter she had just been talking to was talking to a large man, on the heavy-set side. That's right. She recognized him now. Danny Wingfield was talking to Marcus Harris, homicide detective assigned on the Richardson case.

Marcus Harris was glad he had attended Richardson's funeral. Danny Wingfield would prove to be an asset. Sometimes these newspaper reporters could be a pain in the ass; but this kid seemed okay. Seemed to think that Pavolich's secretary, Isabelle Nick, had read some report that Richardson gave to Pavolich the night before his murder. But then she had denied knowing of it. And Bram had denied knowing of it. Harris made a mental note to take Miss Nick out to lunch soon.

Now, he was following up on the only leads he had. First, neighbors of Richardson reported seeing a cab stop in front of the Richardson's home at approximately the time of death, while a costumed man proceeded to the Richardson's house. They had thought nothing of it until, of course, they had learned of Richardson's death. Then, today, he had received a phone call from another neighbor, Erma Krumple, who had found just such a Halloween costume in her trash container. The lab was running blood tests now to verify if the blood on the costume would match Richardson's. A Frankenstein costume with gloves. Well, he now had the name of the costume shop, Treats 'n Tricks, and would have them check out their rental receipts to see who had rented the costume.

He checked his cell phone with the shop ad on it. "Treats 'n Tricks. Hundreds of costumes and unique party novelties. Corner of Roosevelt and Wabash." Just two miles from SynCor Foods headquarters, Harris noted. A short cab drive. Harris made a mental note to check local cabs, Uber or lyfts for any points of departure from SynCor Foods on Halloween night. Of course, the killer could have walked to the costume shop from SynCor if he or she was in good physical shape.

Harris was a seasoned professional at linking clues of a homicide together to form a one-way pattern pointing to the killer. Today was no exception. And now he would begin solving his jigsaw puzzle with a Frankenstein costume. The first, and only, clue he had in the Richardson's murder case that, hopefully, would lead to others.

"Good day," Harris addressed the middle-aged man standing behind the check-out counter at Treats 'n Tricks. "Detective Harris, homicide."

"Tom Jagger. Owner, manager, whatever you want to call it. In other words, I own this joint," he said, with a grin.

Harris continued, "I'm investigating a homicide that took place in suburban Oak Lawn on Halloween night. A man named Dan Richardson. He was employed as chief researcher for SynCor Foods, headquartered here at 200 S. Wabash, Chicago. We think the murderer was wearing a Halloween costume that was from your shop. I have the label here . . ."

Tom Jagger's interest perked further.

"Murder. Holy Cow. Hey, I never even knew this Richardson character!"

"No. Don't misunderstand me, Mr. Jagger. You or your company are not suspect in this case. It is most likely the murderer either rented this costume under a fictitious name or stole it. He (or she) probably used it as a disguise from being identified by neighbors or other people who may have seen him."

"Let me see. Oh, yes. This is our costume #00785." Jagger checked his shop computer and said, "That's our Frankenstein costume. Size X-large. From our records, it should still be in our current inventory."

Harris asked, "And where would that be located?"

Jagger led Harris through the store, to the SW corner of the costume-filled shop.

"It *should* be located right here," Jagger said. "It's not here."

"Hmm," Harris said. "And that was the three pieces: a one-piece vinyl costume, rubber mask, and white gloves."

"No, the Frankenstein costume didn't have gloves with it."

"We did find white gloves along with the discarded costume. Do any other costumes in this area have gloves with them that are perhaps missing?" Harris asked.

Jagger fingered through the racks of hanging disguises.

"Hey, yeah. This #01625 butler's outfit comes with white gloves. They are usually pinned on the sleeve." As Jagger searched the butler's costume for the white gloves, the tissue paper packing in the sleeve fell to the floor. Jagger stooped to pick it up and grumbled to no one in particular.

"Man," Jagger said. "What good is a butler's costume without the gloves? I'll need to get a whole new costume. I hope my insurance will cover it. Speaking of insurance, look at this," Jagger addressed Harris.

"Matches. I have NO SMOKING signs posted throughout the store, and some idiot always decides they need a smoke in my shop. With all these costumes, a cigarette, a hot match, is a lethal weapon. And fire insurance is high. One claim and forget ever being in business again. Oh, you'll get your money back, but don't bother opening a new shop. Fire insurance premium would be so—"

"Matches? May I see them please?" Harris interrupted Jagger. "Mmmm. Mandy's Magic Massage House. Looks like a competitor of yours gives away matches as advertisement."

"No, I ain't in competition with Mandy's Magic House. Or Mandy's Cat House, if you will," Jagger chuckled. Never patronize it myself. Know a few fellows who do, however. Located over on Adams Street. About two miles from here. Hey – it's just down the street from that place you said the murder victim worked at, SynCor Foods. Maybe a jealous girl knocked him off? Or his wife caught him there and offed him?" Jagger continued.

Harris didn't answer him but took out a plastic evidence bag and placed the matches inside it. "Maybe we can pull a fingerprint off of it," he said, as he mentally planned a necessary visit to Mandy's Magic Massage House.

As they walked to the front of the store, Jagger said, "Well, please let me know if there's any way I can be of further help to you."

"Mr. Jagger, do you remember anything unusual about any of your customers on Halloween night? Anyone particularly nervous? In a hurry? Anyone lighting a cigarette, for example?"

"No, can't say I do. Halloween night's always crazy anyways. Anything 'unusual' would blend right in with the craziness," Jagger laughed.

"Anyone else working here Halloween night that could be of help to us?" Harris asked.

Jagger pondered. "Halloween. Halloween. Just me, and – yes, I had my 15-year-old daughter working here with me that night. But she never mentioned anything unusual. I'll be glad to ask her, though. I'm afraid Jennifer was more concerned with all the young boys coming in the shop than with ringing up costume sales."

"I'm afraid I will have to question her. There might be something she remembers that could be of vital help in the case."

"Okay, but please don't scare her. She's just a kid."

"Understood. I have grown children myself. Thank you for your cooperation. I'll be in touch."

Harris walked out the doors of Treats 'n Tricks already planning step two of his investigation. A visit to Mandy's Magic Massage House. The next step in his search inspired by a tiny insignificant package of matches. Matches that could simply be smoke in the wind, or a lighted path guiding his way.

Taxi driver Pete Wrangler was exhilarated. It was that same exciting feeling he felt whenever a racehorse he had a $50 across the board on came in by a nose.

It was his good fortune to know information pertaining to a murder he had read about in today's Chicago Sun Reporter. Just a tiny article by a reporter, Danny Wingfield, regarding a murder that occurred on Halloween night.

Apparently, the newest clue in the case was the fact that they believed the murderer had been wearing a Frankenstein costume and mask. The article stated that anyone with information on the case should call Homicide Detective Marcus Harris at 756-7800.

Well, Pete Wrangler intended on doing just that. He clearly remembered that character he picked up at the greasy spoon The Bee Hive with that ridiculous costume and mask on. In fact, he had looked up the route sheet from Halloween night and verified the destination address as the same address listed in the newspaper article as the murder victim's home. He smiled as he remembered the $100 bill the character had pre-paid with, and the $55 tip he had earned since he just jumped out of the cab.

And now, he intended to earn even more money on the poor bloke. He was sure that his information was worth the $1,000 reward for information.

Forget the good Samaritan shit. He knew what he knew alone, until, and only if, Harris came up with the cash for the info. And now, in just a few more minutes, after calling 756-7800, Pete Wrangler would know if he would be $1,000 richer soon.

Somehow, he could feel the green warming his pockets already.

Chapter 8

November 5

M ichelle Heywood looked forward to ad agency presentations as her moment to shine. And today's 8:30 a.m. ad meeting with SynCor Foods where she would present the Nature Plus Formula campaign would be one of the finest moments in her career.

Her stage was set. Bram Pavolich emitted an air of control and power as he sat with outstretched legs in his black leather oversized chair located at the head of the conference table. Michelle sensed his air of eager anticipation, reminding her of a child awaiting the presentation of a birthday cake at a birthday party.

Marketing Director Chet Hartman and his new assistant Pam Pritthouse sat on one side of the diamond-shaped conference table, while David Adams balanced out the other side.

Michelle felt coolly confident as she took her position of prominence at the alternating head of the conference table, directly facing Bram Pavolich. A confidence earned by around-the-clock days and nights of hard work at Ackerly, Adams & Associates this past week, cumulating in a first-class ad program for Nature Plus Formula. Days and nights with Hawk.

Michelle felt the "presenter" was just as important, or more, than the actual ad presentation. That's why she had taken great care in "packaging" herself today for the presentation. And she was pleased with the results. Her new tan mid-knee dress was professional yet feminine. She had pulled her shoulder-length hair up and away from her face, adding a look of sophistication to her fresh, youthful appearance.

"Well, it looks like we're all here. Shall I begin, Mr. Pavolich?" Michelle asked.

"Please do, my dear. I'm eager to see what you have come up with."

"Thank you. We at Ackerly, Adams & Associates, feel the key to success of the Nature Plus Formula campaign will be to capture the market's attention in a big way, for maximum, immediate impact and momentum. The fact that we have a Friday-after-Thanksgiving kick-off date and little more than three weeks to put together a national ad campaign poses us with some basic logistics around which this campaign has been developed. Media selection was led, in part, by this anticipated kick-off date. Ads in major women's magazines require anywhere from one to three months advance ad deadlines. Therefore, at this point, they are not a consideration in the first initial ad phase for Nature Plus. Newspaper advertising will be utilized in a minor capacity, basically using a medium-space back-up ad to run near the lifestyle sections of the paper.

"There is a mass media available that is readily accessible and creates immediate impact, image and product recognition. National television. We have chosen national television, along with social media targeted to the female 18-35 demographic for our primary media, complemented by select radio in targeted chief market areas –Chicago, New York, Boston, Houston, San Francisco, and Miami.

"Social media advertising and television media are a magical combination. The right combination can allure the potential consumer with both sight and sound. The correct message can also elicit touch and smell to seduce and capture the viewer. We feel the ads we are proposing for Nature Plus are of such a high-impact quality, they will capture the marketplace by force – oh, ever so subtly (who said, 'if you want to capture someone's attention, just whisper')" Michelle whispered for dramatic impact.

"And now, let's consider, as any good ad message does, **who** we are trying to reach with this magical message? What makes her tick? Today's mother is classified as a Millennial, also know as Generation Y. They are children of the baby boomers, born between 1981 to 1996 being the range of birth years for our market. These women are considered digital natives since they have elevated usage of the internet, cell phones, and social media. This demographic in many cases have delayed marriage and childbirth, so we are dealing with a sophisticated consumer who wants the best for her baby. These children will be part of generation Alpha. Here's a detailed report of our targeted audience for your further review at your convenience," Michelle said as she passed around printed materials.

"While understanding the uniqueness of a typical millennial mother, you need to realize one thing – she still embodies the human instinct and drive to be a good mother and to love her child unconditionally. This constant thread throughout all of humanity poses her with many dilemmas. Although millennials have had two significant periods of economic disruption since they began in the work force, the latest being the COVID-19 pandemic, many of these new mothers are at the peak of their careers, where they can be torn between the current trend for breastfeeding without shaming and the satisfaction that continuing a career can hold. This is where Nature Plus Formula can play a vital role in satisfying both needs. The best that nature can provide, mother's real breast milk, plus the convenience of a feeding method that a caregiver outside the home can give. Our name, Nature Plus, does say it all. My commendation to whomever selected the name."

Michelle continued, while her spectators watched her as if totally mesmerized.

"Therefore, to focus the consumer on name recognition in a very short time period, we have developed as our slogan, 'Nature Plus Infant Formula. Our name says it all. Designed for your Generation Alpha Baby.'

"Studies have shown that advertisements solving problems have the highest degree of approval. Adding a testimonial from a trusted celebrity adds credence to our viability. We have selected Amber Greene as our spokeswoman for Nature Plus. As an Instagram and twitter influencer with over 1.5 million loyal millennial followers, she has agreed to be our face of the product." She could feel the excitement rise in the enclosed conference room. She dimmed the lights and previewed the video of the ads that would be blasted across social media and prime time television. She showed them the 10-second teaser first. It began with a slow pan of a new mother feeding her baby with a bottle. The baby was a picture of contentment, the mother a reflection of confidence. The announcer, Amber Greene asked, "Why is this baby so happy? Why is her mother so confident? Hush, baby's asleep now. Nature Plus Formula. Our name says it all. For your Generation Alpha baby." The other commercials and ads focused on the benefits of Nature Plus, with Amber Greene interviewing leading nutritionists and medical experts. They all ended in the same way, "Sshhh. Baby's sound asleep. And dreaming about bunny rabbits and sunbeams. The answer to my question – why is this baby happy and mother confident? Because mom feeds her baby new Nature Plus Infant Formula, the only infant formula that is enriched with 25% real breast milk. New from SynCor Foods. Available now in the refrigerator and freezer sections of your grocery or online. Nature Plus. Your Generation Alpha baby deserves nothing but the best."

"Magnificent!" Bram Pavolich exclaimed, as he practically leaped out of his chair. "Brilliant. It's perfect for Nature Plus. Exactly the image I'm looking for."

Michelle felt empowered by the display of enthusiasm from Bram. Others joined in: Hartman praising the unique messaging; Pam Pritthouse saying it was so convincing; Adams stating that it was a superb campaign that guaranteed results.

The rest of the meeting proceeded swiftly. Pavolich signed the multitude of legal papers that would enable the ad agency to proceed: contract with Greene, social media contracts, production cost estimates, copy, and media schedules.

Michelle was exhilarated that all had gone so well. She believed in the campaign herself and was happy to have been instrumental in its creation and development. When the paperwork was completed, Adams and Michelle packed up the art boards in the large, black artist portfolios, while the signed contracts were gathered. Promises of scanned documents to be emailed were made.

"Great work, Michelle," Bram said, as he escorted Adams and her from the conference room door. "When can I expect –"

Pavolich was interrupted by a disturbance outside his office. Isabelle Nick was standing up, her desk chair directly behind her, and leaning across her desk with both hands squared in front of her.

She said, "If you don't get out of here – and I mean NOW – I am prepared to call security." She resembled a pit bull protecting her master.

"What's going on here?" Bram ordered. His jovial mood changed instantaneously.

Michelle recognized the man Isabelle was confronting. He was one of the reporters who had been covering the Richardson murder case.

The reporter turned from Isabelle's desk and looked Pavolich squarely in the eyes. "I'm simply asking this woman about a research report on Nature Plus Formula that the late Dan Richardson wrote and presented, I believe it was handed to you, sir, on the afternoon prior to his murder."

"OUT! Get out of my office." Bram charged at the man, grabbed his arm and twisted it up, jerking it at an awkward angle from his shoulder socket. "If I ever see you in my company again, you'll be arrested for trespassing and harassment."

Bram physically dragged the reporter into the hallway and finalized his display of anger with a hard shove between the reporter's shoulder blades. "Enemy of the people. That's what you are." Turning, he jetted toward his private office. With a look back at his guests he stated firmly, "Good day, David, Miss Heywood, good work. Hartman, you've got your work cut out for you."

Isabelle couldn't remember the last time she had felt so nervous and scared. Pavolich had just summoned her to his office through the inner-office hot line. It had been a brief command.

"Isabelle. I would like to see you in my office. Now."

What would he ask her? Should she mention that she had slipped when talking to the reporter at Richardson's wake and told him the report was on Nature Plus Formula? And if she told Bram that, wouldn't she have to tell him that she had opened the report and had seen words that had bothered her. Words like "murder," "life and death," "Stop Nature Plus Formula immediately." How could she explain her meticulous "attention to detail" trait that was responsible for her retyping the envelope? Would he understand?

After she walked into his office, he motioned for her to take a seat in the chair in front of his desk. Now he looked at her directly.

"Isabelle, one of the main considerations an employer has when hiring an administrative assistant is, 'Whose side is she on?' In other words, is she 'For us, or against us?' As my administrative assistant, really my partner, you are privy to a lot of company information. Personal, confidential, often controversial information. Now, if the woman is a gossip, someone who likes to boast to everyone about what big juicy scoop she knows about, there is a problem. You know the saying, 'Loose lips sink ships.'"

"But sir," Izzie interrupted.

"No, no, let me continue," Bram said. "But you're not like that Izzie. You're different. You have class. That's why this matter with that reporter is especially disturbing to me. What exactly had transpired between the two of you?"

"Bram, you know me. I've worked for you and SynCor Foods for over 20 years. I'm a company person. I'm 100% loyal. This reporter is a snoopy bothersome pest. As you often say, enemy of the people."

"But why would he pester you, of all people? Why should he think you would know anything about some so-called research report on Nature Plus Formula?"

"Sir, I did a stupid thing. And I might as well tell you all about it and clear my conscience. I have a trait that is my blessing as well as my curse. I am meticulous. I pay attention to the tiniest of details You know the saying, 'A place for everything, and everything in its place.' Well, last Thursday after Dan Richardson interrupted your marketing meeting, he placed an envelope in your in-basket. The envelope was wrinkled, soiled, and had your name and the word 'confidential' scrawled haphazardly across it. Well, my curse of meticulousness, if you will, would not allow such an unprofessional display to reach your hands. So, I opened the envelope, set the report temporarily aside and retyped a fresh, clean, envelope with the information. Since I had to refold the report to fit into the new smaller-sized envelope (a penny saved is a penny earned, sir) I couldn't help but notice a few words from the report that were typed in bold caps and underlined."

Pavolich's face seemed to turn to an opaque white, cast with gray.

"And what did these words say, Isabelle?" Bram asked.

"They were odd. Words like, 'DANGER TO BABIES… ANTIBODIES…CHANGE IN CONTENT…ONLY A MATTER OF TIME, BUT IT'S A MATTER OF LIFE AND DEATH.' And then it said, 'MUST STOP NATURE PLUS DISTRIBUTION AND MARKETING IMMEDIATELY!' Naturally, I knew these words were not intended for my eyes, but they still bothered me."

"And why is that, Isabelle?"

"I guess because the day after I read the report, I attended the funeral of my best friend's daughter's baby twin, who had just died of Sudden Infant Death (SID). And I know this sounds foolish, but that baby was being fed Nature Plus. I had convinced his mother, Sofia Ruiz, to sign up for the free research program that provided free formula."

Bram stood up. He leaned forward on his desk, palms down.

"Isabelle, this is serious. What you are saying is slander. Do you actually think there is any connection between that twin's death and Nature Plus Formula?"

"No, no, no, sir," Izzie's voice cracked. "I just feel it was upsetting to me because of the proximity of the two events happening."

"And I suppose you told that reporter all your suppositions and conclusions on all these events?"

"Oh no, sir. None of it. I merely mentioned to him at Richardson's funeral that the report was on Nature Plus Formula because he had stated it was on a personal matter of Dan Richardson. I simply corrected his misconception. It's that darn trait of being meticulous that is my blessing and my curse I'm afraid. I'm sorry, sir."

"Izzie, sorry isn't enough. The mere fact that even in your mind you could connect such an awful occurrence, the death of a baby, with

Nature Plus displays a frightening side of your personality. Matters like this are usually handled by termination of employment."

Termination of employment? Fired? I'm being fired? Me, Isabelle Nick, first class employee? Fired?

"But because of your solid record with SynCor Foods for over 20 years, I will simply put you on a one-week probationary period where your behavior will be watched very carefully. Any contact with reporters, police, will be grounds for immediate dismissal. Now, Izzie, you and I have been friends for years. Please put all these silly thoughts away. I assure you, Nature Plus Formula is the finest product on the market."

"I'm relieved to have told you all this, Bram. It does all seem so silly now that I've expressed it. But there's still one thing that I don't understand. I know I put that report in your in-box Thursday evening, and I remember your taking all your materials in with you following the marketing meeting. Yet you don't remember ever seeing the report?"

"Well, yes, Izzie, now that you bring it to my attention, there was a confidential piece from Richardson, but it had nothing to do with Nature Plus. Richardson had some personal problems, something about a bad gambling debt. Richardson was a troubled man who played the ponies. And he did have some words capitalized in it, like 'Danger.' The fact that he, personally, was in danger because of the debt. I read it and tossed it out. I'm presuming the gambling debt could have something to do with his murder."

"But shouldn't the police know about that?"

"Isabelle," Bram said, raising his voice like a parent reprimanding a child. "Let's leave police work to the police, and newspaper work to the reporters, and our business to us."

"Right. I absolutely agree. Bram, I'm a company girl, 100%."

"You won't regret it."

Danny Wingfield could not believe his luck. The small crack that had been left open in the door of Pavolich's office had provided him with just the access he needed to sleuth in on Bram's conversation with

Izzie. How convenient it had been for him to go into the men's room until all the people (from what looked like a marketing meeting) were gone, and then slither back into the office hallway, to place his ear against the crack in the doorway.

So, Izzie *had* read the report! He had instinctively known that she knew something more than she was saying. But it was more than he had hoped for. "Danger to babies. Antibodies. Only a matter of time, but it's a matter of life and death." Danny reviewed the notes he had written from their conversation. Several leads to be pursued and brought to the attention of homicide detective Marcus Harris. Like this bit about Richardson having a bad gambling debt, and Bram saying that *that* was what the report was on. Wingfield instinctively knew that was a figment of Bram's imagination. Or defense. What was he hiding? And why? If Richardson had found something wrong with Nature Plus that could be dangerous to babies, why wouldn't Bram listen and respond to the findings?

Profit. Of course. Wingfield had seen the value of money take priority in dozens of incidences in his life. Money brought power, and life, after all, was just life. Wingfield felt it was a cock-eyed world he lived in. In fact, that was why he was drawn to the world of journalism. He had found out early in life that the power of the pen was mightier than the sword. His style of journalism had more than a touch of the muckraker, and that's why Danny never grew bored with his job.

And now, he had some definite leads to the Richardson case that could crack the case.

Like this woman, Sofia Ruiz, who Isabelle mentioned. He'd set up an interview with her and see if he could find any connection between Nature Plus and her baby's death.

A dead baby. Danny allowed his mind to ponder the thought for a moment. In his mind, there could be no greater grief to bear.

Danny's ears pricked up. He recognized the sounds of the meeting between Bram and Isabelle being over: the sliding of chairs, the shuffling of feet.

Danny closed his spiral-bound notebook and slithered several feet down the hallway, then scrambled to the stairwell.

What had Bram said? If he ever found him in his office again, he'd have him arrested for trespassing and harassment.

Well, thank you, Mr. Pavolich, for this juicy new information you've provided me with.

Because now maybe it will be you who's being arrested. For murder.

Isabelle was glad Wednesday was finally over. First there had been the big advertising presentation and then her confrontation with that newspaper reporter. Then her reprimand by her boss. She was glad he had finally left the office. 4 p.m. Earlier than usual. But she knew it had been a long day for him, too.

Well, she was through for the day, too. Anymore typing, filing, could wait until tomorrow. She was drained. She couldn't wait to get home, soak in a hot tub, devour a turkey sandwich, curl up with a good book, and drift off until tomorrow. She would just straighten up his office as she always did at the end of the day.

Isabelle was glad Bram was quite organized himself, as she sifted through some papers on his desk. Some bosses she had worked for just couldn't throw anything away. Now, Izzie wanted Bram's office to look particularly bright and organized for tomorrow. To ingratiate him to her once again and move on from this current grievance he had with her.

As she tidied around his desk, Isabelle's eagle eyes noticed a piece of paper protruding from the top drawer.

Izzie pulled at the drawer, which she found, to her surprise, to be locked. Hmmm, she thought. She could not remember that drawer ever being locked before.

"Well," she said aloud, "Just leave it alone. It's locked because he apparently wants it locked."

After Isabelle had finished with her work in his office, she gave it the final once over, checking it for final appearance and organization. It was immaculate except for that tiny, curled piece of paper protruding from the drawer. A tiny detail prohibiting Isabelle to take pleasure in a job well done.

She poked at the paper with her finger, trying to push it back into the locked drawer. It sprang back each time.

"Damn," Izzie said aloud. Damn if she could just leave it alone. But she could not tolerate untidiness. It was that one little misspelled word, that one little hair out of place that bothered her until she *had* to do something about it.

"Well, that's what has made me such an excellent administrative assistant."

With that statement, Izzie pulled a bobby pin from her hair and picked at the lock to the drawer. The lock moved. She opened the drawer and was shocked at what fell upon her sight. The envelope she had typed to Bram Pavolich, torn open! Mr. Pavolich had assured her that he had seen this envelope, read the contents on Richardson's gambling debt, and discarded it! And now here it was. Locked in his top drawer!

Isabelle quickly looked around the room. She knew Bram's office could lock from the inside. She locked the door, and returned to the open drawer, bearing that mesmerizing envelope.

She picked up the envelope and looked around. Isabelle imagined invisible eyes watching her. Cold eerie haunting looks staring at her. Bram's words seem to echo through the room. "Isabelle, there are certain matters that are personal, confidential."

He's right, Isabelle thought to herself. This is a company matter that I have no business getting into.

She dropped the envelope and its contents back into the drawer like a hot potato. Quickly, she shut the door of the drawer, the tiny piece of paper no longer protruding. The key! Where was the key to lock the drawer! If the drawer was unlocked tomorrow morning when Bram came in, and the office was obviously tidied up, he would know it had been Isabelle who had been in the office and pried open the locked drawer! *Certainly, that would be grounds for immediate dismissal.*

She searched and found keys, but none that fit the drawer. She tried to relock the drawer with her bobby pin, but that didn't work.

Then, as if receiving a bolt of fresh insight, why would Bram say he threw out this report with supposedly meaningless personal information about an employee, when here it was in a locked drawer in his private office! Why was he lying? What was he denying?

Isabelle took the envelope in her hands and sat in his chair. Its massive height and still warm seat gave her the impression of Bram's presence in the room.

With shaking hands, she proceeded to read the contents of the report in its entirety.

My God! God, it couldn't be true! But if it *was* accurate, what about the twins? Sofia Ruiz's twin? Could that be why little Anthony had died? And hadn't she, Isabelle, had a hand, however indirectly and innocently, in that death? Izzie's mind was flying. She put the report back in the drawer, shut it, and returned to her own desk.

Her mind raced at an accelerated pace, trying to formulate correlations, consequences, and a plan of action. Who should she tell? The reporter? The detective? No one? What had Bram told her? "You're a company girl, Izzie."

Izzie had never been so confused in her life. Surely, she must be overacting. How could it be that she, Isabelle Nick, Administrative Assistant, should be privy to the knowledge that this new formula could harm approximately 2% of the babies who would use it.? Harmful unto death. By natural causes. Totally without a trace to Nature Plus. Why, if it was true and Bram Pavolich was going to disregard the findings, eliminate the findings, if you will, well, that made him a mass murderer of innocent babies and probably of Dan Richardson, as well!

She needed time. Time to think everything over. Everything was going fast. Too fast. Hadn't Bram said he wanted Nature Plus available to the public fast? A matter of weeks.

"But it's a matter of life and death," the words of Richardson's report pierced her consciousness.

When exactly was Nature Plus Formula scheduled to hit the public? She had to know. She would ask that girl from the ad agency, Michelle Heywood. She had her number right here on her list of contacts: Ackerly, Adams & Associates. Senior Account Executive, Michelle Heywood.

She'd call right now and then she'd know what to do.

Michelle answered her line at Ackerly, Adams & Associates in her customary manner.

"Michelle Heywood speaking."

"Is this Michelle Heywood, the young lady who was at SynCor Foods today?" a soft voice asked.

"Yes, speaking," Michelle said.

"This is Isabelle Nick, Bram Pavolich's Adminstrative Assistant."

"Yes, Miss Nick. Hello. How nice to hear from you. How may I help you?"

"Well, I was wondering exactly when the advertising for Nature Plus is to begin? When *exactly* will mothers be able to buy Nature Plus for their babies? I'm – uh, I'm planning some events – company events – around those dates, so I **need** to know exactly when my last chance is, I mean do you know those dates, Miss?"

"Why, yes. Of course. National social media and TV will break on November 25, the day after Thanksgiving. Nature Plus Formula products will be on the grocery shelves one week prior. A teaser campaign will also be airing beginning Nov. 18.

"Oh, my. That's only a little over a week. I don't have much time."

"Much time for what, Isabelle?"

"I have to do something. But who? Something **must** be done, Miss. Poor Sofia Ruiz. And her poor baby!"

"Something must be done! About what?"

"Nature Plus," Isabelle's voice got higher and louder, and then the volume lowering, she said secretly, "It's just a matter of time."

"What is, Miss Nick?"

"I have to go. I have a lot of thinking to do. I must plan what I must do. Good day, Miss Heywood."

The dead tone echoed in Michelle's ear. Hauntingly.

It was only five days since Sofia Ruiz had buried her son, Anthony, yet it seemed like years. Eternity really. Her head felt cloudy, like a mass of fog had descended upon her brain and nothing she could do would clear it. She was tired, oh so tired, constantly. Her back ached, stinging when she picked up and carried her only living son, Andrew, twin brother to Anthony. Yet, holding and cuddling Andrew was the only thing that brought her peace, however brief and fleeting, yet peace, nonetheless.

She was enjoying this momentary flight of happiness now as she rocked Andrew in the big old comfortable rocker of her mother's, lined cozily with a handmade afghan.

When the phone rang, she heard herself answer in a cheerful manner. *I'm feeling better. I'm going to be okay.*

Her cheerful hello was returned with a sharp interjection of a man's voice.

"Hello, is this Sofia Ruiz?"

"Yes. Yes, it is."

"Mrs. Ruiz, you don't know me—"

"Who is this?"

"My name is Danny Wingfield. I'm a reporter with the Chicago Sun Reporter."

"Reporter?"

"Yes, Mrs. Ruiz. I'm covering the Dan Richardson homicide. Mr. Richardson had been employed as research director at SynCor Foods, where your friend, Isabelle Nick, works. One day prior to his murder, Mr. Richardson disclosed research on Nature Plus Formula, stating that there was danger to babies . . . antibodies . . . that it was a matter of life and death."

"What are you talking about? What do you want? Leave me alone."

"Wait, please, Mrs. Ruiz. Let me explain. Isabelle Nick thought that Nature Plus Formula could somehow be related to your son's death. I know this is a bad time for you, Mrs. Ruiz, but please tell me, did your son ever seem to have any type of reaction to the formula? Was an autopsy done on your son?"

"Autopsy? I've had enough of this talk. You've upset me with all this crap about formula causing Anthony's death. Don't you ever, and I mean ever, call me again, or I'll report you to the police. Leave me alone. Just leave me alone," Sofia screamed.

After hanging up the receiver, Sofia's prior feeling of peacefulness seemed like a figment of her imagination. *Formula? Isabelle Nick? Was there something wrong with Anthony's formula? Had I poisoned my own baby? Had Isabelle known? Why hadn't Isabelle called if this was true?*

As Sofia Ruiz rocked her son with great sweeping movements, her sobs bellowed throughout her entire home.

The information from cab driver Pete Wrangler had been well worth the money he demanded, Detective Marcus Harris reflected. Besides for the fact of verifying that a costumed man with a briefcase had taken a cab from a restaurant located just two miles from SynCor Foods to Dan Richardson's house, he had also learned that the cabby had found matches in his cab that were from Mandy's Magic Massage House. He had been using them since Halloween and gave them to the detective for evidence.

Mandy's Magic House had been tied to the murder two times, first from the costume shop and now by the cab driver. And now it was time to give ol' Mandy a little visit.

"Welcome to Mandy's Magic Massage House, sir, where you're guaranteed to have a magical experience," a middle-aged woman addressed Harris.

"Hello. You Mandy?"

"Who's asking?"

"Homicide detective Marcus Harris." Harris showed Mandy his badge.

"What business have you got with us?"

"I'm investigating the murder of Dan Richardson, who had been employed as research director for SynCor Foods, located just down the street from here. You familiar with that company, Miss?"

"Maybe I am."

"Well, we have reason to believe that the murderer may be a-uh-customer of your-uh-shop. You and your girls could be in danger, Miss, and any information you could provide us with would help capture this murderer."

"Murder? We may get some scum bags in here, but I don't think a murderer–."

"Look like the rest of us, Mandy. It is Mandy, isn't it?"

"Yes." *She seemed to warm a little. Become more human.*

"Are any employees of SynCor Foods customers here? Dan Richardson perhaps? Bram Pavolich?"

Mandy's eyes seemed to reflect recognition at the sound of Bram Pavolich's name.

"You know Mr. Pavolich, Mandy? Was Mr. Pavolich here on Halloween night?"

"We don't disclose the names of any of our customers. For all I know, you could be investigating a divorce, adultery charges. No, sir. Our business is not catering to murderers. Discussion closed. Our business is massages, sir. Magical massages. $25 first half hour. After that, any arrangements can be made between yourself and our hostesses."

"Thank you, Mandy. But I've got to go. Oh, by the way, do you happen to have any matches? I'm out."

"Sure. They're free to our customers, but I'm sure I can make an exception in your case."

Chapter 9

November 6

Detective Marcus Harris liked to get into the office early. At 7:30 a.m., the world belonged to him. With feet outstretched atop his paper-strewn desk, he thoroughly enjoyed his first cigar of the day, and a steaming hot cup of black coffee.

His mind was clear in the morning, allowing him to review the facts in a case, and creatively link clue to clue, leading to patterns and solutions.

Today his mind was engrossed in the Richardson homicide. Slowly, the pieces were starting to come together. It had all started with the retrieved Halloween costume found in an alleyway garbage can by Erma Krumple. The blood found on the costume had matched Richardson's blood DNA. One could presume that the murderer had selected Halloween and the costume as a disguise. However, it seemed likely that Richardson had known his assailant because there had been no forced entry. After interviewing the daughter of the shopkeeper of *Treats 'n Tricks*, he had learned that she vaguely remembered a man who asked to see their assortment of large costumes. She had led him to where the large costumes were located. The only reason she could even remember him was because he had seemed very nervous and had lit a cigarette! It had irked her since the shop had numerous "No Smoking" signs posted throughout. She also had said that she could not remember if he rented a costume. She didn't think so. By the time she was going to check on him to ask if he could use some help, he had been gone.

Then, of course, there had been the matches found at the costume shop from Mandy's Magic Massage House, or house of prostitution, if you will. Harris took a hearty gulp of the hot coffee. He had a sneaking suspicion that Bram Pavolich was a customer of Mandy's. He'd have to see if he could get any other information from any of the girls who worked there.

He took a deep drag on his cigar. And what about the cab driver? Pete Wrangler, wasn't that his name? Pinpointed the costumed man at a restaurant just down the street from *Treats 'n Tricks*, and just two miles from SynCor Foods. And another package of matches from Mandy's Magic House was also found in the cab. Harris laughed out loud. Seemed like the murderer was doing a bit of advertising for ol' Mandy.

And then what about that report Richardson supposedly presented to Bram just the night prior to his murder? Danny Wingfield had told him that he had learned Isabelle Nick thought the report was pertaining to the new baby formula Bram would be introducing soon. Yes. He'd talk with Izzie more, privately.

But now it was Bram Pavolich who commanded his attention. Harris finished the coffee. Yes, today was the day to pay Bram an overdue visit. He wanted to know just how physically fit ol' Bram was … on the jogging trail, and in the sack at Mandy's House.

Michelle Heywood gained deep satisfaction from the processing of an approved ad campaign. Yesterday's grand sweep of approval by Bram Pavolich for the new Nature Plus Formula campaign was just the ticket she needed to turn ideas into realty. And the new campaign would certainly add importance and weight to her career portfolio.

Today she did all the routine procedures which set the total campaign into motion. Processing social media and other media buys through the media department. Proceeding with production arrangements with the studio. Signing the talent contract which booked Amber Greene as the exclusive representative for Nature Plus.

They were all the gratifying steps toward turning thoughts, ideas, and concepts into powerful messages that would, quite without invitation, enter the subconscious and conscious minds of millions of people, affecting their buying habits and lives. It was an exciting thought, yet somewhat frightening, Michelle mused.

Michelle's own personal code of ethics set guidelines for her career. She had to believe in the goods, products, and services she advertised. And she had to believe in the ad treatment they received. For example, she insisted that portrayals of women's roles in commercials be non-sexist. In the male-dominated world of advertising and production, women were customarily portrayed as men saw – or wanted to – see them. It was only through Michelle's proven track record of marketing successes that she had influenced men to modify their rigid stereotypical treatment of women's roles.

That was one of the reasons she was taking so much enjoyment in the Nature Plus campaign. It was a wholesome natural product that benefited both the woman and the baby.

She found, however, that thoughts would creep into her consciousness, clouding her enjoyment on the campaign. Like yesterday, when Bram Pavolich threw out that newspaper reporter. The reporter's accusations seemed to repeat themselves in her mind. And then there was that phone call from Isabelle Nick, later yesterday after she had returned to the ad agency. She had sounded so, well, anxious and nervous. Somehow Michelle could not shake the feeling that Isabelle had wanted to say more to her but didn't.

But she knew it was just her creative mind getting the best of her. She had always loved mystery novels and considered herself a bit of a sleuth. She had never even seen a murder before, and now to relate to the Richardson murder, even in an indirect manner, piqued her curiosity. *It might not be such a bad idea to talk to that reporter.* Just to see what exactly he was basing these accusations on.

But that would have to be later. Right now, Michelle had an ad campaign to complete. A campaign that would be seen by millions of people in just a few weeks.

Bram Pavolich felt like he was sitting on top of the world. Life was being good to him, very good. SynCor Foods stock had gone up double digits in the last week. Instead of being a negative influence, the publicity on Richardson's murder had helped publicize the new Nature Plus Formula line. Bram leaned back in his executive chair, the smell of genuine leather enveloping him. *Aahh.* The king's cut of prime rib from *Beef 'n Ale* had been satisfying. The two martinis, extra dry, easy on the vermouth, had added to his overall ambiance of well-being. Soon, in just a few weeks, Nature Plus would be available to the public on a nation-wide scale. Soon he would claim the champion of titles for himself. Let Simi milks and Lac-alikes go to hell. Within six months, Nature Plus would command the Number one position in the infant formula competition.

His genius idea would be fulfilled. First on a national level. Following the first year, he'd expand operations on an international level, reaching Japan, China, Europe. Everything was going remarkably well. That girl, Michelle, was first rate. Where the hell had Adams been hiding her? She was different, Bram mused. Confident to the point of almost being cocky. Bold. Knew her shit.

Her main talent had been in her intuitive treatment of the product. In less than a week, she had presented a campaign that worked on many levels, that would reach people. It was as if she had been meant to market his genius. It was all coming together so beautifully. He allowed the bombardment of self-satisfying feelings to overtake his psyche, knowing that in the competitive business world, feeding his ego was as important as feeding his body.

His total composure was starkly interrupted through the inner office "hot line" ring between Isabelle and his executive suite.

"Yes?"

"Mr. Pavolich. There's a Mr. Harris here to see you. Detective Marcus Harris. Homicide."

"Tell him I'm in a meeting. He must make an appointment."

"Yes, sir. Thank you, sir."

Harris, shit. What the hell did he want? Nosy son of a bitch, get off my ass, he mused, his pulse rising.

The "hot line" ring pierced his thoughts. Bram lunged forward from the comforting folds of his supple leather chair.

"Yes?"

"Sorry to disturb you again, sir. Mr. Harris says it's imperative that he see you, now. Those were his exact words."

"All right. All right. Give me a few minutes."

Bram turned in his chair, facing his credenza. He reached into a side drawer, pulled out a pocket mirror, combed his hair, and took a breath mint.

The report, Richardson's report. Out of reflex more than anything, he checked the drawer containing the report. He was stunned when it coolly opened, unlocked, the report lying unguarded, facing up.

Bram could feel panic rise. His throat tightened. It was all falling apart. Apart. Was this a trick? Who had opened this drawer? Harris? Did he know about the report? This report? Had he been snooping around here when he had been out to lunch? No, no, Izzie had been here the whole time. Izzie? Izzie? What did she know? His desk had been perfectly organized this morning, as usual. Had Izzie opened the drawer? And if she had, did she read the report? Had he left it open?

No, no, no, he was sure he had locked the drawer. Now calm down, he told himself. You must not, repeat, must not show nervous agitation when talking to this Harris. I did nothing wrong, he said to himself. He was going to ruin everything, his dreams of a lifetime. It had been justified. *I am not guilty!*

"Everything is fine," he said aloud, gaining composure. "I'll simply lock this drawer and see what Marcus Harris's business with Bram Pavolich is all about."

"Izzie, you can show Mr. Harris in now."

"Mr. Pavolich, my pleasure to meet you again. You know I couldn't help but notice that the stock in SynCor Foods is going up. Looks like all this publicity about Dan Richardson didn't hurt your company at all."

"Don't see why it would, Detective Harris. Dan Richardson's murder had nothing to do with SynCor Foods. Afraid ol' Dan was a gamblin' man, detective. A pony, or lack of money if you will, brought Dan to his final days, if you want my estimation."

"Was Richardson a ladies' man?"

"No, no. Not ol' Richardson. Too much with his head in the test tubes and his fingers in the ponies."

"Hah! Too bad," Harris said in a tone more appropriate to a saloon. "Some men never learn that a fine young woman is like a fine cigar, one of the simple pleasures of life," Harris laughed a "good ol' boy" belly laugh, offering Bram a fine Havana cigar.

Bram could feel his guard go down, quite against his better judgment. The saucy talk seemed to bring back his prior self-satisfied mood.

Harris continued. "You know what I mean, eh, Mr. Pavolich? Eh? In fact, I'll let you in on a little secret of mine. There's a favorite place I like to go myself not far from here. Mandy's Magic Massage House. Ever hear of the place? Real great little ladies over there who really know how to take care of a man."

Bram laughed and felt himself being drawn into this spirit of comradery.

"Yes, I guess I know the place. Have a favorite gally of mine there myself. Stacked in all the right places, if you know what I mean. And always so eager to please."

Harris snorted. "Sure do. They're the best kind. Never a shortage of women here at your company, I guess. How about giving me a grand tour? I've never seen a human milk production plant before."

"Sure. I was just about to call it a day anyway."

"I have to see how my company is doing. I bought stock in SynCor Foods this morning. Think it's gonna go up."

"Up is the only way for SynCor Foods," Bram said with the confident air of a champion.

As they were walking out, Harris said, "You sure are up, Bram. You know, you sure keep yourself in good shape. Jogger? Or walker? You know they say walking is one of the best forms of exercise . . . say you should try to walk two miles a day to keep in tip top shape. Me, I don't think I could walk two miles if my life depended on it. What 'bout you, Bram?"

"Well, I tell you, detective, I pride myself on good natural physical health. I could easily walk even more than two miles."

"You don't say."

Isabelle Nick was surprised. Instead of a somber interrogation of Bram Pavolich by Marcus Harris, it sounded more like they were a couple of college boys at a frat party!

Isabelle could hear loud boisterous laughs coming from Bram's executive office. Whatever was going on sounded more like a celebration than an investigation!

Well, no matter, she had made up her mind over lunch.

Izzie's train of thought was interrupted by Bram Pavolich leading Marcus Harris from his office.

"Izzie, I'm going to show Detective Harris around the Nature Plus milk production factory."

"Yes, sir," Izzie smiled automatically. "You'll be back today?"

"We're leaving our things in my office. But then I'm calling it a day. It's been a long week."

"Yes, sir."

When the men were out of sight, Isabelle knew this was her time to act. Now or never. Later could be too late.

She went into Bram's office. With her back facing the door, Isabelle pulled on the drawer holding the secret report.

It was locked! Oh, my God, it was locked again!

Bram must have relocked the drawer. That meant he knew that it had been opened. Did he suspect she had opened it?

Izzie could feel a numbness overtake her. With shaky hands, she searched Bram's desk for keys to the drawer. She found them! They had been under some papers. Carefully, she unlocked the drawer.

The report was still there! Somehow between all her restlessness last night and this morning, she had thought the report had been a figment of her imagination. It is real, feeling panic rise. Real! And she had to do what she had to do.

With shaky hands, she removed the report, and wedged it between two manila folders. Looking down the corridor, she stealthily made her way to the executive copy machine.

In a twilight limbo state of consciousness, Izzie saw herself making a photocopy of the five-page report. It seemed that every nerve in her body was turned on in an electric on-guard awareness of danger and caution.

After the copies were made, she hurried back to Bram's office. She replaced the original report back into the drawer. The keys? Now where the heck were the keys to relock the drawer? If the drawer was found open again, Bram would know it had been her!

As she nervously searched the desktop for the keys, she could hear the men's voices returning to the office.

She found them! With a second's motion, Izzie locked the credenza drawer, tossed the keys back into the desk with a clunk, and secured the copied report under a large manila folder.

She was just exiting his office as they returned, manila folder tucked protectively under her arm.

She had done it! By the grace of God, Nature Plus Formula would be stopped from its deadly course.

Bram Pavolich had the eerie feeling that his desk had been tampered with. Call it premonition, ESP, or whatever, Bram felt that something was just not right.

He checked the drawer holding the report. It was locked; however, there was tiny fragment of paper protruding from a corner. It hadn't been there before. He would have noticed.

And how oddly Izzie had acted when he and Harris had returned from the factory tour. With her head down, she had shuffled out of his office, arms covering some papers and a folder under her arm. Protectively. As a mother might protect her child. And then when Detective Harris had left his ID card, Isabelle had swept it up in a second's motion.

Bram had turned his head briefly before entering his office to see Isabelle place the card in a large envelope that she had in her top drawer.

Things were not right. And then his credenza drawer had been opened prior to today. Last night, it must have been. Who had opened it? Izzie?

Bram buzzed Izzie on his inner office line.

"Izzie?"

"Yes sir." Bram thought he noticed her voice quiver.

"Please do me a personal favor and report to purchasing. I guess that new employee we hired has got something screwed up, and, as usual, they think you are the only one who can help. They're waiting for you, now."

Of course, Mr. Pavolich."

Bram pressed the numbers 456 on his desk phone, purchasing department.

"Purchasing? My personal executive assistant Isabelle Nick will be there in a minute to review any problems you may be having with your new employee. What? Well, create some. She will be there in a minute to help you with a problem. And make sure it is a thorough review of about 15 minutes."

Bram went out from his office and stood over Isabelle's secretary desk. How small and insignificant it seemed in comparison to his. He opened her top drawer and pulled out the large manila envelope.

Copies of the report! And atop it all, the ID card of Detective Marcus Harris! Bram swooned back on his heels, feeling air leave his body. His head felt light, like he was going to faint.

Poor sweet Isabelle. His dear sweet Izzie. She was such a fool.

A fly had landed in the half-filled cup of black coffee, now stone cold, left on Detective Harris's desk from this morning. Harris stared at the fly while his mind reviewed the Richardson murder. It was as if the stagnant fly represented Harris's stalemate progress on the Richardson case.

Sure, he had found out that Bram frequented Mandy's Magic House, but that wasn't enough to arrest him for murder. Sure, Bram could easily walk two miles, the distance from SynCor Foods to the costume shop, but, again, that wasn't real evidence against him.

Yet, Bram had taken to his interrogation like a fatted calf leading to water. Harris laughed aloud. What a narcissist! He wanted the success of Nature Plus Formula very much. Perhaps too much? What about that report that Richardson supposedly presented to Bram the day before his murder? Surely it must contain key evidence against him. But who else would know of its contents except Pavolich and Richardson. Perhaps Richardson's wife? Isabelle Nick?

His train of thought was interrupted by the phone ringing.

"Harris, homicide," he answered.

"Hey, Marcus. It's Danny Wingfield. What have you got on the Richardson murder? Any arrest yet?"

"Nope. Not yet."

"Any suspects? Pavolich?"

Harris laughed. "Remember, Danny, you said that, not me. Hey, Danny. You know anything about Richardson playing the ponies?"

"I heard that, too. No apparent truth to it. I talked to his wife, but he could have kept it from her, I guess. But not likely."

"How did you hear about his playing the ponies, Danny?"

Danny laughed. "Well, coach, I know this isn't exactly kosher, but I sleuthed outside Bram's office door yesterday and learned a bunch of good stuff."

"Like?"

"Like the fact that Isabelle Nick had seen that research report Richardson presented to Bram just the night before he was murdered. She hadn't read the whole thing, but key phrases of the report were in all caps, and she did see those."

"What were they, Danny?"

"Wait, let me get my notebook. Okay. Here. 'Only a matter of time, but it's a matter of life and death.' 'Danger to babies. Antibodies.' That's when Bram told Izzie that Richardson was, and I quote, a troubled man who played the ponies, unquote. Only troubled man, I see in this case, is ol' Pavolich. Do anything to protect his little Nature Plus. That the way you see it, Marcus?"

"Danny. You know, you're good. Ever think of being a detective instead of a reporter?"

Danny laughed. "So, do you have anything I can report for Sunday's paper?"

"I did pay Pavolich a visit today. Got the grand tour of the new Nature Plus production plant. What a weird set-up. Women in rose pink cubicles hooked up to high-tech breast pumps in a Barbie Doll setting. I saw the new line of packaging. Looks like milk cartons. Going to be available in the refrigerator and freezer sections of grocery stores. Mothers will be picking up a quart of formula just like a quart of milk. He has a formula line with breast milk for newborn to the first year. Going to initially distribute nationally. Phase II calls for a new whole milk product enriched with human breast milk for children aged one to three, and expanded markets on an international level. Says the potential for human breast milk products is unlimited. Regular fountain of youth. Good for you in all sorts of natural ways. Possibility of one day expanding to adult consumer. Someday, Danny, you might go to a bar and get a creamed drink made with human breast milk!"

"Weird times we're living in. I sure would love to see that production plant and take some pictures of the women breastfeeding, the new packaging . . ."

"Whooh, Danny. Take it easy. Pavolich guards that plant like a great Dane protecting its master. Don't you have any other stories to work on to keep you out of trouble?"

"I'm making grounds on my Freddy Mack story. Definite drug/mafia connections there. It's keeping me busy. But, come on, detective, crack this case already."

"I'm working on it, Danny. Working on it."

After he hung up, Harris stared at the cup of this morning's cold coffee. He'd give Isabelle Nick a phone call tonight at her home. Yes. He needed to know what Izzie knew.

And the sooner the better.

Isabelle was ready to call it a day. She knew what she had to do, and, wearily, set out to do it.

She grabbed her hat, coat, and scarf to prepare herself against Chicago's traditionally cold November winter night. Bundled up, she secured the manila envelope containing the copies of Richardson's research report in the crook of the arm of her wool coat.

She was temporarily startled by Bram Pavolich calling out from the door of the executive office.

"Are you leaving for the evening, Isabelle?"

"Yes, sir. Time to call it a day."

"Fine. Have a pleasant evening." Then, his head protruding from the door, his eyes fixed upon the manila envelope she was holding, he asked, "Why, you're not taking work home with you, are you, Izzie?"

"Oh, no, sir. Just some magazines and reading materials I need to catch up on."

"Fine, Isabelle. See you tomorrow. Oh, Izzie, did you ever get a new car, or are you still helping our nation's climate change crisis by using the public bus system?"

"Still taking the bus, sir. Serves my needs very well. Only $2.25 to get home with the free transfer on Highland Avenue."

"Ah. But do you have to wait long for the transfer?"

"Oh. Just a matter of minutes, usually about 13 minutes to be exact. But I enjoy it. The long bus ride relaxes me after the day's activities. Well, I must be running, sir, to catch the bus."

"Good night, Isabelle." And then he added after a moment, "Thanks, for everything, Izzie."

Izzie pulled the scarf tightly around her neck. 5:32 p.m. The bus would be here any minute. *Sure was dark out already.* Just like night, ever since daylight savings time had been changed back. And it wasn't even dinnertime, yet. Ah, the windy city, Chicago.

Isabelle got on the 5:33 p.m. bus. It seemed unusually crowded, and she hadn't been able to get a seat. As she held the cold steel bar above her head, she balanced her stance to the rhythmic movement of the bus's stops and goes.

She had wanted a seat so she could have used the time of the 12-minute ride to review, once again, Richardson's report. She knew what she had to do. As soon as she got to her apartment, she'd kick off her shoes and call the detective. Harris was his name. She had his ID card in the manila folder she was holding.

Izzie felt as if she was in a half dream-nightmare state. *Was this reality? Was she working for a madman murderer who would stop at nothing to launch his new line of baby formula?* The thought sent shivers up her spine.

Finally, the bus arrived at Highland street. Izzie's hand ached from clenching the iron bar above her. She exited through the back bus door, stepping over the curb to the intersection of Fern and Highland. Izzie checked her watch. 5:48 p.m. The bus usually got here at 6:01 p.m.

God, it was dark out. The streetlight cast an eerie glow to the unusually empty intersection. Izzie could feel tension building up inside her. Never in her life had she been such a key factor in the destiny of life. Here, under her arm, she held the evidence pointing to Bram Pavolich as the murderer of Dan Richardson. The report also told how Nature Plus Formula would kill 2% of the babies who used it, without a single trace to the "silent murderer." She shuddered. Thousand of defenseless babies, helpless infants that depended upon others to provide for them. And she was the only one – living! – who knew!

Dan Richardson had discovered the fluke in Nature Plus that caused the antibiotic systems of 2% of the babies who used it to break down. And, eventually, cause them to die. And he was dead! It was only she, Izzie, that could now save the world's infants!

The ride on the transfer bus seemed to take forever. The bus was almost vacant except for a Hispanic mother and her two children, and a homeless man slouched in a seat with a fedora hat over his face. After taking a seat in the back of the bus on the long bench seat in a corner, Izzie felt she couldn't wait one more minute and had to call Detective Harris. *Oh, dear God, please let him still be there. I must reach him.* She reached inside the manila envelope for the card he left at SynCor Foods. Here it was, 756-7800. Izzie dialed, carefully, her hands shaking from nervousness and the brisk November night air. Four rings and no answer. No answer machine either. Damn, she'd have to go on google to get his home number. First, she had to call Sofia Ruiz to warn her. Her inner self told her to call Sofia Ruiz. NOW! Her fingers nervously scanned her contacts for "R", Ruiz, Sofia Ruiz. She pressed the number.

Please be home, Sofia. Sofia, please answer.

"Hello?"

"Hello, Sofia?"

"Yes?"

"Sofia, this is Isabelle Nick. I can't talk right now. I want you to stop using Nature Plus Formula immediately. There is real danger to baby Andrew if you continue using it. I'm going to the police, detective Harris with the facts of Dan Richardson's research report."

So intent was Izzie on her vital message to Sofia that she didn't see the "homeless" man in the fedora hat get up and walk slowly down the aisle to the back of the bus to a seat directly in front and to the left of her.

"Izzie, what are you saying? How could formula hurt Andrew? Are you saying Nature Plus killed my baby twin, Anthony?"

"Sofia, my God, I don't know. I don't know what it all means. I'm sorry I ever told you about Nature Plus Formula in the first place. But now, promise me, you'll stop using it. You must promise me. There's great danger. I must go now. I'll call you later from home. I'm sorry if I'm upsetting you, but I felt I had to call you now. Goodbye, Sofia, and God bless you. I'm sorry."

Izzie had been huddled in the corner of the bench seat facing toward the window. She felt a jab in her side. She turned to see the homeless man slouched over her like he was passed out.

"Hey, get off me," Izzie commanded, but she felt dizzy. Time and space were spinning around her. She looked up at the homeless man's face, and then, it could not be mistaken. It was the face of Bram Pavolich. A gloved hand came over her mouth. Suffocating her. Stopping her from shrieking out. Stopping her from crying out to save the innocent babies who were going to be killed by the hand of this cold-blooded murderer, Bram Pavolich. *She needed to cry out, MURDER! Cry out, Murder, for the innocents. Cry out, murder, for little Anthony. Cry out, murder, for Dan Richardson. Cry murder for her own life.* She saw a gun in Bram's hand. Was she going to be shot? The Hispanic bus driver seemed like miles away, and his radio was on loud. From what Izzie knew about guns, this one had a silencer on it.

"Izzie," Bram purred into her ears. "You have disappointed me."

And then, it was over.

Sofia Ruiz stared blankly at her cell phone. She had never heard Isabelle sound so strange. Almost hysterical. What did it all mean? Danger? What had Izzie just told her? Stop using Nature Plus? But why? Had it somehow been responsible for her little Anthony's death?

She went to recent phone calls on her cell. She called Izzie back. Something was bothering her. Izzie's phone went right to voice message.

Sofia felt her body begin to quiver. She felt heavy on her legs. She placed both hands squarely on the kitchen table. She hung her head down, like a rag doll. She needed to clear her head. It was all going too fast.

God, she wished Antonio was home already. Soon, she told herself. He'll be home, soon. He's always home by 6:30 p.m. She tried to calm herself. *Think logically!*

She smoothed her hands down the sides of the oversized extra-large T-shirt she was wearing, and through her short curly dark hair.

It couldn't be possible! Nature Plus a danger to her babies? So, she had fed little Anthony – what? Poison. To her sweet baby twin as he looked up to her trustingly for his only source of nourishment!

And who was this detective that Izzie said she was going to call? The name sounded familiar. It was the same detective mentioned by that reporter who had called her – when? Just yesterday.

Sofia lifted the lid on the pork chops she was cooking for dinner. Their sweet aroma rose to her face, brightening her momentarily. Sofia poked them with a fork, shifting their positions in the pan.

It seemed like ages since she had received that other phone call from the reporter. Time was going so slowly for her lately. Almost like slow motion. Her train of thought was interrupted by baby Andrew's familiar cry.

Sofia smiled to herself. Whenever Andrew smelled supper cooking, he became hungry. She laughed softly to herself. She instinctively picked up a baby formula bottle she had left on the kitchen table and walked into the baby's nursery. She settled herself into the comfy Afghan-lined rocker, cuddling her baby softly in her arms.

"Here, my big boy. Here's what you wanted. You were hungry."

As Sofia fed the baby, Izzie's words came into her mind, hauntingly. "You must stop using Nature Plus."

Sofia jerked the bottle from Andrew's mouth, startling him into a piercing cry. She felt herself crumble. The tears flowed down her cheeks. *What was happening? Was she going crazy?* Now she couldn't even feed her only living son.

"Get a hold of yourself," Sofia said out loud. "Antonio will be home, soon."

The tiny grey hippopotamus clocks the twins had received from her brother read 6:25 p.m.

Well, baby Andrew would just have apple juice tonight, Sofia thought, as she carried the tiny baby into the kitchen. As she propped Andrew onto her lap with the warm apple juice bottle, she decided to call Izzie again. Once again, it went to voice message.

She had to talk to Isabelle. She had to talk to her. God, where was Antonio? Sofia dazed off into space, automatically feeding and comforting her living son.

It would take Izzie 45 minutes to get home. She had called about 6 p.m. She'd call Izzie back at 6:45 p.m.

She had to reach her. It was a matter of life and death!

Pretty slow for a Thursday night, Mandy mused to herself, as she sucked a long drag of her cigarette. Tonight, she just had Marie and herself, of course. Mandy only worked when she wanted to, one of the chief benefits of being in this business as long as she had been. She fluffed up the sides of her dyed red hair. *Hmmph.* It felt dirty. She'd wash it tonight. Ah, here comes someone, old regular. Bram Pavolich.

"Hello, Bram. How's life treating you?"

"Fine, Mandy. Fine."

He seemed like he was in a hurry. Maybe him tonight? She could use the extra money. Naw, she really wasn't in the mood. Anyways, she had heard that Bram could be pretty rough in bed. And that he was a "tit man." Looking down at her average-size chest, Mandy responded, "Only have Marie tonight, Bram. Slow night. That okay with you?"

"Fine, fine."

Bram was definitely in a hurry, Mandy thought as he moved quickly up the stairs to where Marie was. Seemed out of sorts, too.

As Bram bounded up the stairs, Mandy saw something protruding from his back pocket. Something metallic and shiny. Was it a gun?

Mandy, girl, don't let your imagination get the better of you.

Ever since she had been questioned by that detective about whether any of their customers were employed at SynCor Foods, Mandy could not stop thinking about Bram Pavolich.

Should she have told the detective? Could Bram be a murderer? Mandy laughed out loud.

No, Mandy. Old detective Harris was barking up the wrong tree.

It was a slow night. Slow for a Thursday. She'd close up early. She wanted to wash her hair. It felt so damn dirty.

It was 7:30 p.m. Sofia checked her last cell phone message to her friend, Isabelle Nick. She had tried repeatedly, and it always went to messages.

"Antonio, Isabelle should be home by now. She runs her schedule like clockwork. I'm scared. Something's not right. I can feel it."

"Sofia, please calm down. For your own good. You're so worked up, it's not good for you." And then he added, his voice slightly lower, "Not after everything we've been through."

"But that's just the point," Sofia refuted. "Isabelle said to stop using Nature Plus Formula, that it was a danger to Andrew, and that it could have caused Anthony's death!"

"But that's insane," Antonio said. As he unbuttoned his pale blue work shirt, he continued, "Honey, I know the last week hasn't been easy. Let's try and forget. We must go on. We have baby Andrew to live for."

He wrapped his arms around her, gently raising her chin up. She felt herself warm at his touch, as she always did. She looked into his eyes and found kindness and understanding. She and Antonio were linked together forever, in love and tragedy.

"I know it sounds insane . . . I probably sound insane . . . but if you could have heard her voice. She was so scared of something. Or someone."

"Okay, Let's forget about it for tonight. Call first thing tomorrow. Tomorrow, everything will fall in place. You'll see, love."

"I only hope you're right, Antonio. I truly do," Sofia said, softly, almost prayerfully.

Chapter 10

November 7

Thank God it's Friday! Michelle Heywood laughed softly to herself, letting herself enjoy the waves of self-satisfaction that filled her. She knew this total at-one-with-the-world-and-herself feeling didn't come often, and she loved every second of it.

She felt on top of the world. The Nature Plus Formula campaign was moving along smoothly. The client was thrilled, and Dave Adams made no qualms about letting Michelle, and the entire ad agency, know that he was thrilled with its success.

Michelle suddenly found herself the recipient of dozens of compliments. Comments like, "Congrats on Nature Plus! You deserve it."; "Good work on the new account, Michelle. Good for the agency."; "Heard the client flipped for the Nature Plus campaign. Good going, Michelle! Worked some of that magic of yours, eh?"

When she felt good inside, it seemed her looks never seemed better. Her natural strawberry blond hair took on a lustrous shine and bounce. Her complexion looked well-scrubbed and glowed with wholesome freshness.

"Well, being in love doesn't hurt either," Michelle said aloud, after appraising her appearance in the full-length mirror of the lady's restroom at Ackerly, Adams & Associates.

Michelle felt a rush of thoughts and feelings come upon her, making her feel nicer than she ever had in her life. And the reason? Hawk Wilder. She couldn't believe that it had finally happened to her. Her! Michelle Heywood! Happily, oh so joyously, in love!

Just thinking about Hawk, his warm brown eyes, his lean tall body, the way his brown hair fell haphazardly over his forehead, made Michelle feel good inside.

And I have Nature Plus to thank. She smoothed her khaki-colored tunic over matching slacks, checking her profile in the mirror. Her mind couldn't stop thinking of Hawk. Working together on the campaign, creating magic in words and images, linked her and Hawk in a world of their own, a world that only they shared.

The interaction, give and take, always seasoned with laughter and caring, weaved them together, to this magical wonderful state she was experiencing.

Their first "official" date at her sister's Halloween party had had the gory event of Dan Richardson's murder as part of it.

Yet, that, too, seemed to draw her and Hawk together. He had stayed the night with her, and although they hadn't made love that night, Michelle had never experienced such sensual feelings from being held, caressed, and kissed. It was as if every cell in her body glowed at his every touch and stroke.

And today, Michelle could barely stand to consider her good fortune. She and Hawk were going on a company-paid convention for Valu-Mart Drug Stores in Boca Raton, Florida. Four glorious days and nights in balmy, sun-drenched Florida.

Michelle checked her watch. 11 a.m. Time to leave the office. She and Hawk had a 4 p.m. direct flight from Chicago to West Palm Beach. She straightened the items on her account executive desk – notepads to the left, pens neatly lined up to the right.

Just one last thing before I go. She called her sister on her IPhone.

"Hello, sister. This is your sister," Michelle said jovially. "Do I have a new niece yet?"

"Don't you sound like you're in a good mood. Wish I could say the same about myself. I'm so depressed. It's 14 days late. I can't stand it. I can't sleep at night. I'm up seven or eight times going to the bathroom. It's awful. I'm totally gigantic."

"Well, it should be any second. Just hang in there. I'm just calling to let you know I'm going out of town for a few days. Company convention. In Florida."

"Don't make me sicker."

Michelle laughed. "Guess who I'm going with?"

"Who?"

"The art director. Hawk Wilder. You met him at your Halloween party."

"Oh, yeah. He seemed really nice."

"I think this is it, sis. It finally happened. Another one bites the dust."

"Oh, Shell, I'm so happy for you. What a hottie," Mary added, seductively.

"He's just the greatest person I've ever known. I'm so thrilled! I just don't want it to stop."

"It won't. If it's for real, it just gets better."

"I'll text you where I'll be staying just in case you have the baby. We'll be at Boca Hotel, in Boca Raton, Florida. Bye, sis. I'll pick up a T-shirt for you in Florida."

"Better make it an extra-large," Mary retorted.

After hanging up, Michelle grabbed her belongings in her leather attaché and headed out the office. She had a 4 p.m. plane to catch. A plane to Florida. With Hawk.

Once he had become chief homicide detective, Marcus Harris's Fridays were just like any other day of the week. The thrill of knowing the workweek was over, looking forward to two days of rest and relaxation just weren't part of a homicide detective's lifestyle. His was a 24-hour job, ever-changing, ever-new.

Still, he was looking forward to tonight. Friday night professional wrestling was on at 8 p.m. and he intended to stretch out on his worn lazy boy recliner with a few beers, his remote control, and relax.

He and his wife, Kara, would make their usual Friday night dinner, steak and garlic mashed potatoes, his favorite. And for dessert, apple pie topped with a generous dollop of fresh vanilla ice cream.

For 25-years and through raising five kids (three grown and married, four grandchildren, two teenagers still living at home) their family dinners were just as much a tradition as going to mass on Sunday.

He smiled as he thought of Kara. After 25 years of marriage, the thought of her still brought an exciting warm glow to his heart. His Kara. His refuge from the daily pressures and stark realities of his job.

His momentary flight from the cold moss-green walls of police headquarters, homicide division, was abruptly interrupted by the sharp ringing of his desk telephone.

"Hello, Harris, homicide."

A soft shy voice began. "Hello? Hello, is this homicide detective Marcus Harris?"

"Speaking."

"Hi, you don't know me, but my name is Sofia Ruiz. I believe you know a friend of mine, Isabelle Nick. I'm scared, detective. Izzie (that's her nickname) called me last night and told me that she was going to call you. Did she? I'm worried because I tried to call her all last night, and she never answered. There's still no answer this morning. Have you heard from her?"

"Is this the same Isabelle Nick that works at SynCor Foods?"

"Yes, yes," the voice answered anxiously, and then with a note of relief, said, "Good, so you *have* heard from Izzie?"

"No, the last time I saw Izzie was yesterday at about 4 p.m. at SynCor Foods. In fact, I tried to call her last night at about 6:30 p.m. and it went straight to messages."

"May I ask why you called her?"

"We're investigating the murder of a former SynCor Foods employee, Dan Richardson."

"Yes, that's right! That's the name Isabelle mentioned. She said she had information about some report. It had to do with Nature Plus Formula." And then, her voice lowering slightly, she said, "Nature Plus could have contributed to my infant's death."

"What time did she call you?"

"It was about 6 p.m. She was on the bus to her home. She said she was going to call you right after she hung up. You mean she didn't call you?"

"No, she never called me last night."

"Detective. That's odd. So strange. She sounded so determined like it was a matter of urgent importance."

Something clicked in Harris's mind. Something from this morning's reports of area homicides from Thursday p.m.

"Can you hold for a moment, Mrs. Ruiz?" Marcus requested.

He searched his screen for the homicide report. *Here it is. Hhhmm.* He returned to his call with Sofia.

"Mrs. Ruiz, do you think you could come to police headquarters this morning?"

"Police? Why–?"

"I'm sorry, Mrs. Ruiz. There was a murder last night on a CTA bus at approximately 6 p.m. The body was found at the end of the driver's shift. Female, approximate age 50, weight 120, 5 ft., 3 in. tall. She was shot in the chest. I need a positive identification from you, Mrs. Ruiz, but I'm sorry to tell you that I believe that murdered person is your friend. Your friend – Isabelle Nick."

"Lovey, oh Lovey," Norma Pavolich called out to her husband in a sing-song voice, like one that would be used to call a young child. "Your chicken soup is done. Come into the kitchen."

Bram ambled into the kitchen, his spirit weakened. Although it was 11:30 a.m., he was still dressed in a checkered bathrobe, wrapped over beige flannel pajamas. His vinyl-bottom slippers shuffled on the sleek linoleum floor. His hair, uncombed, stood up around his head, masking the growing bald spot on his head. He hadn't slept well the last few nights, and his eyes were surrounded by folds of puffy skin. The side jowls of his face hung lackluster, like they possessed not an ounce of strength. His sickly-looking appearance only seemed worse compared to the perky, wholesome, appearance of his wife, Norma.

The two-week visit at her sister's had done her good. She had arrived back home this Friday morning early, ready to resume her domestic duties. When Bram had told her he was sick and had no intention of going to the office, she had said, "Just as I thought. Here I go and leave you a poor helpless thing for two weeks and you've worn your health down. Lovey (her pet name for Bram), you just stay in bed and I'll make you some fresh homemade chicken soup. That will fix you up in a jiffy."

Now, as Bram spooned down mouthfuls of the delicious soup broth, tender chunks of chicken, celery and carrots, it almost seemed as if last night had never happened.

Having to kill Izzie sickened him. He had loved Isabelle, a loyal worker who had stood by his side for over 20 years. He'd made his decision to kill her so fast, and it had happened so fast, it just didn't seem real.

The look of betrayal in Isabelle's eyes as he covered her mouth with his gloved hand had haunted him all night, and still haunted him now.

"Why, Bram. Your hands are shaking so, it's a wonder that chicken soup stays on the spoon," Norma said, jerking his thoughts to reality. "Why, you're a nervous wreck. I knew I shouldn't have gone away for two whole weeks at a time. And I never shall again," she concluded, while perpetually fussing around the kitchen, straightening a dish towel here, re-arranging the kitchen countertop knick-knacks.

Bram's thoughts focused on the moment. *Yes, it had certainly been an eventful two weeks without the constant chatter of his wife.* But, honestly, it was good to have Norma back. She seemed to keep him adrift towards port, rather than drifting aimlessly through life's sea.

"Well, did you call into the office yet? Izzie's probably wondering why you're not in yet."

At the sound of his wife saying "Izzie," Bram shuddered. "Right, right, call the office," he muttered to himself.

"Absolutely," Norma continued in a chirpy voice. "The president of one of the biggest food companies in the nation, soon the world, is allowed a sick day, too!"

Bram retreated to his private office. There was no need to make a phone call. Izzie wouldn't be there to answer his call. Just the thought of her death sent shudders down his spine, making the already chilly air in his home feel even colder. *I'll make a fire. Yes, a nice warm fire is what I need right now. I'll burn Dan Richardson's report and be done with it finally.*

The copy that Isabelle had made was still in a manila envelope tucked securely in his briefcase. But today was the day to destroy all of it, forever. SynCor had cost him two dear employees already, and he wanted an end to it. *He wasn't a murderer! He was a protector! SynCor Foods must be protected, at all costs!*

He decided to call the office anyway. It might look suspicious if he didn't call Izzie to let her know he was staying home. *After all, if he hadn't killed her, she would be there, wondering why he wasn't in.*

Bram called his office line. *It was answered on the third ring. Good. The employees do pay attention to the rules.* If a phone rings more than five times, the employee is put on automatic probation, and if a second incident occurs, it's grounds for immediate dismissal. It was his attention to the little details of customer satisfaction and image that had made and continued to make SynCor Foods a success.

"Good morning. SynCor Foods."

"Good morning. This is Bram Pavolich. Who is this, please?" He immediately recognized the voice.

"Oh, hello, Mr. Pavolich. It's Pam Pritthouse. How are you?"

"Not very well, I'm afraid. Touch of the flu bug, so I won't be coming into the office today." And then, playing dumb, he continued, "Where's Izzie? Why are you answering my direct executive line?"

"Well, sir, Isabelle isn't in yet. She hasn't called in either, which is strange. They asked me to man her phone and duties until we heard from her. Said it was odd for Izzie not to call. She said she had been here 20 years and had never missed a day of work."

Bram involuntarily swallowed, loudly, creating an audible nervous sigh into the receiver. It had been bad having to kill Izzie, he thought. He had liked her so much. She had been the perfect employee.

"Sir, are you okay?"

"Fine. Like I said, I have this damn flu bug." And then, changing the subject, "Have there been any messages?"

"Yes, just one. Detective Marcus Harris called at 11:15 a.m. Said it was urgent that he reach you. If he calls back, should I give him your home number?"

"No!" Bram barked. Gaining composure, he continued, "No. Don't tell anyone my whereabouts today. As far as you, or anyone else knows, I'm simply out of town on business." And then, in a condescending tone, he added, "You see, Pam, to my clients and customers I'm never sick. It's important to my image."

"Oh," Pam said. "Well, that's all the messages. Now you stay in bed today, Mr. Pavolich, and get well."

"That's exactly what I intend to do," Bram concluded the conversation.

After Bram hung up the phone, he decided it was time to get the wood for the fireplace. He'd burn all the copies of Richardson's report and be done with it. Yes, a burning fire is just what he needed right now.

Danny Wingfield wanted a fresh new story for Sunday's paper. Oh, sure, he had two stories "in the can" – one on teenage gangs in Chinatown, and another on a drug half-way house on the North Shore with certain high-profile celebrities rumored to be there. Both had non-dated information so they could be used at any time within the next month or so. It was a practice a seasoned journalist had shared with him when Danny had first started in the newspaper business.

"*Always* have something in Sunday's paper, and preferably something good," he had told Danny.

Sunday exposure counted, and a fledgling reporter who wanted to create a name for himself should stockpile at least two good stories for off weeks when, either by sickness or other reason, the customary Sunday feature story wasn't completed.

And it had paid off. Since then, Danny had begun the practice of developing three to four stories at the same time. Now, his editor counted on Danny's three to six pages of copy and two to three photos for the Sunday Tempo section of the Chicago Sun Reporter. This week Danny had the Chinatown gang story scheduled for publication.

But that could always be changed as late as Saturday at 5 p.m.

There was still time to develop a new story. He regarded the Friday 11:30 a.m. digital reading on his watch. Well, maybe not a whole new story, but a new slant on a prior story? A definite possibility and Danny felt in his gut instinct that there was more to the Dan Richardson murder than what was already reported. In fact, he felt it could be the biggest story of his life. He decided to call Detective Marcus Harris to see what, if any, new developments in the case had occurred.

"Detective Harris, homicide."

"Hello, Marcus. It's Danny Wingfield. Anything new on the Richardson murder I can put in Sunday's paper?" Danny leaned back in his chair, and pulled his fingers through his hair, as if preparing his brain to think, a habit he had developed since being in the business.

"Don't know if it's ready to be in the paper yet, but remember Bram's executive assistant? Isabelle Nick? Dead."

"Dead?" Danny found himself gasping out loud.

"Yep," Harris continued. "Dead as Sofia Ruiz's baby twin."

"Sofia Ruiz? You mean she's involved in this, too?"

"Well, it seems like Izzie called her friend Sofia just before she was murdered. Supposedly told her not to use Nature Plus Formula. That it might have killed her baby."

"Weird," Danny said.

"Sure is. And then Sofia Ruiz tells me that Izzie was going to call me right after hanging up. I never got the phone call. She was murdered in a CTA bus. We're not sure exactly when it happened. The driver, Jose Rivera, didn't discover the body until the end of his night shift."

It took Danny about 10 minutes to get all the particulars on the case. After concluding the conversation with Detective Harris, Danny allowed himself a few minutes to digest what he had just learned. Isabelle's death would be treated like just another routine murder in the "streets of Chicago." Or would it? What could an interview with Bram Pavolich add to the story? Perhaps photos on the SynCor production plant with the breastfeeding mothers? What about an interview with Sofia Ruiz?

Danny searched his phone and found the number for Pavolich's executive direct line.

"SynCor Foods," a sing-song voice answered.

"Yes, may I speak with Mr. Pavolich?"

"Mr. Pavolich is out of the office on business. Who may I say is calling?"

"Danny Wingfield of the Sun Reporter."

"Oh, Danny, yes, I think I remember you. Were you the -uh, gentleman that Mr. Pavolich threw out of the office just the other day?" There was a little flirtatious laugh.

"The one and the same. You were there?"

"Yes. I was in the marketing meeting on Nature Plus Formula. Hi, I'm Pam Pritthouse, assistant to marketing director Chet Hartman."

"Hi," Danny said warmly. "So. you're temporarily taking over Isabelle's duties, eh? Damn shame, isn't it?"

"What?" Pam asked, inquisitively.

"Oh, then you haven't been told. I'm sorry to have to be the one to tell you, but Isabelle Nick is dead. She was murdered last night."

"Murdered?" Pam said, the shock evident in her voice. "Does Mr. Pavolich know?" she asked.

"I don't know."

"Hmmm, it didn't seem like he knew anything about it –"

"Oh, he's in the office?" Danny leaped on the statement.

"Oh, no. Like I said, he's out of town on business. I just spoke to him this morning when he called in."

"And how about you? Do you get a lunch hour? How about if I take you out to lunch? Hannigans is great on Fridays. TGIF all day."

Pausing momentarily, then, "Sure, why not. Sounds good. Should I meet you there?"

"No, I'll pick you up. I'll be at SynCor Foods, in say, just about one-half hour."

"Great. I'm getting hungry already," Pam said.

"Good. I'm starved," Danny replied.

Bram Pavolich felt himself unwind with each crackle of the fire he had built in the old stone fireplace located in his study. He stood in front of it, still dressed in his robe, wrapped securely around flannel pajamas. He stared at it. The glistening colors of red, orange, and yellow drew him to it, creating one presence, one entity.

He had just burned the entire research report of Dan Richardson. Five pages of facts, illustrations, and diagrams. He burned it slowly, page by page, feeling himself becoming more serene with each page destroyed, turning to ash.

He was so totally engrossed in what he was doing, he barely paid attention to the sing-song high-pitched voice of his wife, Norma, crying out, "I'll get it," in response to the doorbell.

The clarity and calm of his mind was abruptly disrupted as he turned toward the study doorway in response to his wife saying, "Here he is! Now what did you say your name was? Oh, here it is on the little card you gave me, Detective Marcus Harris, homicide. Homicide. That means murder, right? What an unusual way to make a living. Lovey, someone is here to see you. Oh, I should have warned you, darling. I wasn't aware you weren't dressed yet. I thought when you said you were going to build a fire, you would have dressed to get the wood from the backyard shed. I'm sorry."

Then, continuing her monologue over the faint interruption of Bram's voice, "A fire is so nice in the afternoon, don't you think so, Detective Harris? May I call you Marcus?"

Not waiting for an answer, Norma said, "Bram had some old papers he wanted to burn, so he said, 'Norma, I'm gonna build a fire.' I said fine, would give the home a nice cozy feeling. Bram's not feeling good today. A touch of the flu. Bad cold. I've been at my sister's house for two weeks. Never do it again, mind you. No one to take care of Lovey. Got himself a touch of the bug. But better tomorrow, right? Well, I'll leave you two boys alone."

Norma exited, leaving the atmosphere in the study remarkably quiet except for the sounds of the fire.

"Nice lady," Marcus said.

"Loves to talk. Ol' Norma doesn't need anyone to talk to. Five-minute recitations are her credo," Bram said, trying to force a casual-sounding laugh.

"Sorry to disrupt you at home, but I have a matter of great importance to discuss with you."

"I *did* tell the-uh-girl at work not to tell anyone I was sick at home," Bram said.

"Oh, she said you were out of town on business," Harris said. "But I didn't believe her. When you've been in the detective business as long as I've been in it, you can tell when someone is lying. No, I thought I'd try you at your house."

Bram felt himself involuntarily stiffen.

"So, you say you are here on a matter of great importance. Explain, please," Bram took control of the situation. His mind was clearing again, thinking methodically.

Meeting the challenge head on, Harris said, "Your executive assistant Isabelle Nick was murdered last night." And then stating in a strong affirmative question over Bram's startled, "What?", the detective added, "But that doesn't surprise you, does it, Bram? Because you were there. Did you murder Isabelle Nick?"

"Don't be absurd. Why on earth would I want to murder her? I loved Isabelle. She was the best employee I ever had. Worked for me for 20 years. I'm greatly saddened to hear of her death."

"Where were you last night at seven o'clock, the time of Izzie's death?"

He had killed her at six, Bram mused to himself. Good, let them think it was later. Because he did have an alibi for seven. Lowering his voice as if taking someone into his confidence, Bram said, "At 7 p.m.

last night, I was at Mandy's Magic House. Check for yourself. I was with Marie."

And then, as if sharing a joke with a buddy in a locker room, Bram chuckled, "Please don't tell Norma. What she doesn't know won't hurt her."

"I'll check your alibi. Bram don't bother leaving town. On business. Or for any other reason. You and I will be doing some more-uh-talking before the week's over."

Harris reached down to button his overcoat and noticed something leaning against a manila folder, resting up upon the fireplace mantle. Something familiar. Very familiar.

"You weren't going to burn my business card, were you? Along with all the other papers that were in this manila envelope that you just burned?" Harris asked halfheartedly, noting the freshly curled pages in the fire, just turning to ash. Harris swooped the card and empty manila envelope under his arm.

Bram, momentarily losing composure, leaped at Harris. "Hey, give that to me."

Then, more in control, he said, "I won't burn it. I'll need it to call you if I hear of anything on Isabelle's case. I want to find the killer just as much as you."

"Just the same," Harris answered, still looking at the business card. He noticed another phone number written neatly on the card in pen.

"Bram, whose number did you write on my card?"

"Number?"

"Bram, I don't believe this is the card I gave you. I believe this is the card I gave to Isabelle Nick, and I believe this is the phone number of her friend, Sofia Ruiz."

Then, passing a new business card to Bram, Harris said, "Here's a new one for you, Bram. For you to call me – uh – with information of Isabelle's murder."

And then, in a statement declaring the finality of the meeting, Detective Harris stated, "The other is police evidence in the murder investigation of Isabelle Nick."

It had been remarkably easy to get corporate authorization to visit SynCor Foods, Danny thought. The rectangular-shaped sticky note printed with "Guest Pass. Hello, My Name Is . . ." had been quickly awarded to him by SynCor Foods security when Danny had announced that he was there to take marketing assistant Pam Pritthouse to lunch.

Taking Pam to lunch was the biggest benefit of his venture: not only for all the newsworthy information he had learned from her, while amiably chit-chatting over a carafe of wine at Hannigan's; but also, for the information that was vital to the story he planned to write today for publication in Sunday's paper. Danny had learned that Nature Plus Formula was 25% human breast milk. The breast milk was gathered from lactating women in the production factory at SynCor Foods. Pam had said it was quite odd to see women lined up in rosy, pink cubicles with sophisticated breast pumps attached to them. Most of the mothers were young and poor, but they needed a way to support themselves and their new babies. SynCor provided a generous salary, plus onsite day care, which was a benefit many of them couldn't afford to turn down.

She had told him about the superb ad campaign conceived by Michelle Heywood of Ackerly, Adams & Associates that would use Amber Greene as a celebrity sponsor.

He had also learned that Bram Pavolich was not out of the office on business as she had originally told him, but was at home, sick with the flu.

She hadn't meant to break the confidence of Bram Pavolich. It had sipped out quite innocently.

They had been waiting for their lunch orders of a crabmeat crescent with avocado for Pam, and a half-pound bacon cheeseburger for Danny. The carafe of wine had flowed as easily as their conversation. Pam had been explaining about the usage of Amber Greene as the Nature Plus celebrity spokesperson.

"It's mostly for the image of Nature Plus. To lend credibility to an otherwise unknown product."

Danny had replied, "Yeah, image. Corporations are always so concerned about their image."

"Yes, that's why Mr. Pavolich didn't want anyone to know he was sick at home today."

"He's not out of town?"

"Oh, I'm sorry I said that. It just slipped out. Please don't tell anyone. No, he doesn't want anyone to know he's sick. He said he's never sick to his customers and clients. He has to preserve his image."

Danny had his work cut out for him. After returning Pam to her office, he had found his way to the breast milk production factory. A sign marked the doorway, "Authorized Personnel Only." Pam had pointed it out to him on the way back to her office. He had photographed the entire scene, all vividly depicting this revolutionary new method of making baby formula. First, he had taken general shots showing the outline of the factory with its numerous cubicles that housed the breastfeeding women. Then, when he had known he would be leaving SynCor Foods shortly, he had gotten bolder.

He had taken photos of individual ladies. One woman, Sandra Nesskey, was about 29 years old. She was in "free time," as she had explained to Danny, which meant she was free to play with her four-year-old son, Sean, and six-month-old baby daughter, Krystal. When free time was up, her children would go to the professionally staffed onsite childcare center, and she would, once again, recline in the comfort of her specially-designed chair and press the button to activate the high-tech whisper smooth breast pump. She had said she produced six quarts of breast milk daily, for which she was paid a generous salary, all meals, and childcare. She was new to our country, originally from Poland, and she appreciated her job and felt "lucky" to have it.

The second woman was Freda Monner, an African American woman about 21 years of age. Freda's man had left her when she had her now two-year-old baby girl, Trina. She had been on aid to dependent children when she had replied to the ad placed in the paper which had stated, "Attention – Breastfeeding Mothers. $$$$ TOP PAY, FREE meals for you and your child(ren), FREE Child Care. Apply in person, SynCor Foods, 200 S. Wabash, Chicago."

Both women had signed the photography release forms when Danny had explained that he was doing a "positive" article for the Sun Reporter.

Yes, it had been a very productive afternoon. This exclusive feature could award him the Journalist of the Year award, as well as other coveted national journalistic awards.

He planned out the rest of his day. First, an interview with Sofia Ruiz. Then, a phone call to Michelle Heywood. And, finally, a statement from Bram Pavolich. He would process the photos himself, tonight, at the Sun Reporter.

It had been his good fortune to have taken Pam Pritthouse out to lunch, professionally and personally.

He could not remember ever having seen a prettier girl. Her beautiful oval face, large blue eyes, and easy smile had quite enchanted him. Yet, her manner was so easygoing, he had felt totally at ease with her. He felt it had been a mutual attraction.

Yes, it had been a great Friday. Thanks to Pam. He knew that he would be seeing her again. It seemed to be in his stars.

The aroma of chiles, cooked beans, and tamales in the tiny kitchen of Sofia Ruiz smelled tantalizing, Marcus Harris thought. In fact, it made him realize that he had skipped lunch entirely and was famished. Well, it was almost six, and he was ready to call it a day. He wanted to watch professional wrestling at 8 p.m. and was looking forward to his usual Friday night dinner shared with his wife Kara – steak with garlic mashed potatoes – washed down with two, three, maybe even four beers.

It had been a long week. A frustrating week. The Richardson murder, and now the Isabelle Nick murder, were connected. Bram

Pavolich probably killed them both. But "probably" wouldn't stand up in a court of law. What concrete proof did Harris have against Bram? First, Bram was tied to Mandy's Magic House. He had used Mandy's as his alibi for Izzie's murder. Marcus had purposely told Bram they thought the murder occurred at 7 p.m. instead of 6 p.m. He had a hunch that if Bram had murdered Izzie, that he might go to Mandy's afterwards. Bram had testified that he had been at Mandy's at 7 p.m. Then there were the packs of matches from Mandy's found both in the costume shop and the cab of taxi driver Pete Wrangler. He would visit Mandy's tomorrow, Saturday, to see what else he could learn. Second, there was the business card and manila envelope that Marcus had just taken from Bram. Perhaps if they fingerprinted the envelope, they would find Isabelle's prints on it. But again, that was circumstantial evidence. Of course, an executive assistant's fingerprints would show up on a manila correspondence envelope.

So why did Bram Pavolich commit murder? There had been opportunity. Bram's wife had been out of town during both murders, so any change in pattern of lifestyle – coming in late, or not at all – would not have been noticed by anyone.

But the chief evidence that Marcus could prove against Bram was motive. Ah, motive. Marcus Harris had found that motives could "move mountains." And, unfortunately, cause murder.

Marcus remembered a saying he had learned when he was a young cop in training, "Beware of a man running scared." Marcus felt that Bram Pavolich was "running scared." And Sofia Ruiz had a key to what Bram was running scared about.

The windows in her kitchen cast an eerie glow. Then, the loud clap of thunder.

"Ah, a thunderstorm," Sofia said, bringing his train of thought back to reality. "I love thunderstorms. Always have. While other kids said they were afraid of them, somehow, they would calm me, soothe my soul." Sofia reached to the stove and turned down the burner to low.

"It's helping me deal with the news about my friend."

Marcus realized that he liked this new mother and dreaded his next words.

He began, "Sofia, I think – unofficially and off the record – that Isabelle was killed not so much because of who she was, but because of what she knew. I believe you were the only person she gave any hints about what she knew. She had intended on calling me after speaking to you yesterday, but unfortunately the killer got to her before she got to me. It's almost certain that you were the last person she spoke to before she was attacked. That's why it's extremely important that you try to re-enact in your mind that entire phone conversation. As close to word by word that you can."

The voice recorder ran about 30 minutes as Sofia related to Marcus the conversation she had had with Isabelle Nick last night, as well as her other contacts with her the past week.

"Now, is there anything, anything at all, the tiniest thing, that you think you might have forgotten?" Marcus asked her.

"No, this is the second time today I've re-enacted the phone conversation," she said, her brow furrowing with tension.

The thunderclap sounded so loudly, Marcus found himself jumping up out of his chair. So did Sofia. They shared a nervous laugh at their shared experience.

"Mrs. Ruiz, please do me a favor. No more interviews. Talk to no one. Same thing for your husband. I'm going to assign you police protection until this case turns. You are a key witness in this murder investigation, Sofia."

His voice, indicating a turn in topic, continued: "And now, if I take the expressway, I'll be home just in time for my Friday date night dinner with my wife, Kara: steak, garlic mashed potatoes, and apple pie."

Sharing his lighter tone, Sofia said, "Mmm, sounds good!"

Yes, Marcus needed a good dinner. Because his day was not yet over. He needed to talk to Danny Wingfield. Before it was too late.

Danny Wingfield held all the aces in the deck, and he knew it. It felt good to have Bram Pavolich under his power . . . to be in control of the situation. Yes, the power of the pen was mightier than the sword.

Now, even on Bram Pavolich's own turf, his home, Danny felt power over him. Bram had been just about to sit down to his Friday night dinner when Danny had knocked on his door.

His confrontation had been direct. He disliked Pavolich. He thought all along that he had killed Dan Richardson and Isabelle Nick. Now, he, Danny Wingfield, would expose him.

Bram had tried to capture the situation. He attacked Danny with, "What do *you* want?"

Danny had been coolly professional in his response. He had explained to Bram that he was extending him the courtesy of any equal statement covering a story that would appear in Sunday's paper.

It was then that Bram's tone had changed. That he had become remarkably friendly, even helpful. He had asked Danny into the study, where a fire was burning in a mature stage of white glowing wood. The fire offered a nice contrast to the thunderstorm outdoors.

Bram asked Danny, "So what exactly will your story be on?"

"You."

"Me?"

"Well, I should say Nature Plus Formula. But that is you, isn't it? I mean the success of Nature Plus is your success. I guess you want – or need – that badly right now." Danny flipped on the audio recorder he always carried with him for interviews.

"Tell me more," Bram said, calmly, his eyes taking notice of the taping.

Remembering the journalist's rule of advising the interviewee that they were being taped, he said, "Right. I see you consent to the recording of our conversation." Then, he continued, "It will be a business feature story in Sunday's business section. It will note your company's history, including its highs with the successes of Perky Plus Popcorn and Grandma's Butter Cookies throughout the '60s and '70s. It will also note the drop in your company's net worth and stock during the '80s. All up until your public launching of Nature Plus Formula."

"Sounds like the article will be good. For you, and for my company."

"There is a downside of the article, which is why I am here. To offer you the courtesy of a response. Or, you may simply say, 'No comment.'

A fairly large portion of the article will deal with the facts regarding Dan Richardson, Isabelle Nick, and Sofia Ruiz."

"And what are those *facts*?"

"I have a source who states that Dan Richardson interrupted a marketing meeting the day before his murder, telling you that he had to see you, that it was a matter of vital importance. I have two sources who say that Dan Richardson had been working on a research report on Nature Plus. One of these sources said that the report warned you to stop marketing Nature Plus, that it could cause great danger to babies."

Danny added, with a flair of the dramatic, "The person who told my source that information is dead. Murdered in a CTA bus. As well as the writer of the report."

Danny continued, "The public may view you as, say, irresponsible, to manufacture and market a baby formula that could hurt babies."

"I would not make any false allegations, or your paper will be in for a substantial libel lawsuit."

"I intend to clear this article with our legal department tomorrow morning, as well as with my editor."

"So, you have not written it yet."

"No. I've compiled all my facts and interviews," Danny said while patting his journalistic notepad. He continued, "With the exception of ours, the last one."

Bram smiled to himself, sharing an attentive look with Danny. "So, what do you want me to say? I want the public to know that they will soon be able to purchase the finest baby formula ever created, the only formula available fresh in the dairy and freezer compartments of their grocery stores. The *only* baby formula that gives their babies the extra super advantage of real breast milk. Our research with newborns that we've conducted over the past eight years shows that babies fed with Nature Plus Formula are healthier, bigger, and have a stronger resistance against disease due to the benefits of receiving natural antibodies available in the breast milk."

Danny interrupted, "Does this, say 'superbaby phenomenon' occur in *all* babies using the formula?"

"All is a very vague term. Nothing is 100%," Bram countered.

"Then would you say your ratio for infant mortalities is less, equal to, or greater than the national average?"

"I don't know the specifics, but I would say we are about equal to the national average."

"Who would know? Dan Richardson? But of course, he's dead. He knew though. Perhaps he knew that this 'superbaby phenomenon' didn't occur in all babies. An infant mortality ratio of 1% more, say, than the national average, wouldn't be enough to make a substantial claim against Nature Plus. Maybe Nature Plus caused an additional 1% of babies to die – to react negatively – to these antibodies."

"Mr. Wingfield. I believe you've listened to a few too many conspiracy podcasts. Our research program was conducted in full accordance with the federal standards, which are very strict."

"Standards that would not be exact enough, however, to point to any unusual deaths. After all, one baby's death in 200 is – business as usual?"

"I am not here to be harassed by an impertinent reporter who doesn't get all the facts. Your paper will hear from me. It'll be your job, boy," Bram barked. Then, his mood pivoting 180 degrees, "So, will there be any photos in this story?"

"Yes, three or four," Danny said. "I have a few good ones of breastfeeding mothers in your production plant. Then I'll use the photo of Dan Richardson's corpse in his home the night of the homicide. Plus, a photo of Isabelle Nick I got from her own personal photo album. She's wearing a bright red SynCor Foods shirt. We even have a stock photo of you from our photo morgue, as they call it. Receiving an award from the head of the Food and Drug Administration for your success with your national household food products, Perky Plus Popcorn and Grandma's Cookies. Oh, and one more. I have a picture of Sofia Ruiz with her living twin baby; the other twin died while participating in your infant research program."

Bram's face blanched. It was as if a fury was going to explode, but intense self-composure held it all in. He said, "The fact that this story is nothing but rumors, innuendoes, conspiracy theories, and libel remains. Your editor agrees with your running it?"

Danny replied, "I have a filler story on Chinese teenage gangs scheduled for Sunday. I intend to write this story tonight, select the photos, and present it to my boss prior to the 12 noon Saturday deadline. The space is already reserved. They will have time to switch to the new story. I know he will want to run it. Journalistically, it's a fine piece of work."

"So, there's nothing I can do to change your mind on this, Danny, before you complete your story tonight? Hey, it is TGIF and you'll be in your office at the paper working instead of out with friends."

"I don't mind," Danny said. "I do my best work under pressure. Most of the regular reporters leave on time on Fridays. There's only a few of us who go the extra distance."

"You sound like you have your mind made up. Say, Danny, an ace reporter like you causing trouble for anyone else in town?"

"In fact, I am. I hope to crack a story on the Chicago mafia before next week."

"Is that a fact." It wasn't a question. It was a statement. Bram Pavolich had concluded the conversation and walked Danny to the door.

Bram Pavolich had always felt just a little more secure in life knowing he had "Rick" to fall back on. And today, he needed him. He had learned about Rick through Mandy's Cat House from Marie. It had been a few years ago on his regular night at Mandy's. After he had feasted on her body, devoured her sumptuous breasts over and over, they had lain next to each other, perfectly at ease. It was then in idle conversation that she had told him about a guy she knew who was a professional killer. "Rick" is what he called himself.

"Rick, the Dick. You know, a real macho man," she had said, laughing.

Through a little extra coaxing and a $500 tip, Bram had obtained Rick's phone number. It had been stashed away in his top bureau drawer since that time, waiting. Waiting for necessity. Because Bram did not want to personally kill Danny Wingfield. Yet, Danny Wingfield had to be dealt with. Tonight. And along with his elimination would be the disappearance of the news article and photos on Nature Plus.

"Norma, I do not want to be disturbed, by or for anyone," Bram called out to his wife in a command, as he entered his private library with the worn piece of paper, simply stating, "Rick 879-2111." His breathing was coming faster now. Almost panting. He could feel his heartbeat quicken, almost jump. His stomach tightened, involuntarily. He called the number on the burner phone he kept in his office for situations like this. The line on the other end rang.

"Huh." It was almost a grunt.

"Is this Rick?"

"Who's asking?"

"My name's not important. But I think you may have a service I'm interested in."

"What kind of service?"

"We have a mutual acquaintance, Marie from Mandy's Cat House. She recommended you for the job."

Silence. Then, Bram continued, "Are we communicating?"

"We're communicating," the gruff voice on the other end stated.

"What are your charges?"

"$30,000. Cash. Are we *still* communicating?"

Bram kept $100,000 cash in a safe under a painting in the library. No one knew about it. Not even his wife.

"We're still communicating," Bram answered.

"Who, or what, are we talking about as the recipient of this service?"

"Danny Wingfield. Reporter for the Chicago Sun Reporter. He's there right now, working on a late-breaking story. The services include him, the photos, notebooks, papers, recorder, anything on or near him. His computer, I-phone, all digital devices. I think he should be found in a Chicago canal. Preferably looking like a mafia job."

"I need the money first. No money, no Rick. Got it?"

"Where can I leave it for you? I don't want to meet you."

"Where are you?"

"North shore area."

"All right. Since we both know where Mandy's is, put the money in a plastic garbage bag behind the electric sign. You know the sign I'm talking about?"

"Yes."

"How fast can you be there?"

"Twenty minutes."

"Okay. $30,000. Remember, no less, no job."

"How can I be sure you'll do it?"

"Don't worry. Danny Wingfield will not see the sun rise tomorrow."

Danny was filled with the feelings of excitement and anticipation that only fulfillment in his career as a writer could bring. It was as if he was a force of nature, bringing together all the different elements of life in a cohesive manner, creating a unique one-of-its-kind story. His cubicle was the furthest away from the elevator and the editors' offices, and he liked it that way. Almost everyone had cleared out for the night and the quiet solidified his laser focus on his story. The SynCor Foods story was his best. The photos of the two women who were employees in the breast milk production plant at SynCor were amazing. The photo composition, study of contrasts in light and dark, and human-interest appeal made them exceptional photojournalism. As he put the final touches of his story before sending it, he relaxed and allowed himself to soak in all the good feelings of achievement he was experiencing. A few more lights went out in the office and Danny was satisfied with his final product.

A voice called out into the air, momentarily stunning him. "Danny Wingfield?"

"Yes?"

"Danny, where are you?"

He didn't recognize the voice. "Who's there?"

A moment of fear passed over Danny. Then, it was over. The shot had been expertly executed, piercing Danny in his chest. There was only a moment of recognition, and then, total darkness.

Marcus Harris kicked his shoes off and rested his legs up on the lazyboy recliner. Ah, that second beer hit the spot after his delicious steak dinner. The combination of food and ale was the perfect mixture to put him in a most wonderful state of being.

He was almost glad he hadn't been able to reach Danny Wingfield. He had tried to call Danny after he had finished his dinner, but it went straight to voice messages.

Well, maybe it was better. Sometimes it was time to leave business alone. And after all, professional wrestling was on and "The Animal" was next.

Marcus took a long glug of his beer and stretched out in his recliner.

Ah, it's a good Friday night to be home, he thought to himself, happily.

Chapter 11

November 8

The Boca Raton Hotel was far grander than Michelle had ever imagined. Giant majestic Royal Palms lined the circular entryway leading to the over 100-years-old hotel. It had all the grandeur and formality that was Palm Beach yet possessed a rare ambiance since it was in exclusive Boca Raton, some forty miles south of Palm Beach. Yes, Palm Beach, the city that had been the exclusive tropical hideaway for the world's richest and most famous people.

Tonight, it was all hers to enjoy and share with Hawk. Michelle's questions of whether she and Hawk should share a life together besides their professional life at Ackerly, Adams & Associates, had faded. She was happy. Yes, she was in love with Hawk, and she felt that he was in love with her, too. They hadn't expressed those words yet, so Michelle was hoping this weekend would be the moment she had been waiting for.

It had been an eventful Saturday, the second official day of the trade show for Valu-Mart associates. After continental breakfast of coffee and Danish in the main meeting area, Michelle and Hawk attended the day's events of speakers, workshops, and open marketplace. The first speaker spoke of the new role of manager as cheerleader, hero finder, motivator, respect giver. Then, a 15-minute break before the next speaker, a marketing researcher who spoke of the changing family, citing that the typical family of father as breadwinner, mother as homemaker with three children had gone the way of the Beanie Baby craze and burned CDs. The American family was evolving, changing, diversified, encompassing a multitude of different family groups and blended families.

Michelle had been famished by lunchtime, and had feasted on the grouper in fresh tomato, new potatoes, baked acorn squash, and key lime pie for dessert.

The afternoon was free, enabling Michelle and Hawk to roam the marketplace, filled with venders' products, samples, and advertising co-op programs. Mini informal workshops, consisting of a group leader and Valu-Mart associates, gave them a unique opportunity to meet other associates from throughout the US, and learn, first-hand, of their concerns and problems.

At 4:30 p.m., Michelle dragged herself to her room, arms loaded with plastic shopping bags overflowing with boxed samples and papers. As she threw herself on the bed, she found herself relaxing amid the fragrant freshly cleaned bed linens.

Silly as it sounded, the things Michelle loved the most about the room were all the little personal touches. The shell-shaped soaps, wrapped in chocolate brown tissue with gold accents, the bath amenities of lotions, shampoos, and of course, the chocolate mints resting on freshly made beds.

Michelle had submerged herself in the huge, oversized tub. She found herself floating off to another world amidst the luxurious bubbles surrounding her, as the day's excitement, as well as some of the tension, melted away.

Afterward, she had stretched out on the bed, wrapped in a fluffy, white bathrobe, pondering what she was going to wear to dinner poolside with Hawk. She selected a tangerine sun dress which was off the shoulders but held up by spaghetti straps. There was knock on her door. It was Hawk, holding two tropical drinks.

"Wow, you look unbelievable," he said, his surprise apparent. It was one of the first times he had seen Michelle in anything other than a business suit or casual wear.

"You come with libations," Michelle said, as he passed her one of the tropical concoctions.

"It's the hotel's signature drink, the Dolphin Delight, a cooling concoction of rums and liqueurs, blended with a touch of lime sherbet to a creamy aqua color, topped with a slice of Florida Key Lime."

As Michelle sipped the luscious drink, her lips became glazed with the froth.

Hawk moved closer to her and said, "Here, let me help you," and he kissed her, licking the frothy goodness. Michelle returned his kisses with equal ardor and soon they were lying next to each other on the bed.

"You know, Hawk, a girl could get used to this lifestyle really easy," Michelle quipped. "It's a shame we have to leave tomorrow and go back to the real world in Chicago."

"Maybe we don't."

Michelle laughed. "I don't know about you, but I have to pay my apartment bill."

"No, not now. I mean in the future. Maybe some day you and I could move to Florida and open our own ad agency. I'd handle creative, you'd handle clients and business development. We'd be great."

"Sounds kinda, uh, permanent?"

"Yeah, I know," Hawk said. "I guess that's the way I've been thinking about us. Along permanent lines."

"You have?" the words purred out of her.

"Mmmmhmmm," he said as his lips brushed her neck, her cheeks, her face.

"Babe? This is real, right? I mean sometimes I feel like I'm in a fantasy, it feels so good. I'm falling in love with you," Michelle spilled the words out easily, the libations easing any hesitation.

"Oh yeah. It's real. I love you babe. I have for a while."

Suddenly, Michelle leaped up and started making a call on her cell phone.

"What's up?" Hawk said, surprised.

"I made dinner reservations for 6 p.m." Then, to her phone, "Yes, this is Michelle Heywood. I had reservations for 2 for 6 p.m. Something has come up, so we won't be there until 7 p.m. Thank you."

Chapter 12

November 9

Sofia Ruiz always strived to make Sunday breakfast special for her and Antonio. Sometimes she would fix pancakes, French toast, or homemade waffles, always accompanied by generous servings of thick-sliced bacon or pork sausages.

Today, Sunday, she had awakened early, earlier than usual. Perhaps it was her anticipation of seeing the feature story on Nature Plus Formula that Danny Wingfield promised would be in Sunday's business section.

It was still dark out. Sofia checked to see if the paper might have been delivered yet. She poked her head outside their apartment door. *No papers, yet. Of course, it's only 6:00 a.m. It's usually not delivered until about 6:15 a.m.*

Sofia decided to make an egg casserole, using leftover ham she had from last week. She sliced fresh mushrooms, shallots and green pepper into a medium saucepan. Homemade hot biscuits would go perfectly with it. Just the thing to brighten this very chilly November morning. Sofia reflected on how good she felt. Very cheerful, and yes, even optimistic. She was finally coming out of her depression over the loss of her baby and her friend, Izzie. And, crazy as it sounded, she felt it was because of her interview with Danny Wingfield, and the printing of today's article.

She had first been apprehensive about talking to Danny about Anthony. Sharing her tragedy with people who would read the newspaper, people she didn't even know, people who possibly didn't care, had at first scared her. But, seeing the determination in Danny, feeling, along with him, that her son's death could be a key pointing to a public hazard that could save other babies' lives, maybe thousands of lives, had strangely calmed her. Given her the feeling that her son's death was no longer in vain, that some good could come of it.

She heard the familiar thump of the morning newspaper landing on her front doorstep. She turned the burner that she had been using for the mushroom mixture down to low. With anticipation, almost excitement, she pulled the rolled newspaper out of the clear plastic bag containing it.

Unlike her customary procedure of first reading the Accent section, with the advice columnists, Sofia quickly scanned the various mastheads, picking out the Business Section.

Odd, she thought. Danny had said it would be the cover story of the business section. But this Sunday's cover story was captioned, "CHINATOWN. MERCHANTS TERRORIZED BY TEENAGE STREET GANGS." The featured cover photo was a close up of two gang members, looking menacing with shaved hair and warrior-type make up.

But where was the feature story on Nature Plus Formula? The photos on the breastfeeding women Danny had told her about? She searched the rest of the business section. The article on Nature Plus was not to be found. Her mind panicked. She felt some of the darkness that had momentarily cleared in her mind, return, uninvited. She searched through the papers in the kitchen "catch all" drawer to find the business card the reporter had left for her.

Here it was. Danny Wingfield. Sun Reporter. He had written his cell phone number on it for her. With shaking hands, she dialed his number. One ring. Two. Direct to messages. Nervous tension filled her. Now, where could he be? Where would Danny Wingfield be at 6:15 a.m. on a Sunday morning?

Am I going crazy? Did this article even exist? What was Danny doing to her? Was someone trying to hurt her and her family?

As she stared blankly at the kitchen wall, darkness, now greater than ever, permeated her very being.

Chapter 13

November 10

Monday mornings were bad enough but returning to the stark cold Monday morning workday after a fabulous convention weekend in Boca Raton, Florida, was the worst, Michelle thought. It was as if her mind was functioning under a different wavelength, swaying rhythmically in motion as a palm tree in a refreshing tropical breeze. Somehow, the hustle-bustle of the agency surrounding her was totally out-of-sync with her own body rhythm. She rang Hawk's extension.

"Hawk Wilder speaking."

"Yes, is this the same Hawk Wilder who seductively licked tropical cream off my lips?" Michelle whispered, laughing.

"One and the same. What can I do for you today, my tangerine dream?"

"Rescue me! I can't function today! I think I left my brain at the swimming pool at Boca Hotel."

"Mine, too. Except my brain is dancing in the palm trees. Why don't you and I escape all this and spend the day in bed."

"Sounds tempting. But by any chance are you inheriting a fortune you haven't told me about?"

"Not exactly."

"Sorry, me neither. Guess that means we keep working."

"Until we escape to Florida and open our own ad agency," he added, somewhat seductively.

Warmth filled Michelle's heart. "See you at lunch?"

"You got it. Hey – I forgot to tell you something important today."

"What?" Michelle asked, putting on her "work hat" once again.

"I love you."

"Love you too. Can't wait for lunch. Gonna run now. Gotta call Bram Pavolich."

Michelle dialed her direct line to Bram Pavolich's executive office.

"SynCor Foods. Bram Pavolich's office." The words came out stilted, as if the person were reading them off a piece of paper.

"Yes. This is Michelle Heywood from Ackerly, Adams & Associates." Then, following a brief pause, Michelle added, "Is Isabelle Nick there?"

"Whom may I say is calling?"

"Michelle Heywood. I'm with the ad agency for SynCor Foods."

"Oh, so no one had told you yet?"

"Told me what?"

"Miss Nick was murdered last Thursday night. They found her in a CTA bus she took on her way home."

"Thursday night? Thursday?" Michelle automatically flipped her desk calendar back to the prior week. She had nothing marked on the sheets marked, "Thursday, November 6." She flipped back one sheet to "Wednesday, November 5."

"Why I was there just last Wednesday and had seen her. We had a big advertising presentation. My, what a shock! Have they found the murderer?"

"I'm just a temp, but from what I heard, no, they haven't found the murderer. It's quite the topic of conversation around here. Everyone is shocked. You know, you hear about these things happening, but you never think it can happen to you."

Michelle was quiet.

"Did you want to speak with Mr. Pavolich?"

"Uh, no. No. I'll call back later."

Dead? Isabelle Nick dead? Couldn't be. But it was. What did it mean? This was the second murder of SynCor Food employees in just one week. First, Dan Richardson. Now, Isabelle Nick. What was the connection? Was there any connection? But what was it? What was the link? The answer seemed to present itself to Michelle with decided clarity. Nature Plus Formula. And then, as a co-existing thought to Nature Plus, Michelle listened as her mind simultaneously presented the following: Bram Pavolich.

Michelle shuddered. She felt so odd. The hairs on her arms stood up, and she felt as if something was gripping her throat, causing her breathing to become irregular. Was she losing her mind? Maybe she had overdone it in Florida. Because now she was thinking of Bram Pavolich, not as the client she was supposed to strive to help achieve his marketing goals for a new innovative product, but as a cold-blooded murderer. And if Nature Plus was the reason he would murder, what was wrong with Nature Plus? Could it harm babies? Possibly kill them? And since she, Michelle Heywood, so-called superstar ad genius, had created the perfect ad campaign to make millions of women select Nature Plus to feed their babies, didn't that make her an accessory to murder?

Michelle's mind was spinning. Thoughts and facts were flooding her mind, like a computer being fed data in search of a conclusion. Thousands of details. All seemingly tied together now, with the bloody tie of murder. Dan Richardson's interruption of the marketing meeting. Was that only a week ago Thursday? Those pleading eyes, haunting Michelle. The same look she had seen reflected when she and Hawk had driven Mrs. Richardson home during her sister's Halloween party to find her husband in his murder setting. He had mentioned a report. But then Bram Pavolich denied any knowledge of just such a report. And then, last Wednesday, that funny little reporter had accused Bram Pavolich of having knowledge of that report and Bram had physically thrown him out of the office.

Michelle stared at her desk calendar which still had "Wednesday, November 5" on it. She had a habit of scribbling while talking to people on the phone, a habit she got into from taking accurate notes during college seminars and later at ad/client meetings. That practice was always supplemented by her desk tape recorder.

Now, she stared at the calendar sheet that marked the day before Izzie was murdered. Scribbled on the bottom of the page were some haphazard words. They were, "Commercial's air dates – Friday after Thanksgiving." Something clicked in her mind. That's right. Isabelle Nick had called her at the ad agency last Wednesday afternoon. She had sounded strange. Almost bizarre. She had asked Michelle when the ad campaign for Nature Plus was to run. She had sounded desperate. Michelle examined her notes carefully, for any other clue to the conversation. Scratched to the side of the page were the words, "Sofia Ruiz." What did that mean? Michelle repeated the words in her mind. Didn't Isabelle say that something had to be done. And then she had muttered something about Sofia Ruiz.

She punched in 411.com on her computer. Sofia Ruiz. There was a number for an Antonio and S. Ruiz. Michelle called the number.

"Hello?" The voice was soft.

"Hello, may I speak to Sofia Ruiz?"

"Speaking."

"Hello, you don't know me, but let me introduce myself."

"We're not –"

But before Michelle would let her say the anticipated word, "interested," she blurted out, "I'm a friend of Isabelle Nick."

There was a brief silence on the other line, and then, "What do you want?"

Michelle explained who she was, how she had heard of Isabelle's murder, and how Isabelle had mentioned Sofia's name to her in her somewhat hysterical phone call last Wednesday.

Then, Sofia said, "I really don't know you. I'm under police protection."

"Police protection. My God, what's happening?"

"I received it after Danny Wingfield talked to me. And then he disappeared. Funny little Danny Wingfield, the ace reporter." And then, as if in a faraway place of thought, Sofia continued, "Everybody's going away. Anthony. Isabelle. Danny." Then as if a damn broke from too much pressure, the words spilled out. Emotional words. Loaded with fear and grief.

Michelle learned how Isabelle had called Sofia the night she had been murdered and had only left her with her final death wish. To stop using Nature Plus. Michelle heard how Danny Wingfield had said he was doing a major feature story on Nature Plus Formula for Sunday's paper, and then he and the story disappeared off the face of the earth.

Sofia said, "I don't know why I'm telling you all this. I guess I needed someone to talk to. People think I'm crazy. They think I'm losing my mind over the death of my twin son." Sofia paused, and then said, "Maybe I am."

"No, you're not. I was thinking about a possible connection between Dan Richardson and Isabelle's death. But now, Danny Wingfield's disappearance is definitely too much of a coincidence."

Sofia had not known the particulars about Dan Richardson, so Michelle told her all about his mysterious death.

Suddenly, feeling somewhat unprofessional talking about a private happening at a client's business, Michelle said, "Well, I'm glad I got to talk to you. I'm going to be going through a lot of decisions. You see, I'm the one who created the ad campaign that will make Nature Plus Formula fly off the shelves. It will be available to the public and on grocery shelves in less than a week. We're spending millions of dollars to promote it."

Sofia's voice raised in pitch, almost sounding hysterical. "But something must be done! That's what Izzie was trying to tell me. To stop Nature Plus. It was her dying words."

Michelle heard sobbing. "Now, please, try and calm down. I'll speak to my boss right away. If there's something wrong with the product, if it harms babies, we won't market it. Period. Corporate profits aren't worth it. Now, please, trust me. I'll do whatever I can."

"Please, please. Be careful. I can only feel we all are in danger."

"I will," Michelle said, confidently.

But then, after hanging up the receiver and milling over her thoughts, Michelle seemed to remember a statement she had heard first thing this morning. Something the temp girl had said: "You never think it can happen to you," seemed to stay with Michelle, even over everything else she had learned today.

She would have to be smart. Smart and careful. But not too careful. In just less than two weeks, millions of women would be brainwashed by Amber Greene, toting the benefits of Nature Plus.

Yes, Michelle thought, out loud, "You never think it can happen to you."

David Adams wondered if maybe women should have stayed in the kitchen and the bedroom instead of the boardroom. This *thing*, this episode with Michelle Heywood just a few minutes ago really threw him for a loop. What had happened to transform the sleek sophisticated professional who pitched the perfect ad campaign to the client last Wednesday into a raving emotional *female* ready to throw away the biggest new account and the best thing to happen to Ackerly, Adams & Associates in over 10 years? What had happened? Too much pressure? Maybe he had been wrong to have promoted her to senior account executive? No, if he hadn't, he surely would have lost the Nature Plus account altogether. Bram Pavolich *liked* her. And now, she was accusing him of being a murderer!

David Adams rose from the oversized high back leather chair and paced the floor of his office, like an animal stalking its prey.

Shit, who would have thought this would happen? Here he was, anticipating the biggest quarterly volume and profits in the past five years, and he gets a call, a *frantic* call from Michelle Heywood.

"Mr. Adams. Oh, I'm so glad you're in. I must speak to you. It's a matter of great importance," she had said.

Upon her entrance into his office, Adams had sensed something was not right. Michelle was all worked up over something. Her face was flushed white, while her hair matted in tiny strands around her face. Her eyes were both wildly excited and yet filled with fear.

It had all spilled out from her in a manner of minutes. A potpourri of words and images . . . disconnected, random thoughts. Accusations! Adams had no idea what Michelle had been leading up to with her piercing statements concerning the research man's murder, the secretary's murder, and the reporter's disappearance, until she had stated, with apparent authority, "Mr. Adams, I know you'll agree with me that we cannot allow the Nature Plus ad campaign to run until we are *positive* that it cannot harm babies. That the campaign, indirectly, and Bram Pavolich, directly, are murderers!"

David Adams had reacted as strongly to that last statement as if someone had slapped him hard across his face.

"What?" he shot back at Michelle. "Whatever are you saying, Michelle?" He stared at her as if she were a murderer. Because if she wanted to pull the Nature Plus advertising campaign, she would, indeed, be a murderer. Of Ackerly, Adams & Associates. His company could not withstand the financial loss of the projected media commissions from the Nature Plus campaign. It would be dead. Along with David Adams, President. All washed up.

He had stared at Michelle with contempt. How dare she accuse a client of being a murderer? After all he had done for her. After *he* had given her the generous raise, company car, and complete creative control on the Nature Plus account. And now? Due to what? An over surge of female hormones? Irrationality? Irresponsibility? Emotionalism? She had turned on Nature Plus, turned on his agency, turned on him, David Adams!

He felt his face gain control once again. His muscles hardened. He had looked her squarely in the eye and said, "I don't know what your problem is, but I won't stand for it. This is *my* ad agency and *my* account and *you*, Miss Heywood, are not calling the shots. I don't know what has led you to these obviously inflamed and probably libelous claims, but whatever has, I suggest you forget it. NOW. Because the Nature Plus ad campaign will run in less than two weeks, with or **without you!**" Then, his tone lightening a little, he had continued, "Maybe a woman shouldn't push herself so hard. You did a damn good job on the account, but maybe I overworked you. Take the rest of the day off, Michelle, and come in tomorrow with a new attitude on this whole thing. Talk to no one at A, A & A about this! I don't need a bunch of hysterical creative people overreacting to your claims." And then, his tone reflecting the finality of the conversation, Adams had said, "You're a good worker,

Michelle, and I want you on my team. But remember, no one, not even *you*, is irreplaceable."

Hawk had just reviewed the final digital layout for Valu-Mart's newest ad campaign when Michelle called him.

"Hawk, can you leave for an early lunch? I have to talk to you."

"Michelle?"

"Ssshhh. Not so loud. Don't let anyone there know I'm calling you. I'm so scared. I have to talk to you."

"Okay, okay. Are you all right? I'll come pick you up and we'll –"

"No!" she interrupted him with force. "You can't be seen with me just now. It could cost me my job."

"Your job! Michelle, what the hell is going on?"

"Meet me at Hannigan's. Leave in a few minutes. I'll leave now."

He saw Michelle immediately when he entered Hannigan's. It was only 11:30 a.m. so the usual lunch crowd had not yet arrived. Michelle waved her hand, flagging him to the little table for two next to the bay window, overflowing with lush green plants. She had already ordered a white wine, which was partially gone.

"So, what's up? I've never known you to order wine with your lunch on a workday," Hawk said.

"That's because I'm not going back to work today. Old spineless Adams gave me the day off because, (and I quote) 'A *woman* shouldn't push herself so hard. Maybe I overworked you,' unquote, or something insane like that!"

"Well, that's good. Don't take it as a personal attack, Michelle. You *have* been working really hard. It's great to have the day off. I wouldn't mind it. Take advantage of it. Enjoy."

"Oh, it's not that simple, Hawk. He also said I'm not irreplaceable."

"What the hell does that mean?"

"It means I know Bram Pavolich is a murderer and Nature Plus can harm babies, and there's nothing I can do about it. I created its ad campaign, my Frankenstein, so I'm an accessory to murder!"

Lowering his voice, Hawk said, "Accessory to murder! Michelle, you are talking crazy. Bram Pavolich is a murderer? That's a very strong accusation. Very strong. Has he been arrested?"

"No, no. I don't know what they're waiting for. Probably concrete proof. But it doesn't matter. It doesn't change the fact that Dan Richardson is dead, Isabelle Nick is dead, Sofia Ruiz's baby twin is dead, and Danny Wingfield is probably dead. And the Nature Plus ad campaign is scheduled to run in just under two weeks. It's already on the shelves available for purchase in some markets."

Hawk hadn't known about Sofia Ruiz and the death of her son. Michelle related the whole story to him including the part about Isabelle's final phone call, warning her to stop using Nature Plus.

The change in Hawk's attitude was immediate. With understanding eyes, he said, "I can see why you're so upset. Adams' reaction to the whole thing is typical. He's more concerned about the money in his pocket than anything else. I don't think there's much you can do, Michelle. If you continue to try and stop the ad campaign, Adams will just fire you. And then they'll still run the campaign. It's best to leave these things up to the legal investigators. They're probably hot on Pavolich's trail now. Who knows, they may have a warrant out for his arrest right now!"

"But Hawk, I've got to do *something*! I can't just sit idly back and do nothing."

"But what can you do that the investigators aren't already doing?"

"I don't know. Maybe I can talk to Dan Richardson's wife. She's a good friend of my sister, you know. Maybe there's something she could remember that she hasn't told the cops. Some tiny detail. Or maybe I could talk to some of the people at SynCor Foods who work in the research department. If Dan Richardson found out something about the negative aspects of Nature Plus Formula, maybe some of the other researchers know of them, but have been afraid to talk."

"Michelle, now you are sounding crazy. What are you going to discover that all the Feds in the FDA haven't found? Be realistic, start snooping around at SynCor Foods, and it'll get back to David Adams, and there goes your job."

"Then I don't care. Somebody has to do something!"

"If what you're saying is true, Michelle, don't you know what has happened to people who wanted to 'do something.' Dan Richardson. Isabelle Nick. Danny Wingfield. If Bram Pavolich is the cold-blooded murderer you say he is, you won't have to worry about losing your job, you'll have to worry about losing your life!"

Hawk watched as Michelle placed her fork down next to her spinach salad with shaking hands.

"Let's get out of here, Hawk." As she turned her head around, looking at the growing crowd of people now amassed at Hannigan's for lunch, she said, "This whole thing is getting me paranoid."

Hawk lightened his tone, apparently relieved that he had impressed the danger of the situation to Michelle.

"So, babe. What are you going to do, now that you're a lady of leisure for the rest of the afternoon?"

"Oh, didn't I tell you? My sister had a baby girl. Two weeks and two days overdue. My brother-in-law called me at home last night. A big baby. Ten pounds, one ounce. Had to have a C-Section. My sister is just overjoyed. They wanted a little girl so bad. I'm going to take the afternoon off and visit my beautiful new baby niece, Amanda Michelle!"

Michelle knew that everything Hawk had said over lunch had been rational. What could be gained by her meddling into the Nature Plus and Bram Pavolich investigation?

"Nothing," she told herself firmly, aloud, as if by hearing it aloud she would then believe it. But it didn't help. She felt as if she was being driven, almost by an outside force of nature, to pursue her own investigation. As if, she, Michelle Heywood, was destined to play a role in this life drama.

Suddenly, Michelle laughed out loud. "Destined," she said aloud. "Now I'm starting to sound like a lunatic. My *destiny*! How dramatic! Maybe I am going off my rocker."

Well, enough of SynCor Foods today, Michelle thought. Today she wanted to enjoy the visit with her sister and new niece.

St. Jude Medical Center had a bright cheerful atmosphere. The lady at the reception area was a middle-aged nun. Her warm gracious smile lifted Michelle's spirits.

"Good afternoon. How may we help you?"

"Good afternoon. I'm here to visit my sister. She just had a baby. The baby has my middle name, Michelle. Amanda Michelle, a big baby, ten pounds, one ounce!"

"Oh, my. How proud you all must be. Right down that hallway, and then to your left."

As Michelle walked in the direction that had been pointed out, she was aware of three couples that were apparently heading to labor and delivery to have their babies. A mixture of joy, anticipation, and fear was apparent in them; they seemed to share glances and smiles among themselves, as if sharing a very special secret.

Would she ever know of this moment in her life? Would she and Hawk someday have their own child?

She found the room or "birthing suite" her sister had selected 212. A quick glance revealed the homey feel of the suite, complete with a lighted mirrored dresser for mom, small table for "dinner for two", recliner for dad to sleep over if he wants, and a tiny bassinet on wheels near her sister, who was lying in bed.

"Hi, sis. Congratulations. You did it!" Then, she peered into the bassinet near her sister, her voice lowering to a hush, "Hi little Amanda Michelle. You're so beautiful. You have your auntie's middle name."

"Sis, how are you doing?"

"Let's put it this way, I'm glad it's over. I had been in labor for over fourteen hours and was finally fully dilated. Then I tried to deliver her for two hours, but her head was just too big. Fifteen inches."

"Ouch," Michelle said. And then, "But she's perfect, right?"

"Oh, yeah, she scored top numbers on her Apgar test. That's the test they give the baby right after birth to check for wellness. So, after all my labor – without an epidural – they said they'd have to do an emergency C-section. I said fine. Just end this pain."

"No foolin'," Michelle said.

"Here, see where they cut," her sister said, lifting her flannel nightgown exposing a white bandage running horizontally along her lower stomach. "It's not too bad. It's what they call the bikini cut, about six inches below the belly button."

"Does it hurt?"

"Yes, but luckily, I had a real good nurse last night. An older woman. 'Been a nurse here for 18 years,' she says. 'I'll watch over you as if you're my own daughter.'"

"Can you walk?"

"A little, but very slowly." She rolled carefully from side to side, inching her way up the elevated bed.

"Need help?" Michelle offered.

"No, no. My nurse says I have to do it myself," she answered, laughing.

Michelle looked into her sister's eyes. She saw how happy she was. Two sons, and now, a daughter. A great husband. Imagine, her little sister with three children, and she, Michelle, with none. Well, Michelle thought. I have a great career. A great career that could harm babies. She shuddered, involuntarily.

"I'm so happy for you, sis. I didn't have time to get you anything yet. I just got the afternoon off."

"Oh, that's unusual. To visit me?"

"Yes, that. But also, just to get away for a while. Work has been crazy lately."

Their conversation was interrupted by baby Amanda crying. A nurse came in and said, "Somebody's hungry." The nurse gently picked up the baby and gave her to Mary. "You're breast feeding, right?"

"Yes."

"Okay, well let me know if there's anything else you need. Juice?"

"That would be nice," Mary answered.

After the nurse had left the room, Michelle said, "I'm so glad you've been able to breast feed. I know how much you wanted to this time."

"Yes, I'm really glad too," Mary said. "But I guess it doesn't matter that much anymore. If I hadn't chose to breast feed her, I could have given her almost the same thing, but from other mother's breast milk. Something called 'Colostrum Cocktail.' My nurse told me about it."

Michelle felt herself freeze. "What?" she asked, her voice incredulous. "The Colostrum Cocktail by Nature Plus Formula?"

"That's it! I remember the name. Nature Plus. I liked that. Like I said, I almost chose it, and probably would have, had I not taken those La Leche League classes."

"That's the formula I did the ad campaign for. It's not supposed to hit the market until next week."

"It's possible it's another one, but I'm almost positive that was the name she mentioned, Nature Plus. She said the hospital just got it a few days ago. Supposed to be a great new formula."

That's right, Michelle thought, remembering the distribution plan. Hospitals were to have the formula available a full two weeks prior to the public ad campaign kickoff.

Michelle staggered back on her heels and fell into the bay window of her sister's room, knocking over the single red rose in vase that Mary had received this morning as a congratulatory gesture from her doctors.

"Michelle! What's the matter? Are you okay? What did I say?" Mary said, startling the baby to a piercing cry.

Michelle said, "I'm sorry. I'm sorry for upsetting you. It's nothing. I guess I was just surprised that Nature Plus is already being sold to the public."

"Oh," Mary said, nestling the baby once again against her breast. "You detail-oriented types. Freaking out over an apparent deadline date." Mary added, warmly, "But no matter. It's your brains that got you where you are. After all, I'm proud of the fact that it's my sister that's responsible for creating the ad campaigns for so many products I see on TV. Hey, I bet I'll be seeing all your TV commercials on Nature Plus since I'll be watching all the programs your media department purchases for mommies. I'll be so proud. Hey, I've got an idea. Maybe you could use baby Amanda in a future commercial, huh? Wouldn't that be a winner, Amanda Michelle starring in a TV commercial for Nature Plus. All due to her talented Auntie Michelle!"

Michelle was drawn to the City of Chicago Public Library like a magnet is drawn to steel. She needed data. Hard factual data to fill her mind, until she could feel confident that she was making logical rather than emotional decisions. Her confrontation with Dave Adams really threw her. Was she being a totally irrational female? Or did her innate senses tell her that something was wrong with Nature Plus, and Bram Pavolich! Even Hawk didn't fully believe her. Oh, he was sympathetic to her in some ways, but even he had said to leave the whole thing alone. She had decided during lunch to take his advice.

Until she saw her sister and her new niece, Amanda Michelle. The fact that Nature Plus was already being offered to newborns in hospitals stunned her. Seeing her sister's happiness brought the issue which had seemed somewhat large and impersonal very close to home. It now affected her, Michelle, personally, and she had to know the logical way to proceed.

The huge library filled Michelle with a sense of solidarity and purpose. The rows upon rows of books had a calming effect on her troubled heart. Decorated posters lined the aisles. One featured a huge dragon boldly colored in green marker with the wording, "Pete's Dragon, Children's Library, Nov. 26."

Michelle made her way through the children's library, where a giant Paper Mache dragon, Superman and Kim Possible were a few of the decorations that transformed the children's section of the library into a children's fantasyland. It brought back warm memories to Michelle of her own hometown library that she loved to go to when she was a child. She had not been to a public library in quite some time. Any research materials she needed usually were supplied online or by the ample in-house library at the ad agency. She approached the media specialist behind the desk in the adult section.

"Good afternoon," Michelle said.

The media specialist smiled in a cordial manner and said, "How can I help you?"

"I need research on infant formulas. You know, government restrictions, if there have ever been any cases of formula hurting babies, more in-depth research than what I can find on google."

She walked Michelle to the on-site computer and showed her how to search for scientific studies on infant formula. Michelle's eyes feasted on the information found in the articles. Their titles lured her to total absorption of every word. Titles such as: *Best for Babies, or Preventable Infanticide*; *The controversy over artificial feeding of infants in America*, *The controversy over infant formula*, and *A healthy formula – successful end to Infant Formula Action Coalition Act*. She learned that the World Health Organization (W.H.O.) who voted to adopt a non-binding code restricting the promotion of infant formula products to third world countries, due to studies that had shown there was real misuse among low-income and poverty families using formula, leading to infant deaths and malnutrition. Millions of babies die before reaching their first birthday. Yet, not providing formula to these countries didn't solve the problem, as most mothers in third world countries, who were poorly nourished themselves, could barely provide enough breast milk for their infants past the third month, while some couldn't breast feed at all.

W.H.O. advocates argued that aggressive marketing of formula contributed to a vast shift away from breast milk, the safest and most nutritious food for infants.

Two words she had just read pierced Michelle's consciousness. They were, "aggressive marketing." Wasn't it she who had told Bram Pavolich she would have millions of mothers relating to "Nature Plus" as an everyday household word?

But, she said aloud, calming herself with this thought, "Nature Plus is nutritious because it contains breast milk." She read on, "Mother's milk is the world's original and best fast food, a complex recipe containing more than a hundred nutrients, many which are different chemically from those found in formula products." Again, two words stood out in Michelle's train of thought. *Different chemically.* How did breast milk differ, chemically?

She found herself totally absorbed as she read on, "In most healthy women, these nutrients are enough to sustain a baby's growth for the first four to six months of life." There is a nutrient called "taurine," which the article stated, "may be involved in the early development of the brain."

The article continued, "Mother's milk is also a potent armament against infection. Like a soldier stripped of weapons, a baby at birth lacks many of the biological agents that fight bacteria. While its own immune system matures, an infant acquires antibodies from its mother's milk that are effective against the intestinal infections that are the leading killers of infants in developing countries."

"The immune system in human milk has evolved over millions of years specifically to protect infants, and it's uniquely different from milks used as substitutes." The source of the article was a Dr. Goldman from the University of Texas medical branch in Galveston.

A Dr. Gaull of the Mt. Sinai School of Medicine in New York was quoted in the article as saying, "For us to think that in 40 years we can duplicate what has happened in four million years of human development is very arrogant."

Michelle rubbed her eyes. Reading the tiny letters on the computer had strained her eyes. She took a few moments to ponder all that she had just absorbed. She was interrupted by the media specialist who said, "I'm sorry, Miss, you'll have to wrap up. The library closes in just 15 minutes."

"Closes?" Michelle said, in a startled voice, apparently shocking the librarian who seemed to jump at her declaration. "What time is it?"

As Michelle rose her left wrist to check the time on her watch, something else caught her attention with uncanny force. Her eyes were glued to the item dangling from her wrist, the sterling silver bracelet that her doctor said could someday save her life. The bracelet engraved with the words, "ALLERGIC TO PENICILLIN."

Ashley Richardson had finally resolved to go through the things from her husband's safe deposit box once and for all. After her husband's death, she had gone to the safe deposit box and dutifully unloaded the contents into a brown paper grocery bag. Her husband was a coin collector and kept valuable coin and silver collections in his safety deposit box. She had always assumed Dan had kept some spare cash in there also, for emergencies, but had never known for sure. So, she had not been too surprised when she had immediately seen the $5,000 cash at the very top of the box when she had gone to the bank to clear out its contents.

Ashley had never really seen that much cash in one spot and had gotten a little nervous. So, in the closed quarters of the bank's safe deposit viewing rooms, she had quickly stashed the money in her purse and loaded the rest of the contents in the bag.

She hadn't felt like rushing to the bank to empty the safe deposit box contents the day after her husband had been murdered, but she did. Amid the shock of finding her husband dead on Halloween night, making funeral arrangements, working with the police, helping her daughters with their feelings of loss, the *last* thing she wanted to do would be to run to the bank.

Dan had drilled it into her since they were first married that if anything should ever happen to either one of them the other person should immediately go to the safe deposit box and remove all contents. Illinois had a locked box law, whereupon the safe deposit box of the deceased person was locked, and, in some cases, taxes charged on any monies found in the box.

So, it had been almost two weeks since her husband's murder, and she still had most of the box's contents to still go through. She had started the day after her husband's funeral. She had plopped herself down in the family room with the bag. Instead of dumping out the contents in front of her, she had simply removed one item at a time, reviewed it, and then decided whether it was a document that had to be saved or something that could be discarded.

Ashley had found the job to be a visit down memory lane. Since the older contents were at the top of the bag, the first item she lifted out of the bag had been their marriage certificate. Next, she had found a card she had sent him on their first anniversary. It had touched her deeply that Dan had saved it through the almost 25 years of their marriage. Their daughter's birth certificate had been next. But it was the Easter card that she had found that had been sent to "Daddy" from his little girl that had broke her up. She had remembered how much her oldest daughter, Taylor, loved her dad, and had always been Daddy's little girl. She remembered, vaguely, that little Easter card, yellow chick on the front, and, if her memory served her, remembered holding her hand as she had signed, "Love, Taylor, XOX."

The rush of feelings and emotion, packed with love, hurt, and loss, had been too much for Ashley, and she had quickly left the job for another time.

"Well, tonight, I'll finish it," she said, aloud, dumping the contents of the bag out, lifting the bottom of the bag high in the air.

She had done it purposefully. This time she would go through the more recent items first and not get bogged down by sentimental items.

She glanced at the potpourri of items in front of her. At a moment's glance, she recognized their life insurance policy, stock certificates, and an envelope she had never seen before, with the corporate logo of SynCor Foods on it. *Probably health insurance booklets.*

Her train of thought was interrupted by her phone. She grumbled aloud, "I'm doomed never to get done with this."

"Hello?"

"Hello, Ashley. It's Jack Tillman."

"Hi Jack, good to hear from you. Any news on that new baby of yours by any chance?"

"Just happens to be why I'm calling. We have a beautiful, healthy baby girl."

"Oh, Jack, that is good news."

Jack laughed, good-heartedly. "Yep. She's a real beauty. Ten pounds, one ounce."

"Wow, how's Mary doing?"

"She's fine, fine. She's at St. Jude."

"Do you have the number handy? I'd love to call her."

"Yes, it's 984-8375."

"Okay, great, I've got it. This is the first good news I've had in some time. I'll call her right now. It's not too late, is it?" Ashley said, noting the 8:30 p.m. time on her watch.

"No, no, not at all. I just left her and she's wide awake. You know Mary. Talking to all the patients on the floor, making friends with everyone."

"Good, I'll give her a call, now. Congratulations again!"

Ashley called the hospital. *To heck with clearing out the contents of the safe deposit box now.* She hadn't had any good news in a long time. It would do her some good to hear Mary's cheerful voice.

"Good evening. St. Jude's Medical Center."

"Patient room for Mary Tillman, please."

I'll finish the job tomorrow, right after my 11 a.m. bowling match. There's nothing so important that can't wait until tomorrow.

She warmed inside at the sound of her good friend's voice at the other end.

"Hello?"

"Hello, Mary. Congratulations on your new beautiful baby girl!"

Michelle found herself sitting straight up in bed, emitting a blood-curdling scream. Her room was dark, the usual nightlight bulb that cast a familiar warm glow to the room had apparently blown out. The only light in the pitch-dark room was the red fluorescent numbers on her digital clock radio that flashed on and then off again, apparently due to a power shortage during the night, bolding displaying the time: 3:33 a.m.

Michelle could feel her hair cling to her face, wet from perspiration. She was scared. It had been a horrible nightmare. Her scream had frightened her. It had sounded foreign, and it was only after some moments of staring in the room and seeing no one else that Michelle realized for sure that it had been her own scream.

She was cold. The room was chilly, even though Michelle always kept the thermostat on the same temperature, 77 degrees. Michelle drew a blanket around her, trying to stop her body from shaking.

Michelle immediately threw on the overhead light, which flooded the room with brightness. She stood up from the bed, her silky pajamas sticking to her perspiration-wet body. She walked to her nightstand to reset her alarm clock.

"Damn, why can't this clock have a power shortage battery back-up?" she said, as she went through the familiar but tedious job of resetting the clock. She crawled back into bed, drawing the comforter close around her and looked around her room, now filled with overhead brightness.

But she could not shake this feeling of fear that was deep in her. The nightmare had been awful, and so incredibly real, it was as if it did happen to her.

The dream had begun with her being pregnant and ready to have her baby. She and Hawk were driving to the hospital, but instead of arriving at the hospital, they ended up at SynCor Foods. Hawk suddenly disappeared and Bram Pavolich had appeared as a doctor, looking evil and grotesque dressed in his masquerade of a doctor's costume. Then, she was placed in one of the cubicles that the SynCor mothers used to produce the breast milk. Michelle could feel the labor pains coming on, her baby ready. Where was Hawk? A head protruded into her cubicle. It was Izzie dressed in a white starched nurse's outfit who said, "It's her time. It's her time."

Michelle could feel the baby needing to be born. She pushed and pushed. As she placed her hand down between her legs, she pulled out a baby's leg. She had screamed in the dream at the sight of the bloody limb.

Her labor pains forced her to continue pushing. Since no doctor was around, Michelle had again reached between her legs and pulled out an arm. Again, she had screamed as she lay the dismembered limb down next to her body.

The labor pains continued, and Michelle kept pushing. Out came another leg, moist blood clinging to its white skin. It kicked and moved as if alive.

In her dream, the door of the cubicle had swung open and "nurse" Izzie came in while saying, "It's her time. It's her time."

Suddenly, Bram Pavolich loomed between her legs, his face large and distorted.

"Now just push, push. It's the head. Always the largest part. You're almost there, keep pushing."

Michelle continued pushing in earnest, feeling more the anticipation of seeing her baby, instead of feeling the pain. She pushed hard and felt something between her legs.

As she looked up with eager anticipation, she saw "Doctor" Bram Pavolich holding her baby. But instead of a whole beautiful baby, Bram Pavolich calmly held a baby's head in the outstretched palms of his hands. A baby's head dismembered with no body. It was alive and well, and looked straight at Michelle and said, "Hello, Mommy."

It had been then that Michelle had let out the blood-curdling scream that had woke her up.

The memory of the almost lifelike dream again brought Michelle to a feeling of total fear and panic. She felt alone and scared. Yet she knew she had to go back to sleep. She had to go to work tomorrow. Sitting straight up in her brightly lit room Michelle was wide awake.

Chapter 14

November 11

B ram Pavolich was ready to claim the champion of titles for himself. After all, he deserved it. Creator of the World's Greatest Infant Formula. It felt good just to think those words.

He was sitting in his oversized leather chair in his executive office at SynCor Foods Company. It had felt so good to think his title, he dared himself to say it aloud.

"Creator of the World's Greatest Infant Formula," he said, to no one, shattering the silence in his executive office. Bram felt himself warm at hearing the words aloud. *It had all been worth it.* Certain eliminations had had to be made, but Bram Pavolich was no murderer. He shuddered at the mere thought of the other title he had also earned while creating and launching his innovative formula product. Murderer. But Bram was not a murderer. He was not like one of those "criminal" type profiles with burly bushy eyebrows, closed set-in eyes, and Neanderthal-man build.

Bram Pavolich rose from his seat and observed himself in the full-length mirror to the left of his desk.

Not bad for a 55-year-old man. Lean. Muscular. Strong legs and shoulders. Bram brushed his hand to the sides of his naturally thick and full hair, now more silver in appearance than the medium brown it had been in his younger years. Still can "get it up." It was important to a man. The women at Mandy's knew that. Particularly Marie. Just the thought of her brought his hand to his cock, which he took the liberty of generously stroking. Seeing himself in the mirror embarrassed him, and he turned his stroking into some good deliberate scratches on his balls.

Not that he could – or even wanted to – make it with his wife, Norma. Norma was more a chattering chipmunk or a mere household appliance or servant than someone he would call a sexual partner or even a mate. Izzie was about the closest thing to a true mate with no sexual overtones that Bram had ever experienced. True, dependable, conscientious.

Just the thought of Isabelle darkened his composure, bringing an air of gloom and sadness to his reflected image in the mirror.

Bram returned to his chair, allowing himself the usual comfort and temporary feeling of status he always felt when he smelled the one-of-its-kind fragrant smell of his genuine leather executive chair.

That had been the hardest thing he had ever had to do in his entire life – to kill Isabelle Nick. In retrospect, he had wished that he had hired "Rick" to kill her just as Rick had killed Danny Wingfield. He had done a spectacular job of that, well worth the money it cost. The news said that they found Danny's body in a canal, and just as he planned, they tied it to a professional mafia hit. Unfortunately, with Izzie, there hadn't been time! She was going to contact the homicide detective and give him a copy of Richardson's report. He knew that. Why ever else would she had made copies of the report and hid it in that big manila envelope with the enclosed business card of Marcus Harris?

No, don't feel any remorse. This world is built and sustained by survival of the fittest. Izzie had been out to expose Bram Pavolich as a liar and murderer. She had turned on him. She had been planning on stabbing him in the back, so, he chuckled to himself grotesquely, while quietly whispering aloud, "I shot her in the chest."

Bram recognized this dark feeling within himself. It was as if he were in touch with evil itself, and he lost rational control of his thoughts, actions, and feelings. He had always been "in tune" with the darker side, even from childhood, when waves of evil poured over him and he lost control. Like when he would hang the neighbors' cats with rope nooses from the limb of his backyard tree. He had taken a perverse delight in seeing the cats hanging from limb, helplessly, limply, dead. He had never been caught. Oh, the neighbors had been suspicious. When they found their cats lying dead in their yard or on their doorstep, total mayhem began. An informal inquiry throughout the neighborhood turned up without evidence. Bram had always felt, however, that Mrs. Green, the neighbor with the cats, knew, and was waiting to catch him. He had stopped killing the cats.

But his predator instinct, his sense of survival of the fittest, dominance over others, had never really diminished. In his spiraling career, first as a production assistant and then production manager and online division manager at a middle-size food manufacturing company in Chicago, he had taken every opportunity to stay on top. Challenges to his position had come, and he thought proudly, gone. Firings, rumors, had kept him at the top, and others out of his way.

In his mind (the only one that counted) he was always destined to be on top. Hadn't opportunity presented itself when Bram had been Vice President of Production at Oternoski Fine Foods? Since he had overseen all new products and product development, Bram had had the good fortune of having the first corporate exposure to a butter cookie made by a little Czechoslovakian woman on the South side of Chicago. The recipe was remarkably easy and inexpensive, and resulted in the most deliciously moist and tasty butter cookie.

Bram had known that the butter cookie was a real winner, and certainly, he, Bram Pavolich, had no intention of letting Oternoski Fine Foods have it!

Secretly, Bram had made all the arrangements to start his own food manufacturing company, with Grandma's Butter Cookies as its first food product. His resignation at Oternoski Fine Foods, combined with the launching of his own food company, had instantly earned Bram Pavolich a reputation as a mover and shaker in the food manufacturing industry.

Now, Bram mused, smugly, he was sittin' on top of the world. Corporate stock was up. Industry response to his innovative infant formula had been tremendous. His dreams of a lifetime were about to be realized. No one would stop him, no one.

Bram smiled and said aloud, softly, with the air of a triumphant champion, "Three murders. Eliminations, if you will." And then he added as an additional boost to his ego, "All perfectly executed. Detective Marcus Harris is still sitting it out in left field." He laughed loudly.

Sure, some may call Bram Pavolich an egomaniac, a narcissist, a sociopath. But who cared? When a man has a big ego, it must be filled, at *all* and *any* costs! He sang to himself, "He has the whole world in his hands." Yes, just a week from this Friday, a multi-million-dollar national marketing and advertising campaign would be launched, brainwashing millions of women into using Nature Plus Formula. He sang, "He's got the little bitty baby in his hands." Yes, Michelle Heywood had done her job well, very well. The TV commercial featuring newscaster Amber Greene was first-rate. World-class, really. Now, this afternoon, November 11, he would see the final commercial for the first time. Michelle Heywood was scheduled to arrive at 1 p.m. with the premier viewing. Bram would finally see the apex of his career, beautifully portrayed, with the dignity and respect he deserved. He sang aloud, overcome by the feeling of anticipated excitement:

> *He's got the whole world in his hands,*
> *He's got the whole wide world in his hands,*
> *He's got you and me sister in his hands,*
> *He's got the little bitty baby in his hands,*
> *He's got the whole world in his hands.*

Marcus Harris wasn't fooled by Bram Pavolich. He knew Bram had been responsible for Danny Wingfield's death. When homicide positively identified the grotesquely distorted body found yesterday in a south Chicago canal as Danny Wingfield, all evidence indicated it was a murder by organized crime.

And it probably was: The bullet found in Wingfield was from a sophisticated silencer revolver, a commonly used weapon for eliminations by organized crime. Also, the way the body was disposed of, wrapped in a professional body bag and dumped in a location other than the actual site of murder, pointed to a professional killer. *A professional killer may have killed Danny Wingfield, but it was Bram Pavolich who had paid him to kill. And that was what counted.*

But again, hunches wouldn't stand up in court. With 25% of cases being thrown out of court just on technicalities and most of the rest having charges greatly diminished before punishment was set, Marcus knew the importance of an iron-clad case.

Exactly what he needed in his charges against Bram Pavolich! He was determined to get them right now.

He walked up the concrete walkway to the hole-in-the-wall entrance to Mandy's Magic House. Marcus pulled his scarf close around his neck to ward off the bitter cold winds coming off Chicago's Lake Michigan. He shuddered just at the thought of going back into Mandy's. The odor in the place had a distinctive lingering smell of human body fluids, masked with syrupy perfume and air fresheners. Marcus, who had a loyal happy relationship with his wife, never frequented these places, except for a case. In those cases, it couldn't be soon enough until he could leave. He usually left with the feeling of imaginary germs and diseases crawling on his skin.

He was greeted by the familiar face of Mandy. He had been here several times, building a relationship with her, trying to gain her trust and help in providing any incriminating evidence she might have against Pavolich. But so far, it had all led up to nothing. Either Mandy didn't know anything against Bram, or she simply wasn't talking.

She greeted him in a familiar manner, almost playfully. "Somehow I thought I hadn't seen the last of you."

"I guess you were right," Marcus responded, opening the top buttons of his coat in a *I'm-here-to-stay-a-while* gesture.

"That's why I didn't bother to call you."

"Call me? Call me about what?"

"First, let's talk a little. Sit down over here," Mandy said, indicating a pink velvet loveseat situated at the side of the lobby. He noted Mandy's attitude to be different today. Did she know something? He looked at her with concern and interest.

"How sure are you that Bram Pavolich is a murderer?" Mandy asked, taking control of the situation.

"Damn sure. However, I need more concrete evidence to make a sure-fire case against him."

"I know some things that you want to know," Mandy said. "But first, I want to know how much it's worth to you. I know you guys pay for information. Crime watch, somethin' like that. My information – and testimony – is going to cost five grand."

Marcus tried to control his excitement over what he was hearing. He wanted to stay in control of the situation.

"The usual limit is $1,000 for information."

"Well, you'll just have to increase that for two people."

"Two?"

"Yeah, myself and Marie."

"Marie?"

"Yes, you know her. You've talked to her before. She's Bram's favorite."

"For two witnesses, I think I could swing that. I'm sure I can get it approved, depending on the information." Marcus strained to keep his voice calm and collected, to not reveal his eager anticipation at what Mandy was about to say.

"Remember you asked me if Bram had been here last Thursday, the night his secretary was murdered?"

"That's right. He had stated as an alibi that he had been here at 7 p.m. We've approximated Isabelle Nick's murder to be closer to 6 p.m. that evening."

"And I told you he had been here."

"Yes, verifying his alibi for 7 p.m. but not for the time prior to it."

"Remember you asked me if there was anything unusual about Bram that night?"

"Yes, I did."

"And I told you no?"

"Yes."

"Well, I was thinking about it, and I remembered something I saw. Something odd, you know what I mean? At the time, I blew it off, but when you asked me . . ."

"What? What did you see?" Marcus could not control his anticipation any longer. He wanted this creep arrested.

"I had noticed somethin' shining, protrudin' out from Bram's back pocket. Then, just yesterday, Marie was here for work, and I asked her if she had noticed anything that night. She had seen a gun."

"Gun!"

"That's right. When Bram was taking his pants off, it fell out of his back pocket. Marie saw it. When Bram saw her see it, he had said, 'Forget you ever saw that if you know what's good for you.'"

"And she'll testify to that?"

"Yes. As long as we get police protection until Bram Pavolich is locked away for good."

"That's exactly what I intend to do."

"And Marcus?"

"Yes?"

"We'll want the five grand first."

"Right."

"And the police guard?"

"No problem."

"Do you think you could make them plain clothes-men? We don't want to scare away the customers, you know what I mean?"

"Sure. Gotya. But about the $5,000 bucks you want. As far as I see it, Marie is the only key witness the police will need."

"Ah, but I do have more."

"More?"

"Remember how you told me you found our matches in two locations linked to that first murder of that research man from Bram's company?"

"Yes?"

"Well, Bram Pavolich was here on Halloween night. About 6 p.m. Carrying two briefcases. I gave him a half dozen packs of matches that night. He was all out."

"Mandy, you're great. I knew you would come through for us. Bram Pavolich is a dangerous man. If he should happen to come here today, don't act like anything's unusual. I need to go to police headquarters and work up the paperwork for his arrest. He'll be behind bars this evening."

Ashley Richardson's hands were shaking as she dialed detective Marcus Harris's number at homicide headquarters. *Please be there. Please be there.* Oh, God, what would she do if he wasn't in? Would someone else listen to her?

"Homicide," a bland-sounding voice answered the line.

"Yes," Ashley said eagerly, and then burst out with, "I need Marcus Harris!"

The gruff voice responded back, "Harris's not in."

Ashley's voice rose, tipped with an edge of hysteria. "But I've got to talk to him. It's urgent. It's about my husband's murder, Dan Richardson."

"Mam, I understand your concern, but there's nothing I can do. He's expected within the hour. I'll leave a message for him to call you."

She left her name and phone number with the following message: "Found a copy of Dan's report. Urgent. Call back."

How could Ashley wait a whole hour for Harris to call her back? It was all here, in the copy of Dan's report that he had hidden for safe keeping in his safe deposit box. She paced the house, never taking her eyes off her cell phone. *Call me, damn it, before I go crazy.*

Who would have thought? Ashley could kick herself that she didn't go through the safe deposit contents right away. It could have saved a life! After all, wasn't Bram Pavolich's administrative assistant murdered just a week after Dan? Probably because she had information incriminating Bram as Dan's murderer.

The thought of Bram made Ashley shudder. That tall, rather handsome man. Who would think he was a cold-blooded murderer? Not only a murderer of her husband, but a potential murderer of millions of infants. How grotesque. Her Dan had lost his life trying to protect them. If only Dan had gone to federal authorities with his findings instead of Bram. But that wasn't Dan. He couldn't do something behind someone's back. It was against his good character.

Ashley found herself sobbing at the memory of her husband. "Murderer!" she shouted aloud. "Bram Pavolich is a murderer!" Somehow it released something in her to just shout it out loud. She paced the wooden floors of her spacious home, never taking her eyes off the telephone, somehow hoping that by psychically willing it to ring, it would!

Danger. That's the word Dan had used. Danger. Little did he know the danger was to his own life. Ashley shuddered. It was only 20 minutes after two. Oh, how she wished she had finished the job last night how she had intended. She would have called Harris last night at home, and the whole thing would have been over. Bram Pavolich would be safely behind bars, not able to hurt anyone else. Nature Plus would be stopped by the federal authorities.

But she hadn't finished last night because Jack Tillman had called with the news about their new baby. Ashley warmed a moment at the thought of her. But then her thoughts darkened with the thought of Mary's sister, Michelle. The girl whose boyfriend had driven her home on Halloween night to find Dan. Hadn't she told Ashley she was doing all the advertising for Nature Plus? She could be in danger! Grave danger! She was a smart girl, but what if Bram Pavolich thought she knew too much? He was a dangerous man. At any point, too dangerous for a young woman to be left alone with!

She didn't want to tie up her cell in case Harris was trying to call her, but she had to do something. If she could only warn Michelle! She called the hospital where Mary was.

"Hello, Mary. Ashley Richardson. How's the baby?"

"Fine, fine. You don't sound like yourself, Ashley. Is everything okay?"

"Well, not really. I just got back from an event and was going through some of Dan's things from his safe deposit box. Mary, I found a copy of a research report Dan gave to Bram the day before Bram murdered him."

"Bram Pavolich? Dan's boss?"

"Yes. It had to be him. Dan had evidence that would force Bram to abandon his line of Nature Plus Formula."

"Nature Plus! That's the product Michelle is doing all the advertising on."

"Yes, I know. She told me. Please, I must call her. Can I have her number?"

"My cell phone is dead. I'm charging it, so I can't give you her cell; it's on my phone contacts. But, wait, I have her business card here: Ackerly, Adams & Associates, 986-2573. You don't think she's in danger?"

"That's why I'm going to call her right now. I've got to go. I'm expecting a phone call from detective Marcus Harris." Ashley shuddered. "The sooner Bram Pavolich is behind bars, we'll all be safer."

Ashley tried to compose her manner as she dialed Michelle's number at work. She didn't want to seem hysterical and upset her.

"Ackerly, Adams & Associates," the voice on the other end answered.

"Michelle Heywood, please."

A deep voice answered the line, "Michelle Heywood's office, Hawk Wilder speaking."

"Yes, Michelle Heywood, please."

"I'm sorry. Ms. Heywood is not in. May I take a message?"

"Not in!" Ashley's voice rose, her hysteria starting to surface.

"Who's calling, please?"

"Ashley Richardson, Dan Richardson's wife!"

"Oh, hello, Mrs. Richardson. This is Hawk, Michelle's friend. We met on Halloween, not under the best of circumstances. We drove you home."

"Yes, yes, I remember. Where's Michelle?"

"She's at SynCor Foods in meetings. Been there since 1 p.m. Big final ad presentation."

"Hawk, listen to me. She's in great danger. Bram Pavolich killed my husband. After going through some things in my husband's safe deposit box, I found a copy of Dan's research report. There's a flaw in Nature Plus, Hawk. The antibiotics in the breast milk react negatively to the antibiotic system of 2% of the babies using it, causing them to die a variety of deaths, none directly traceable to Nature Plus. My husband told Pavolich the product production had to be stopped, or he would go to federal authorities. So, Bram Pavolich killed him."

"My God. So, Michelle was right."

"You mean she knew?"

"She had strong hunches. In fact, she told our boss her suspicions, and he threatened to fire her."

"Pavolich is dangerous, Hawk. You've got to warn her. Get her out of there."

"Have you called the police?"

"Yes, but Detective Harris was out, expected back within the hour. I left a message. Please help Michelle. I have a strong sense of danger for her."

After hanging up with Hawk, Ashley reflected on her impending feeing of doom. She trembled as she thought the worst. It was the exact feeling she had felt at 7 p.m. Halloween night, when her husband had been murdered.

Michelle had never seemed so precious to Hawk until now, when he was faced with losing her. He couldn't live without her, without her smile, her laugh that always made him laugh.

But he tried to rationalize to himself, she really wasn't in any danger. It was just because Ashley Richardson had just called that he was getting filled with fear thoughts and feelings. I mean, why would Bram – even if he was a murderer – want to kill Michelle? If Ashley Richardson was right, and Bram Pavolich had murdered her husband, he did it because of his motive: To protect Nature Plus. To his warped mind, Michelle would be seen as a friend to Nature Plus, not an enemy to be discarded of. Or would she?

Hawk brushed his hand through his brown hair, a habit he did that somehow seemed to help him think. He remembered how nervous Michelle was yesterday at lunch. She had been so sure of her hunches that Bram had been responsible for Richardson's death, and even his administrative assistant's murder. Would she somehow, unconsciously, express her fears to Bram? Would her cool professional mask crumble, forcing Bram to murder her in a madman's last-ditch effort to "Protect" his formula line?

Hawk thought that if he called Michelle at SynCor Foods on the pretense of having to talk to her about something to do with the commercial production, he could warn her to get the hell out of there. He'd meet her at her apartment and stay with her until Pavolich was locked away for good!

He sat in Michelle's seat at her desk. Memorabilia on her desk surrounded him: a framed picture of Michelle and her two nephews on a fishing expedition; a miniature plant in a "Thank God It's Friday" mug from a prior client's promotion. Her desk smelled like her, a fresh clean smell not unlike a spring day.

Hawk lifted the phone receiver to be greeted by the tiny construction paper cartoon character in the shape of a ghost he had made for Michelle. He had written in a tiny circle next to the ghost's mouth, "BOO!" Hawk warmed at the memory of this. It was when he was first beginning to experience his first feelings of falling in love with her. It was hard to believe that it was only a few weeks ago. So much had happened.

Hawk looked under "S" in his contacts for SynCor Foods. Michelle had shared it with him out of caution if he needed to reach her at Bram Pavolich's direct executive line.

"SynCor Foods," a cheerful yet professional voice answered.

"Michelle Heywood from Ackerly, Adams & Associates, please. I believe she is in an advertising meeting with Bram Pavolich."

"Yes, she is. But I'm sorry, I cannot interrupt the meeting. I have strict orders from Mr. Pavolich that no executive meetings may be interrupted, for any reasons."

"But, Miss, it is very important."

"Look, it's not me, I have my orders." And then she added, in a familiar manner, "I just work here. I can give her a message when the meeting is over."

Hawk knew that Michelle had the habit of turning off her cell phone during ad meetings. He would just have to leave a message.

"The message is: 'You were right about your suspicions yesterday at lunch.'"

"That's it? Oh, excuse me, I just felt the message was urgent."

"It is. She'll understand."

"Okay, and your name?"

"Hawk Wilder."

"I'll make sure she gets the message."

Hawk had an unsettling feeling as he hung up the line. Sure, he thought, Michelle would get the message, but would it be too late?

Hawk had always been a romantic and had more than a touch of the "hero" in him. *To hell with Ackerly, Adams & Associates.* Dave Adams was a dumb clod anyways. Once the Nature Plus account advertising was pulled, A, A & A would be out of business.

If Hawk left the agency right now, he could be at SynCor Foods in about 45 minutes. That was where he belonged. Michelle needed him more now than ever before.

Although the usual ad/client meetings went from 1 p.m. to about 4 p.m., Michelle couldn't wait to get out of this ad presentation meeting with Bram Pavolich, and it was only 2:30 p.m.!

She had kept her professional cool throughout the meeting, confidently and efficiently displaying all the final details of the massive Nature Plus ad campaign, which would run on social media, national network television beginning the day after Thanksgiving. She had started with the viewing of the final commercial, a technique that had always worked through her years as an account executive. Usually, the client was so impressed with the video commercial that all the necessary paperwork that accompanied production and media was accepted and signed by the client with unquestioning speed. It worked particularly well when the commercial was exceptionally good.

Just like the commercial for Nature Plus. Michelle and Hawk had developed over a dozen quality first-rate commercials, and dozens more of just average quality, and this one was unmistakably the best.

The production studio Hawk had selected for the Nature Plus commercial was the best. It had produced several national Cleo award winners, the "Academy Awards" of TV commercials.

Michelle was positive that the Nature Plus spot would win a Cleo. *If* it ever ran! Michelle was still so mixed up with her feelings about Nature Plus. At one minute, everything seemed fine, normal in every way. Michelle was filled with the contented feeling of knowing she had developed a quality ad campaign. In another moment, Michelle would sense an undercurrent in Bram Pavolich that would scare her. Call it female intuition or whatever, Michelle knew that there was something evil about him.

So now, she packed up her things to go. She snapped off her pocket recorder that she used to record all ad meetings and placed it in her blazer pocket. She packed up her art boards in a large black portfolio, and stuffed numerous papers and contracts in her briefcase. She felt ill at ease with Bram Pavolich, who now walked around in his office with an obviously inflated ego. Michelle had seen this happen many times. A client would so closely identify their personal ego with the ambiance of a quality commercial that their own personal sense of well being was increased. In fact, it was this ego satisfaction of clients that kept A, A & A in business and also kept Michelle Heywood employed!

But Bram Pavolich was definitely the most extreme of the clients she had ever produced for. As he watched the Nature Plus commercial his physical appearance actually seemed to change. He seemed to puff up, much as an inflatable punching bag. His eyes seemed to take on a sense of arrogance, seemingly saying to the world in a haughty manner, "I made it. I'm #1."

So now at 2:30 p.m., just as Michelle was starting to let her professional guard down, and anxiously waiting to leave Bram Pavolich's office, she was surprised when he said, "Can I see the commercial just one more time?"

"That won't be necessary because I emailed it to you so you can watch it whenever you want." She continued packing up.

"Oh, but please. Play it again for me, now. While you're still here."

Michelle thought his plea sounded like that of a child pleading with its mother for something.

"Of course," she answered.

She logged into the computer screen and was momentarily startled when Bram turned all the lights off. He stood behind where she was sitting in the dark, placing his hands on the side of her chair.

"I'm very grateful to you, Miss Heywood, because without your genius, my genius product would not be reaching the public."

Michelle felt the hairs on her arms raise. She could feel Bram Pavolich's hot breath on her neck. She twisted in her seat to get up, but Bram Pavolich placed his large hand on her shoulder and pushed her down. Although Michelle was not easily intimidated, now she felt quite frozen, paralyzed in the seat. Her eyes looked straight ahead at the vivid images on the computer screen. The images seemed to pierce through her consciousness to her innermost soul.

"Why is this baby so happy? Why is her mother so confident? Hush . . . baby's asleep now . . ." the TV commercial began.

Bram Pavolich's voice cracked through the air, "SSHH Shhhh. . . baby's asleep now."

Michelle wanted to run! She wanted to scream! But her mixture of feelings flooding her simply paralyzed her as a computer might crash if overloaded with a virus.

Bram Pavolich continued his verbal critique or comment, reminding Michelle of a sports commentator. He seemed to be talking to no one in particular, more to himself than to anyone else.

"That's right, Amber Greene, the women all idolize you. And now they'll idolize Nature Plus, the champion of infant formulas. And I, Bram Pavolich, am the creator!"

Michelle felt herself being filled with total revulsion for Pavolich. Her stomach was turning as she could feel the remains of her digested lunch rising in her throat. The commercial was nearly over. Amber Greene's whisper again emitted from the computer. "Sshh. Baby's sound asleep."

Michelle jumped in her seat as she felt Bram's hot breath once again on her neck.

"Sshhh," he said, in a grotesque whisper, loud enough to pierce through the dark room.

Michelle leaped out of her chair, darted to the light switch and flipped it on, flooding the room with bright light as the commercial aired out the final message, "Nature Plus. Available in the refrigerator and freezer sections of your grocery. Nature Plus. Our name says it all."

Michelle's body was shaking as Bram Pavolich stared at her from across the room.

"Why, Miss Heywood. You're frightened." And then, after a brief silence, he said, in a tone just slightly edged with accusation, "Why are you frightened?"

Michelle stammered, "The darkness. I guess it was the darkness." Then, not allowing the conversation to continue, she said with finality, "I must go. I'm late for an appointment. Good day, Mr. Pavolich."

There was something funny about that girl from the ad agency. After all, why should watching a commercial on a brightly lit computer screen put her in such a frightened state? Unless if he had frightened her. Unless if she knew more than she let on? Did she suspect that he had killed Izzie? She had seemed to be rather chummy with Izzie. Maybe she knew about the tragic flaw in Nature Plus and was just conning him along like a dumb horse being led to water.

Well, nobody conned him! Nobody turned on Bram Pavolich! He had warned Izzie! He had warned her. But she wouldn't listen. And look where it got her.

Bram Pavolich involuntarily chuckled. He was feeling the power fill him now. The power that he was always in touch with. The evil within that made him lose control and made him do things.

He walked out of his executive office. His new administrative assistant was seated at her desk.

"Did Ms. Heywood find her way out?"

"Oh, I'm sorry. I was getting some office supplies. I just got back. I must have missed her."

"Well, I'm sure she found her way out." Bram began to go back into his office.

"Oh darn."

"What?"

"Oh nothing. I just had a message I had to give her. I hope it wasn't too important. But he did say it was urgent."

"Who said? What message?"

"It was from Hawk Wilder. The message was, 'You were right about your suspicions yesterday at lunch.' It didn't sound urgent to me, but he said it was. Very urgent. He said she would understand."

"How thoughtful of him." The sarcasm escaped from his statement. "Has anyone used the elevator recently?"

"Why, in fact, it was just going down as I returned to my desk."

"Thank you, Miss." Bram Pavolich went into his office, came back out in a few minutes, and walked to the stairwell. He bounded down the stairs four at a time, once again filled with his superhero strength that he always realized when filled with the uncontrollable feeling of power.

He reached the ground floor as the elevator was arriving. He was totally delighted as he feasted on the image of Michelle Heywood standing alone in the elevator.

"Ah, Michelle. I'm so glad I was able to catch up with you. There's a small matter I need to discuss with you in my office, concerning one of the contracts I signed."

"The contracts?"

Bram stepped into the elevator with Michelle. He pressed the number three on the lighted dial section. The door slowly began to close.

"Mr. Pavolich, I'm sorry. Can it wait? I have another . . ."

"No, it cannot wait," Bram said, as he clasped his large hands over her mouth. He quickly maneuvered his other hand into his pocket and withdrew a large handkerchief, which he stuffed quickly into Michelle's mouth. With another lightning-quick gesture, he removed his necktie and wound it around the handkerchief, tying it tightly in back. The bitch's hands were flying wildly now, clawing madly at him. Time was running out. The elevator was almost to three. He inserted a key into the elevator. It jolted to a dead stop. The girl's screams were muffled. He had stuck the handkerchief down far, keeping her from moving too much or choking on it. Serve her right, the traitor.

He said aloud, "So your suspicions were right, your friend Hawk said. Oh, yes, he wanted you to get the message, so I'm telling you now. He said that you were right about your suspicions yesterday at lunch." Bram saw her eyes widen with fear and panic.

So, he had been right. He had understood the message. He could read people like a book. He knew she was a traitor. He needed to think. What to do? What to do? He held her arms closed with his strong hands. He had her legs locked with the firm grasp of his large leg wrapped around her knees.

She wasn't going anywhere. He had stopped the elevator with his executive pass key. Now, what to do? Should he murder her? He had to know what she knew. If the police were onto him, he'd have to bail out! Leave the country. Take the $100,000 he kept in his safe in the office and leave. Go to South America. Just leave. This pretty, little Michelle Heywood would be just the ticket he would need to leave the country. They couldn't stop him with her as his hostage. If the cops didn't know anything, then he'd just have to kill her. He had made a big mistake, and she would have to be disposed of. At any rate, he had to know what she knew. The only way he could find that out would be to get her to talk. But they had to be alone where other people couldn't hear her if she screamed.

Hhmmm. It was almost 3 p.m. Work was scheduled to end at 4 p.m., as always. He could summon the employees and tell them SynCor Foods was closing an hour early due to an elevator breakdown. He'd give them 10 minutes to evacuate. Then, in the privacy of his office, he'd get Michelle to talk. He'd find out what her "suspicions" were, all right.

He pulled out a long hypodermic needle from his pocket, the one he had always kept in his office just for cases like this. The bitch was squirming again, now wilder than ever. Bram raised his free hand and swung his closed fist against her face. She flew to the floor from its impact.

Bram pulled the needle chamber back and tested the ejection of the liquid barbiturate. It squirted out against the elevator side door.

He grabbed her limp arm and twisted it up. He removed the tie from her mouth to use as a tourniquet. She was out cold. She'd be out cold for at least an hour after she received the barbiturate dosage. He squeezed the tourniquet around her arm, tightly, making the veins bulge. He slowly inserted the needle into the vein and released the complete contents into her arm. Her body went completely slack. She was out. Bram Pavolich quickly rose and straightened his clothes. He removed the elevator key from the lighted chamber and pressed the number three. The elevator resumed operation. Bram tried to clear his mind. If someone was waiting to use the elevator, he would carry Michelle to his office saying she had just fainted in the elevator. He'd have to shield the side of her face where he had struck her, and her mouth, still stuffed with the white handkerchief.

But chances were very unlikely that the elevators would be used at this time. Inner-floor communication was rare. Elevators were used primarily for arrivals and departures.

The elevator door opened. No one was there. Bram signed a deep breath of relief. *Gain composure.* Was it his imagination, or did the bitch move? Apparently, the movement of the elevator landing had shuffled her body, but she was out cold. He stepped out of the elevator, leaving Michelle alone in it. The elevator door closed and quickly began to descend floors. It was almost to the second floor. Bram inserted the executive key into the outside control panel, and it stopped, between floors. Good, he thought, it hadn't yet made it to the second floor. No one could start it now. Only he had the total elevator control key, a privilege he didn't award to anyone else, not even his security man. To all apparent on-lookers, the elevator was simply malfunctioning. So, everything was going along well. He had the luck of the Irish, he did. Now, he would announce over the corporate loudspeaker that *all* employees were receiving a holiday. All were to go home an hour early. It was a generous surprise from Bram Pavolich. Yes, he was giving everyone a surprise holiday. No one would ask any questions.

And then, after they were all gone, and SynCor Foods was all locked up, he would simply start up the elevator again, and return it to the third floor along with its passed-out passenger, Michelle.

Then, he would take her into his office and find out what she knew. She had better tell him all. It was a big difference for her. It was the difference between a trip to South America or an eternal trip. Bram emitted a low chuckle.

Yes, being president of SynCor Foods was never boring.

Detective Marcus Harris felt like a marathon runner approaching the finish line. It was the only thing he worked the long hard hours for. This exhilarating moment of knowing he was making a difference in the world. Knowing that he had proven a crime against a criminal.

It didn't happen all the time. There were the cases that went unsolved, and then there were the cases that were thrown out of court because of inappropriately obtained or weak evidence. Harris had few, very few, of those anymore. He was a seasoned professional who had fine tuned his skills over the years, enabling him to experience this great feeling of success he was now feeling.

But he wasn't naïve. He knew the case wasn't completed until: A. The suspect was apprehended and charged with the crime; and B. The suspect was prosecuted, found guilty, and sentenced.

As he walked through the heavy doors of homicide headquarters, he took delight in the new testimonies of Mandy and Marie. He quickly glanced over the tabletop contents: the stacks of incoming paperwork, this morning's coffee cup filled with murky stagnant contents, and a half dozen or so telephone messages.

Although Harris was on his way to pick up the finished warrant for Bram Pavolich's arrest from the judge, he quickly made a point of checking his messages. One commanded his attention with swift comprehension. Ashley Richardson. Urgent. Found copy of husband's report. He dialed the number listed with eager anticipation.

"Yes?" the voice on the other end said, frantically.

"Mrs. Richardson?"

"Yes? Is this detective Harris?"

"Yes, it is. You've found a copy of the report?"

"Oh, thank God you called. I was almost out of my mind waiting."

"Now, Mrs. Richardson. Please, try and calm down. You'll help most if you get a hold of yourself."

"Yes, yes. I'm fine now. As long as I've finally reached you. Something must be done, immediately."

"As a matter of fact, I was just getting the finished warrant for Bram Pavolich on two counts of first-degree murder, one count of payment with intent to murder."

"But it's more than my husband's murder. It's Nature Plus itself. It must be stopped before thousands of babies die. My husband discovered it – the fluke in Nature Plus. It's all in the report I found in his safe deposit box."

"The fluke?"

"Yes, although most babies – 98% in fact – benefit greatly from Nature Plus Formula, approximately 2% of the infants react negatively to it, their little feeble antibiotic systems working overtime to attack the "foreign" antibiotics found in the breast milk. Their antibiotic systems deem it foreign for them. It's like how one body might reject a transplant while another might accept it. Eventually, the antibiotic systems of these helpless infants work overtime leaving them defenseless to fight off ordinary germs and bacteria. These infants eventually die of seemingly natural causes.

"Some are diagnosed as sudden infant death. Some eventually die of pneumonia, meningitis, and any other natural diseases. My husband told Bram Pavolich that all formula production would have to be stopped."

"I guess Bram decided to stop your husband instead. I'm sorry, Ashley. Your husband was a very courageous man."

As if a simultaneous response to his last comment, Marcus heard soft crying on the other end. After a brief silence, she said, "You have to catch the monster. You know he closed early today. Odd."

"Who closed early?"

"Pavolich. I don't know if you can still get him there."

"How do you know they closed early?"

"I called. I was trying to reach the sister of one of my friends, Michelle Heywood, who was alone with the monster. I never got to talk to her. Well, at least she's out of there since they closed early."

Marcus was puzzled. "Which lady is that, Ashley?"

"Michelle Heywood from that ad agency. She's the one who created the advertising for Nature Plus."

Marcus's mind pictured the tall young woman he had seen at the press conference the Monday after Dan Richardson was murdered.

Ashley Richardson continued, "When you weren't in, I *had* to talk to someone. I remembered that Michelle, who is the sister of a close friend, was working with Pavolich. I wanted to warn her of what I had found."

"You weren't able to reach her?"

"That's right. I talked with her friend, Hawk, at the ad agency. He said she was at an ad agency meeting with Bram. He was going to call her to warn her to leave."

"Although Bram Pavolich is a murderer, I don't think he's a madman. I don't think this young lady would be in any danger if she didn't pose a personal threat to Pavolich."

"But that's just the point. She had started to deduce for herself that he was a murderer. In fact, she had told her boss about it and he threatened to fire her. If she let Bram know that she suspected anything . . ."

"But you say she's left there?"

"I don't know for sure. I presume she did. I was getting overly anxious just a few minutes ago. It was almost 3 p.m. I called Hawk back at that agency to see what Michelle had said and he wasn't in. They said he had left the office about a half hour before."

"So he had never reached her?"

"I'm not sure," Ashley answered, her voice rising to a level edged with panic. "I called SynCor Foods to reach her myself and the girl at the general switchboard said that SynCor Foods was closing an hour early due to an elevator breakdown. All employees were notified and were leaving the building as we spoke."

She continued on a more personal note, her tone edged with a plea for help: "But Mr. Harris, please! Hurry up and put that madman behind bars. I can't shake the feeling that this nightmare isn't over yet. I can't shake this horrible feeling of doom, this uncanny feeling of immediate fear. I don't understand it, but I feel the exact way I did on Halloween night when my husband was late for the party. I *know* something is going wrong at this very moment. I know, rationally, that that girl will probably be walking out of SynCor Foods any moment, but I can't help this overpowering feeling that she's in danger."

"I assure you, Ashley, she'll come of no harm. I must go now. I'll call you later when we apprehend Pavolich."

Marcus had said his final statement to Ashley before hanging up with the unmistakable air of total confidence.

As he prepared to drive the 30-minute drive to SynCor Foods, Marcus Harris wished he felt as confident as he had sounded.

The first thing Michelle wanted to do was to tear the handkerchief from her throat and mouth. Bram had stuffed it halfway down her throat, and she couldn't swallow at all, and was having difficulty breathing. It made her feel trapped, trapped with incredible fear. She removed it from her mouth. She rubbed her throat. It ached. The acidic taste of the handkerchief choked her. She couldn't shake the unmistakable smell of Bram's after-shave lotion. Her stomach rolled with a wave of acid and nausea, and she thought she was going to vomit.

Her first instinct was to scream. But then she suppressed the urge. She had to think. Think calmly. And rationally. Her very life was at stake!

She removed the necktie from her arm and rubbed the inside of her forearm where he had jabbed her with the hypodermic needle. Her lifelong curse of not being easily knocked out had come to her rescue. Her parents had learned of her abnormally high tolerance for "knock-out" drugs when she was only 12 and needed her appendix taken out. It was then that the doctors had discovered she had a very, very high tolerance to drugs, and needed a very high dosage for surgeries. It was another medical peculiarity to add to her other medical history fact – her allergic reaction to penicillin.

So, it was to her great fortune today that Bram Pavolich had chosen a relatively moderate dosage of tranquilizer to knock her out. A moderate dosage that would knock out the average person, but only mildly affect Michelle.

It was odd how this medical oddity had really saved her life – or she at least hoped her life was now saved! Just as her allergic reaction to penicillin crystalized her hypothesis about Bram Pavolich as a cold-blooded murderer.

It had been at the library just yesterday that something had struck her about her bracelet engraved with "Allergic to Penicillin." Although she had seen it a million times, it seemed to carry a special message for her. A message that didn't seem clear to her until she had been in Bram Pavolich's office, his hot breath enveloping her shoulders. If she, an individual, could be allergic to penicillin, couldn't a baby be allergic to another mother's antibiotics? The idea had scared her so incredibly that her pervading feeling was to flee from his office and never return!

She couldn't believe it had happened! That it was still happening. The side of her face ached from where he had socked her to knock her out while giving the tranquilizer. She had almost blown it when she had felt herself coming to as the elevator was stopping, but she had played "possum." She had been relieved when Bram had left the elevator.

She had to call 9-1-1! She had to call Hawk! Her eyes searched the elevator and discovered that her purse with her cell phone inside was gone. That monster had taken it and left her here. But why?

Her train of thought was interrupted by the unmistakable voice of Pavolich over a loudspeaker. She strained to hear the words, slightly muffled from behind the elevator doors.

She heard, "This is *your* President, Bram Pavolich. As a special bonus to *all* employees tonight, we are closing the plant an hour earlier due to an elevator malfunction. Please enjoy this special treat for all SynCor Food employees as my way of thanking you for a job well done. Please use the stairways. We are closing in exactly 10 minutes. Your prompt evacuation is sincerely appreciated."

Elevator malfunction! Oh my God, my dear Lord, he's keeping me trapped in this elevator to do what he wants to do with me after everyone leaves! And coming off like some corporate hero or something. A benevolent good-hearted boss, when he was in fact a murderer! A cold-blooded calculating murderer of the worst kind. And who knew? Where was that detective? And Hawk? Had Hawk really called and left her that message that Bram had so eerily recited, "Your suspicions at lunch were correct." Would Hawk presume that she had left, completely free and safe from harm?

If she screamed as every instinct urged her to, chances were that Bram would only attend to her, masquerading as the benevolent boss who alone would handle the matter as everyone else in the factory evacuated.

No, her only hope was to escape from the confines of the elevator to find help! But, as always, the rational Michelle was also calculating her possible death.

"If he kills me, at least I'll leave behind some evidence," Michelle said aloud, as she turned on her pocket-sized recorder with unlimited space. She hid it in her lapel pocket of her blazer and fastened the tiny button closing the pocket. The sleek miniature recorder was completely hidden from sight, apparent only to Michelle through the gentle vibrations of its mechanics.

Or was it her heart! It was beating so strongly! She forced herself to wipe the catastrophic idea of her possible death from her mind, and instead concentrate on survival!

Escaping from an elevator shouldn't be *that* hard. Why she had seen it done a dozen times in movies. The ceiling of the elevator seemed higher than it usually did. She felt herself starting to quicken in intensity of purpose and motion.

The ceiling was a mosaic of inter-fitting panels, translucent to the lights beaming above them. If only she could remove the panel and climb up and through to the ceiling of the floor below her. She lifted her briefcase high in the air, poking it at the panel close to the side of the elevator. It raised up, only to flop back down again in position. Michelle then stood on her briefcase as she lifted her art portfolio high overhead, poking it onto the ceiling panel. The panel lifted in the air. Quickly, she jerked the portfolio to the left, causing the panel to land sideways atop the outer side of another panel.

The force of the movement caused Michelle to lose her balance. She toppled to the floor, landing on her side. She was slightly groggy from the tranquilizer. Michelle forced herself up, mentally clearing her mind to continue with her mission.

I have just a few minutes to get out of this elevator and away to the second floor. I'm going to do it.

She repositioned the briefcase on the floor next to the back elevator wall. She placed the art portfolio along the wall on a triangle, braced against the briefcase. She climbed on the portfolio angle and slid down. She tried jumping to reach the elevator ceiling but was off about two feet.

With her total complete physical, mental, and spiritual strength, she ran up the angled portfolio and leaped in the air. Her fingers connected with the ceiling panel, barely holding on by the knuckles. With her every ounce of strength, she wriggled herself up the panel until she was clasping firmly by her entire hand.

Every muscle in her body ached, but she knew it was her last chance. She wouldn't have time to try to jump up again! She swung her right arm forward and connected at the elbow. She did the same with her left arm.

More in control now, she pulled herself up, up and completely through the elevator ceiling. The force of the movement flung her shoes from her feet, landing on the floor of the elevator. Those years of gymnastics had really paid off!

She took a moment to catch her breath, but the mosaic of wires, rope and elevator mechanics surrounding her filled her with the dreadful fear of being crushed by the moving elevator, which Bram would most likely start as soon as he felt the company sufficiently evacuated! She looked above her to the only apparent way out.

A ledge she could crawl on was about four feet above her head. She reasoned that the elevator ceiling panels below her were delicate enough that if she leaped up to reach that ledge and missed, forcing her down again on the ceiling panels, it would be all over. The delicate ceiling panels would crush from her weight, and she would fall back down into the elevator to be found by Pavolich or get crushed if stuck on top of the elevator ceiling.

With all her concentration and might, she leaped up by forcing her body forward. She landed with the top portion of her chest onto the ledge.

Thank you, dear God. Oh, please help me.

What she viewed around her seemed to be the construction piping of the ceiling to a floor about 20 feet below her. If only she could reach that floor and escape to freedom! On her hands and knees, she peered through the pipes to the scene below. It was the second floor of SynCor Foods! The floor that housed the breast milk production cubicles!

Michelle stared down in search of a breast-feeding mother or someone to whom she could yell for help. But instead, all she saw was a completely evacuated floor with huge stainless steel holding tanks filled with the end results of the day's work. Michelle was staring down at huge circular tanks brimming with creamy white mother's milk.

Bram Pavolich smiled smugly. All was going according to plan. It was only 10 minutes since he had made the announcement about leaving early due to an elevator malfunction, and already the entire third floor had been cleared.

People were such sheep. So easy to manipulate. When you understood human nature, like he did, it was easy to know what strings to pull to get his desired reactions.

He couldn't wait any longer. He had to know what Michelle knew. He needed to know if he was a caught fish dangling on a hook whose only option was to take the girl and escape to South America. Or if he was still in the clear. But then, if so, he would be faced with the unpleasant task of deciding how to dispose of the nosy bitch. That would take some thinking.

She would still be out from the shot of Demerol he had given her. He would carry her to his executive office, and give her a second shot, crystal speed. It would make her come to and bring on a level of anxiety. At that point, it would be up to mastermind Bram to figure out a way to get her to talk. And now, just thinking about it, he had thought of the perfect method that would work! He would lock his office doors to encase her in his domain, under his total control. Then, he would bind her hands and legs to make her unable to retaliate. Although they may appear to be weak, Bram really knew that women were incredibly strong. A woman could throw an object with Herculean strength with enough force to knock out a 250-pound man.

And then, he'd begin. He'd begin to cast his spell on her and get her to talk. To spill out everything she knew and everything the police knew.

He'd begin by telling her the whole story. How he had single-handedly developed the concept for Nature Plus Formula. How he had painstakingly passed all the federal health and food regulations, until, after 10 long years of hard-driven labor, he reached his goal of being the first manufacturer of infant formula that contained human breast milk.

With one problem. A problem that Dan Richardson had pointed out in a research report.

But it didn't matter what the report said. It couldn't matter. All that mattered was Nature Plus. Dan Richardson had been like a thorn in his hand, a thorn that had to be removed.

Then he would relate to her ego. He would tell her they were a team, a team in triumph as well as in murder. You see, although he had created the product, Nature Plus, she, Michelle Heywood aka Ad Whiz Kid, had created the demand and desire for his product, soon making it a household word.

You see, Nature Plus was as much her baby as it was his! She could share in its glory as a world-renown success! Together, they could touch the stars, the glory. If she saw it his way, he felt Michelle would join his forces against those who were trying to stop Nature Plus and would tell him all! If she did not see it his way and could only see the conventional way of looking at murder, then maybe she would be so outraged she would scream and shout and call him a madman and tell him what she knew.

Either way, it would work. Madman? Perhaps he was a little mad. But what person of greatness is not different, out of the ordinary, yes, mad!

He felt his body energizing, becoming transformed for the single purpose of carrying out his plan. He walked out of his executive suite and glanced quickly down the corridors of the third floor, once again. All were evacuated. All the little piglets had scurried home to their mudholes, he thought, while snorting air in, he himself sounding like a giant pig. He looked at his watch. It was now 3:15 p.m.

"Time's a wastin'," he said aloud, in a mock Southern accent. He bounded to the elevator. He inserted his master executive key and turned it. The outside control panel lit up, indicating the elevator movement. The number three lit up, the elevator came to a stop, and the doors opened slowly.

Bram blinked his eyes. He was speechless. He stared, dumbfounded, at the barren elevator, empty except for a black art portfolio, propped at an angle against the elevator wall, executive briefcase lying flat next to it, and two shoes, scattered haphazardly. *Where the hell was that girl?*

"Hey, buddy, you can't park there."

Hawk removed his dark sunglasses. The security guard at SynCor Foods was looking straight at his sleek black car with sunroof. The guard's arm was outstretched in a mildly accusing manner.

Hawk regarded the yellow markings on the curved curb where he had parked. He shut the car door and took a few steps toward the guard.

Hawk hadn't expected any obstacles in his search to find Michelle and take her to total safety. After he had spoken to Ashley Richardson this afternoon, he couldn't get her final words off his mind. "I have a strong sense of danger for her," she had said. The phone call to the SynCor Foods secretary offered him only temporary solace. His message, "Your suspicions at lunch were correct," had been carefully thought out, and delivered. He also left the same message on her cell phone, even though he knew Michelle always turned off her phone for client meetings. But how could he have been sure that she had received it in time? That she wasn't already in danger?

Hawk walked from his car toward the security guard. Tapping on a natural rapport he usually could develop with people, he said casually, "Thank you, officer, but I'll only be a few minutes at the most. I'm picking up someone." He tried to radiate a non-threatening look of complete nonchalance to this man who guarded the entryway to his Michelle.

The security officer responded, "Okay, buddy. You can leave your car there. But you can't go in. Everyone's on their way out, anyway. You can wait here for them."

Hawk dug his hands deep into his jean pockets. In his rush to leave the office, he had forgotten his gloves, and the bitter Chicago winds whipped through his brown leather jacket.

"Closing time already?" Hawk asked.

"Nope, somethin' special," the man dressed in the sky-blue uniform said. He was about fifty with a mop of thick white hair setting atop his head, resembling a wig. He continued, his endless stream of conversation seemingly a personality trait. "Yep, ol' Bram Pavolich – you know Bram?" Taking Hawk's nod of his head as a yes, he continued, "Unusual, it was. Never heard the Prez make an announcement over the loudspeaker before. But he did! Great morale booster, it is. People bounding out of here like kids getting out of school for summer vacation."

Hawk's mind conjured up the old childhood nursery rhyme. *School's out. School's out. Teacher let the monkeys out. One ran in, one ran out, one ran all about.*

The sense of urgency Hawk had felt was increasing dramatically. He had to get in. He had to find Michelle!

"All because the President gave everyone the day off an hour early. Right nice gesture it was. He's a right good man, Bram is. Turned something negative into a positive. Elevator malfunction. So, he gives everyone the day off, an hour early. Probably to get the repairmen in. I asked him if he wanted me to stay on for the extra hour, and he says no." Adding with a chuckle, the security man continued, "So looks like I got me the day off too. Just as soon as I see everyone off."

The stream of people leaving SynCor Foods was thinning now.

"Waitin' on your wife, are ya?"

"What?"

"Your wife? You picking up your wife?"

"My wife? Oh, yes, my wife. I don't see her. Don't you think I could run in –"

Hawk was interrupted by the security officer whose tone had changed from folksy to authoritative.

"No, I have my orders. No one is allowed in."

He turned his attention away from Hawk toward a young mother pushing a baby in a stroller and dragging a squirming toddler behind her.

"Hello, Mrs. Strova," the officer said, politely. "Let me help you there. Looks like you've got your hands full."

Hawk regarded the scene with opportunity. The other glass entry door swung open and out while a young factory worker exited. Shielding his crouched body next to the factory worker, Hawk slipped through the doors, gaining entrance into SynCor Foods. He cast a sidelong glance back at the security guard, who was still absorbed in helping the young woman with two children.

Hawk turned at the nearest corridor, getting out of the view of the security guard. He had never been in SynCor Foods before. He searched the hallways for some kind of directory. *There it was.* By the elevator. It was a square in black with gold lettering.

3RD FLOOR
Executive Offices
Accounting
Marketing

2nd FLOOR
Production Factory

MAIN FLOOR
Reception
Research

At the sight of the word, research, Hawk was reminded once again of Dan Richardson and his research findings. To think it had all happened here. The thought simply filled him with an even greater urgency to find Michelle.

His eye was drawn to something out of place. Something that wasn't right. The panel bar above the elevator was lit up on number three. After some buzzing sounds, the number two lit up, indicating that the elevator had just traveled from the third floor to the second floor. Didn't the security guard say that the elevator was malfunctioning?

Hhhmmmm. Second floor. Production factory. That must be where the unusual human breast milk factory Michelle had told him about was located. Someone had just used this elevator and had gotten off at the second floor. Was it Michelle? It certainly didn't *seem* like the elevator wasn't working.

Hawk pressed the circular fixture with the arrow pointing up, indicating a call for the elevator. With immediate response, the elevator hummed. The number two that had been lit up turned off. The elevator hummed more, and then paused. The number one on the panel lit up. The doors opened slowly.

Hawk was about to walk in when he was stopped abruptly. Not by a person. But more by a missing person.

Here was Michelle's art portfolio, briefcase, and shoes.

But where was Michelle?

Michelle considered jumping down from the ceiling pipes onto the second floor but was unsure what the 20-foot distance would do to her. Would she break a limb? Or become paralyzed, or even die? If it was just a broken limb, she would gladly risk it. After the stark immediate burst of pain she would feel, she would simply drag herself, crawl if necessary, to freedom. She felt a sense of urgency. She felt as if she didn't move NOW, RIGHT NOW, she would be trapped. Trapped by the psychopath!

Where was he now? It had been almost 15 minutes since he had made the announcement for evacuation on the loudspeaker. Surely, he had discovered her disappearance from the elevator by NOW! He would be furious! Michelle shuddered at the thought of Pavolich transformed further into a madman by fury.

She knew she didn't have much time. If she jumped, she could kill herself. Maybe if she just hid quietly here, help would come. Her cell phone was turned off and in her purse. Perhaps Marcus Harris, or Hawk, would come and rescue her from this living nightmare. Every muscle in her body ached. Her feat of escaping from the elevator had been strenuous and she was now beginning to feel muscular pain all over. Her right arm that Bram had attacked with the hypodermic needle was aching and felt pushed to its physical limits just by bracing herself against the long steel pipe.

Michelle peered down and observed three huge stainless-steel containers or vats. The one the furthest distance from her was empty, the one directly under her was filled with a milky white substance, while the vat close to the North wall was about half filled. *Mother's milk. Maybe she could jump in the vat directly below her and the milk would cushion her fall.* But how would she get out? Could she pull herself out of the two feet necessary to get out of the vat? And then, would she hurt herself if she jumped to the floor from the top of the ten-foot vat?

Her mind was racing, trying to process information for the best possible solution to her dilemma when she heard the unmistakable sound of the elevator.

She held her breath. So, he had discovered her disappearance. It had to be that. Bram Pavolich had to be on that elevator, coming to revenge her escape from him! Her only option was to try to hide among the steel ceiling pipes, to crouch as low as possible in a ball, so that he wouldn't detect her. She had to be quiet, very quiet.

Michelle's heart quickened to an incredible pace as she heard the elevator stop on the second floor. Her worst fears were realized when she saw Bram Pavolich emerge from the elevator doors.

Even from her place 20 feet above him, Michelle could tell he was enraged. His mannerisms were aggressive. He moved in large fashion, swinging his arms with forced deliberation.

Michelle froze at the sound of his voice, which he bellowed out, echoing on the deserted floor.

"You think you've won?" A long pause. "You underestimate me. I'll not be undone by a little girl! So, you escaped from the elevator. One point for you. It makes the game so much more interesting. It makes the final victory so much more rewarding.

"It doesn't take a genius – even though I am a genius – to realize that you escaped through the top of the elevator to the ceiling fixtures of the second floor. You heard the elevator door open, and you saw me get out. Now, you're scared. Very scared. Because you know you're trapped." His voice rising to a high almost hysterical pitch, he continued, *"He's got the whole world in his hands. He's got the little bitty baby in his hands."*

Michelle was frightened. She felt like a helpless animal hiding in the forest from a stalking lion. However, she did have had the foresight to remove her miniature tape recorder from her blazer pocket and hold it in her hand, outward, to tape Bram's threatening message.

Somehow, the gesture, as little and possibly useless, made Michelle seem more in control of the situation again.

This feeling of control totally escaped her as she peered down to see Bram Pavolich press a button on a concealed control panel which, evidently, activated a metal stairway from the ceiling to the floor.

She stared in disbelief as she watched Bram climb the stairs rung after rung, until he had reached the top. Michelle felt as if she would explode. She could see him now, standing erect atop the little platform that was perched atop the stairs.

His head stuck out atop his long neck, which he swung in rhythmic motion like a turtle looking to snatch a fly.

Finally, she watched in horror as his head stopped, facing in her direction. She could almost feel the power emitting from his piercing eyes as he feasted on the sight of her crouched in her curled-up hiding place.

"Ah, there you are, my little baby." Then, he sang, "*He's got the whole world in his hands; he's got the whole wide world in his hands. He's got the little bitty baby in his hands.*"

Although the immediate danger of Bram was more than 20 feet away, his presence seemed immense, like evil personified, emerging onto Michelle through a dark black tunnel. She could feel the power of his glaring look.

She told herself to stay in control. To think, but the sight of Bram Pavolich only reminded her of her terrifying dream the night before, when he had delivered her dismembered dead baby, freely holding its head in his huge hands. She could almost hear the macabre words the baby had said. "Hello, Mommy."

She screamed, an involuntary forceful eruption of terror and madness, coming from her innermost soul.

Where was Michelle? Hawk's thoughts were focused. He knew every minute was the difference between life and death. Then, as an answer to his question, he heard what sounded like a woman's scream. Was it Michelle? It had to be. All the other women had been led out by Bram's phony evacuation. Elevator malfunction, my ass. He entered the elevator and pressed for the second floor. The doors closed slowly. The elevator hummed, and moved upwards, toward the second floor.

Hawk's mind worked methodically. What was going on here? Bram must have had Michelle locked in the elevator. But Michelle had apparently outsmarted him; by constructing a pyramid with her briefcase and art portfolio, she had escaped through the elevator ceiling. It must have been Bram who got off on the second floor just a few minutes ago.

The elevator stopped abruptly. Second floor. Every nerve and muscle were on guard, ready for anything. He mentally prepared himself for the worst: he could find Michelle, but instead of finding the warm, beautiful woman he had fallen in love with, he might find her bloody corpse. He hadn't heard anything since that last mournful scream. It could have been Michelle's last.

He pressed his body against the wall and maneuvered his way towards what looked like an open area. He found what looked like a giant Barbie dream house with cubicle after cubicle of bright pink rooms. Outside one of the cubicles, he read:

DONER TS46778
RODRIGUEZ

So, this is where the breast feeding mothers nursed their babies and their milk was stored in these stainless steel tanks. He heard people talking in the main open area. He stepped out of the cubicle and looked in the direction from where the sounds were coming from.

Up, in the ceiling, were two figures. One crouched low, limbs wrapped around adjacent ceiling fixture pipes. Another, standing upright on a little platform against the wall.

He had found Michelle, all right, holding onto a ceiling pipe as if holding onto her very life as Bram Pavolich loomed over her, about 20 feet away.

At least she was still alive. There's still hope! He had to do something. But what? He couldn't stand by and watch the woman he loved die. Or was it too late already?

Michelle knew she was going to die. Even though she tried to keep the thought from her mind, it kept coming back. *This is it. I'm really going to die. Never to see Hawk again. Or my new niece or have children of my own.* If it was her time, she was ready to die, but she would leave evidence incriminating Bram after her death.

She was determined to get as much of a confession from Pavolich on her pocket recorder as possible and then secure it in her inside blazer pocket where, most likely, it would go unnoticed by Pavolich.

It may have been a silly idea since Bram could destroy her body and clothes beyond recognition after he would kill her. She shuddered at the thought. Involuntarily, an imaginary headline rose in her mind, "Decomposed body found in Chicago Canal identified as Michelle Heywood, recently listed as a Missing Person." She'd have to hide it somewhere away from her clothes and body with the hopes of someone discovering it if the worst happened.

Dear God, give me strength. Let me walk and not faint. Michelle vowed to stay in control of the situation until the end, whatever it would be.

"So, you are going to kill me, just like you killed Dan Richardson, Isabelle Nick, and Danny Wingfield?" Michelle shot the question directly at Pavolich while making sure the microphone speaker of her pocket recorder faced in his direction.

"I haven't decided yet."

"But you did kill them, didn't you?"

"My dear Michelle. Certain sacrifices have to be made in the name of science and the common good of mankind."

"You call the common good of mankind killing innocent babies? There was a tragic flaw in Nature Plus Formula, wasn't there? A flaw that Dan Richardson discovered."

"Dan Richardson was a fool!"

"His only foolish mistake was telling you about it first. It was his fatal mistake."

"Fatal mistake. Ah, I do admire your dramatic style, Miss Heywood. You have such a way with words. You could have been such an asset. It's such a shame such a brilliant mind, and may I add, beautiful body, must go to such a waste."

He took a step forward on a flat horizontal ceiling beam toward Michelle.

"It's all over. I'm sure the police are onto me. I had hoped to take you with me. But no, you're too ingenious. You'd just cause trouble."

"No, I won't! I promise. Take me with you. They won't hurt you if you have me as your hostage."

Michelle suddenly felt a strong urge to live. She didn't want to die. She wasn't ready to die.

She peered below her. The huge open vat of formula loomed upward at her. Should she jump? Would the thing automatically turn on or something if she did, crushing her with huge steel blades like a giant blender?

Pavolich strode onward toward Michelle.

"Michelle, you're a good actress. But not good enough. No, I'm afraid you won't be going with me. In fact, you won't be leaving SynCor Foods today."

Michelle screamed again, this time so loudly her throat ached. She scrambled backwards a few steps on the horizontal beam. Instinctively, she placed the recorder back inside the pocket of her jacket.

Then, something hit him. Michelle saw a rather large shiny silver object smack him across his body. She watched as he fell through the air, downward, until he fell in the vat directly beneath him filled halfway with the milky formula.

"Michelle, are you all right?"

"Hawk. Thank God, it's you. Thank God this nightmare is over! How do you think I should get down from here?"

"Same way Pavolich got up."

"But that means I have to crawl over the vat he just fell into. What if I slip and fall in?"

"You won't. Concentrate. Concentrate on getting to the stairwell landing and down the steps. You can do it. Let's get the hell out of here and get the police."

"What about Pavolich?"

"I hit him pretty hard with that formula tank. He may stay under and drown. But I don't want to stick around to find out."

Michelle was eager to get down to Hawk. It seemed every muscle in her body ached from being in the crouched position on the pipes. She forced herself to mentally sharpen her mind to face the task ahead of her. She maneuvered her way down to the little landing against the wall. She thought she saw movement in the vat that Pavolich had just fallen into but wouldn't let herself look down for fear of becoming dizzy, losing her balance, and falling.

Hawk's words were music to her ears, and she gained strength with his every encouragement as she stepped down the steel ladder.

"That's it, Michelle. You're almost down. Just a little more, and we're out of here."

Michelle reached the floor and fell into Hawk's arms. No one, nothing, had ever felt so good.

"Honey, let's get out of here."

"What about Bram?"

"He's still in the vat of formula. Even if he's strong enough to swim in that thick fluid, it's doubtful he could get out of there."

"Yeah, it was only half full, so he'd have to reach up and out over six feet."

"To hell with Bram. Let's get out of here. My car's parked out front. We'll call the police once we get out of here."

They ran down the corridor toward the elevator. Hawk pressed the arrow going down. It was quiet now. Michelle knew everything was going to be okay. She had so much to do. She had to contact the police and give them the tape recording with Bram Pavolich. Then she would contact the FDA. And, of course, all advertising and marketing of Nature Plus would have to be stopped.

"Hawk, how did you find me?"

"I had to after Ashley Richardson called me."

"I got your message."

"Good."

"But it was too late; he was already after me. That man is crazy, Hawk."

As she turned her head back from the arrow on the elevator, Michelle saw a huge figure looming behind Hawk, covered in a shiny white substance. The figure reached a large silver object covered with the same white substance up in the air and smashed it down on Hawk.

Michelle emitted a blood-curdling scream, and the old feeling of pure terror she had thought was gone returned.

But there was no one to hear her scream. Hawk was out, lying blankly in a huddle in front of the elevator, splattered with white formula.

Michelle turned and darted down the corridor. Her face ached and her arm ached, and her head hurt, and she prayed it would be over, but it wasn't. Then, she felt a sharp jab of pain in her right shoulder. She had been stabbed! The pain shot through her entire side. She twisted her head to see a mingling of blood and the white substance on her shoulder.

Pavolich had apparently slipped from the force of the stabbing attack. Michelle placed her other hand on her shoulder and continued.

If only she could find the stairway to get to the first floor. She could lock herself in Hawk's car. She knew he never locked it, so if she could only get to the first floor and outside to the car, she'd be safe! She'd lock herself in and beep the horn until help came.

"Bitch, you'll never get away. You bitch. I'll kill you!"

Michelle felt the force of two powerful hands on her shoulders. They threw her against the wall. The impact shot pain throughout her whole body.

"You think your little boyfriend could stop me. What a fool. I'm a survivor. I do whatever I need to survive."

He pinned her arms against the wall above her head. The weapon was a pocketknife. His body loomed large against her. Most of the baby formula had fallen off, yet it left an eerie remain of white curdle throughout his hair, eyebrows, and mouth. Michelle thought, just make it fast. I don't want to be cut up slow and painful.

'NO ONE, NO ONE, STOPS BRAM PAVOLICH!" It was a scream. A violent scream, accented by his outstretched arm with gleaming knife poised to slit Michelle's throat.

And then, a blast. His body fell to the ground, wrapping itself around Michelle's feet.

Ironically, it reminded Michelle of a little child at his mother's feet. She looked up to see a vaguely familiar figure. Where had she seen him before? Yes, at the press conference. It was the homicide detective. What was his name again?

It was over. This time it was really over.

Chapter 15

November 13

As she cleaned out her desk at A, A & A, Michelle was surprised at how much "junk" she had accumulated: the special monogrammed coffee mug from a media event; the funny birthday card Hawk had made for her from the art production staff. She placed it all in a file box she had brought into work.

Dave Adams had laid her off, as well as Hawk. Even though her common sense had told her that the agency would be facing dramatic cutbacks soon, even to the point of no longer existing or selling out, she still felt that Adams held her and Hawk personally responsible for the collapse of the Nature Plus Formula campaign. It was as if he wouldn't have minded if the FDA had banned production of Nature Plus about 120 days later, after his agency had received the benefits of the media commissions from the multi-million-dollar ad campaign!

It seemed like so long ago that her world had almost ended, yet it was only two days ago. Two days since detective Marcus Harris had shot and killed Bram Pavolich. Two days since she had given the detective the tape-recording incriminating Bram Pavolich in at least three murders.

The Federal authorities were contacted through the police just yesterday and already SynCor Foods Company was closed, indefinitely. It was just yesterday that all the media was contacted to pull all advertising and promotion on Nature Plus Formula. Lawyers were already in place to file class action suits against the deceased Bram Pavolich's estate and company holdings. Sofia Ruiz would get needed compensation for her lost baby.

Hawk popped into her office. "How's it going?" His head was wrapped with a large bandage from the impact of Pavolich's hit.

Michelle answered, "Do you really think we can do it, Hawk? Can we really move to Florida to start our own ad agency?" They had talked all last night about beginning a new life together and maybe even having a family too.

But Michelle would never forget. She would never forget the feeling of Bram Pavolich's breath against her shoulders, or the feeling of his huge hands pinning her against the wall.

Because by never forgetting, she would always remember how she and Hawk had helped save the lives of thousands of newborn infants, being innocently murdered at the hands of their mothers, feeding them Nature Plus Formula.

Hawk replied, "Of course we can do it. After bringing down the biggest potential mass-murderer, we can do anything."

Michelle was changed. She felt stronger inside, more confident. She had gone after the truth and truth had prevailed.

She went over to Hawk and kissed him gingerly on his wrapped head.

"You and me?"

"You and me."

Epilogue

One Year Later

Michelle flipped off her sandals and propped her feet up on her footstool that she kept under her desk. If was nice to be the boss of her own ad agency and wear what she wanted to wear and do things the way she wanted to do them. It had been a huge risk for her and Hawk to move to Florida a year ago, after all the fallout from the SynCor Foods scandal. Bram received posthumous charges for his crimes. She and Hawk had married and moved to South Florida. David Adams closed his agency, but that wasn't the defining moment for Michelle to go out on her own. She and Hawk had talked about their dream to own their ad agency and represent clients in a way that was honest and beneficial to people. After their brief weekend in Boca Raton, Florida, they were drawn to a totally new climate for a fresh beginning. It had only been a few months after moving to Florida that they launched their ad agency, Pro Ad Group, even though the "group" was just the two of them! They had been received in the market with anticipation due to positive publicity from the incident in Chicago and their heroic stance that hindered the catastrophic effects of an ad campaign and product gone bad. Hawk was finally able to realize full creative control of his campaigns and the clients were very appreciative of his fresh approach.

They had planned a little champagne toast for 5 p.m. closing hours to celebrate their 10th month anniversary of Pro Ad Group. Michelle had also purchased a bottle of sparkling apple juice this afternoon, which was chilling in the mini refrigerator.

"Whooo, hoo. It's Friday babe," Hawk exclaimed as he came into her office. "Are you ready for that bottle of champagne for our 10-month anniversary? Did you see *Palm Beach Illustrated* called us the 'Forward Players' in advertising?" He placed a glossy four-color magazine on her desk opened to a spread on their agency.

"It doesn't get any better than that," Hawk exclaimed. He reached into the mini frig and got the bottle of champagne and two glasses. After he poured one glass, Michelle covered hers and asked him to get out the other bottle in the frig.

"Sparkling apple juice?" he asked, incredulously. "Are you on some new South Florida diet, babe?" He eyed her in a colorful floral sundress and said, "You don't need to change a thing."

Michelle placed her hand over her stomach and said, "Well, we will definitely need to change a few things, like we'll need a baby swing, and a rocker for breastfeeding –"

"What? Really? You're sure?" Hawk exclaimed with obvious joy.

"Yep. My own positive test last week was verified by my doctor today. We're having a baby."

Hawk enveloped her in his arms and kissed her. "You've made me the happiest man alive."

"Our dreams are coming true," Michelle said. "But one thing's for sure. Our 'formula' for happiness will not include any baby 'formula.'" Their shared laughter that had been deepened through trial and danger filled the room with unparalleled joy.

About the Author

Writing authentic pieces has been Monroe's hallmark: when she was a teacher for a diverse population of struggling readers, she wrote a trilogy of short, easy-to-read novels in which they could relate. This work comprised of *Miracle at Monty Middle School*, *Milagro en la Escuela Monty*, *Krazy White Girl*, *Tagger*, and *Tagger, Reader's Theater*, which in part earned her recognition in her community and Teacher of the Year for Palm Beach County. Her first nonfiction piece was a true story of her years as a caregiver to her husband of 41 years: *I Didn't Sign Up for This: One Caregiver's Personal Story and How She Survived.*

Monroe continues to delight audiences with her fresh approach on a wide variety of topics. She is currently working on her next fiction piece: *Love After Loss*. She resides in Lake Worth, Florida, with her family. For more information, www.marymonroebooks.com

You won't want to miss Mary Monroe's next exciting
new novel, *Love After Loss*, coming soon!

Cover design by EVE Graphic Design LLC

PGIL2021USA